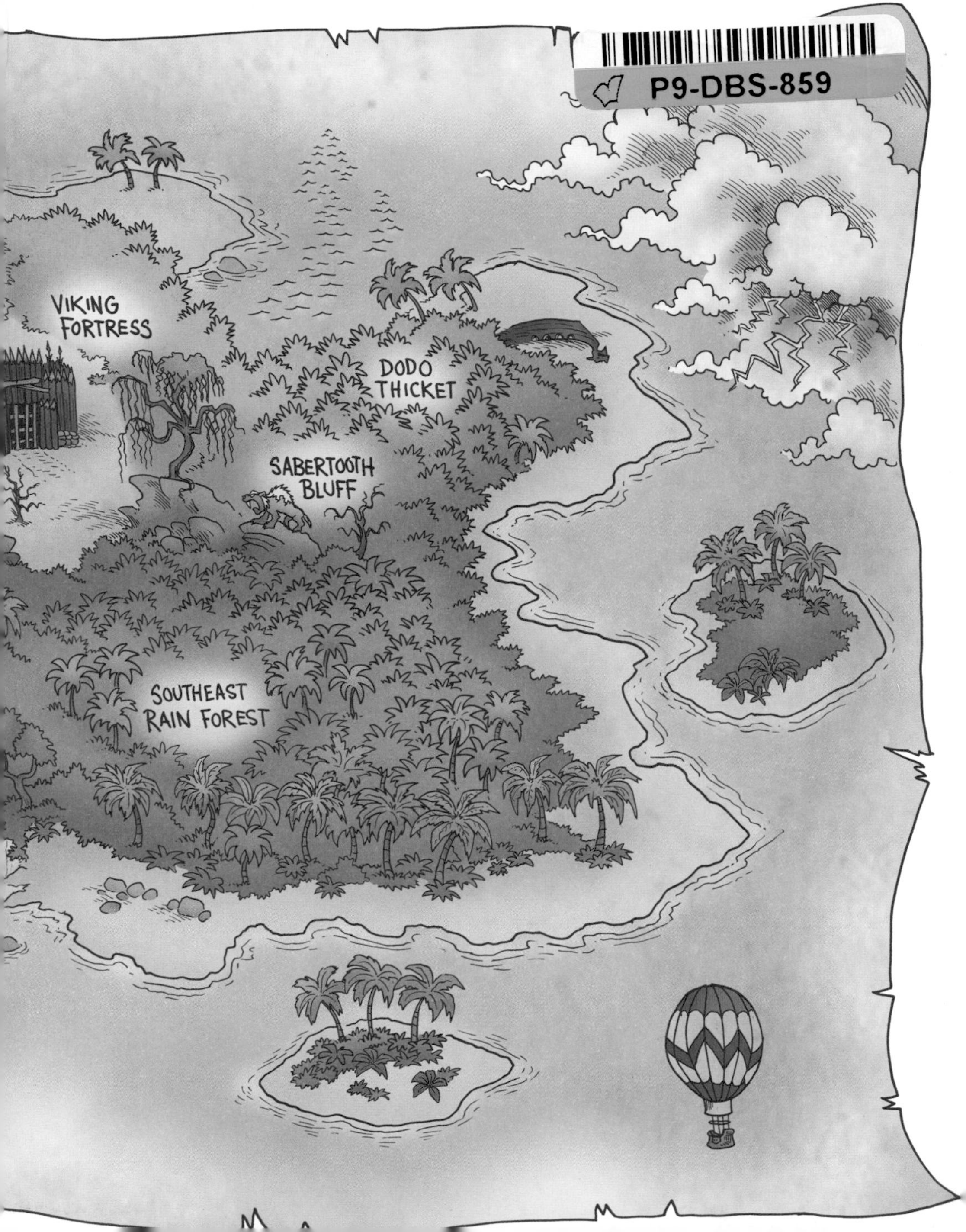
VIKING FORTRESS
DODO THICKET
SABERTOOTH BLUFF
SOUTHEAST RAIN FOREST

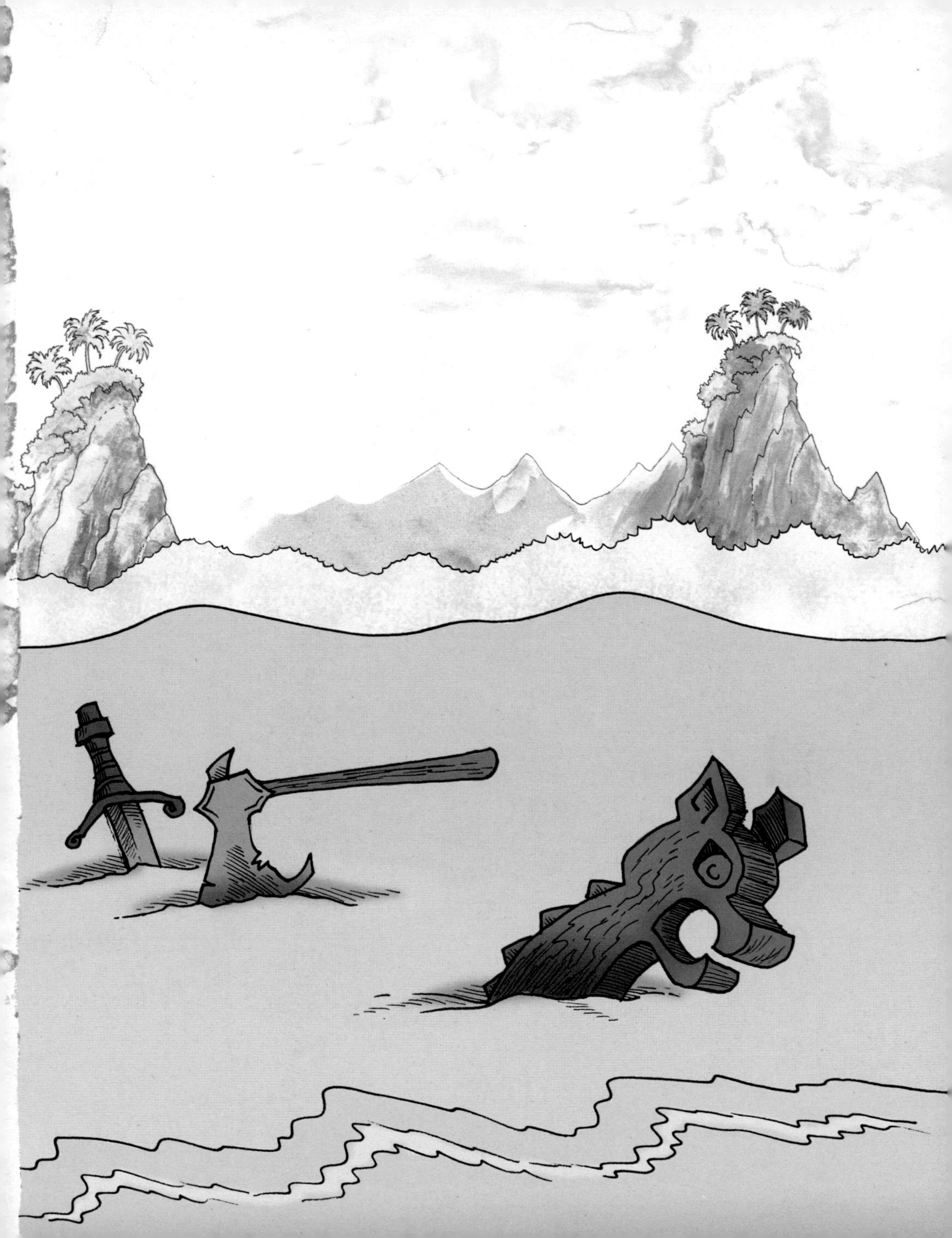

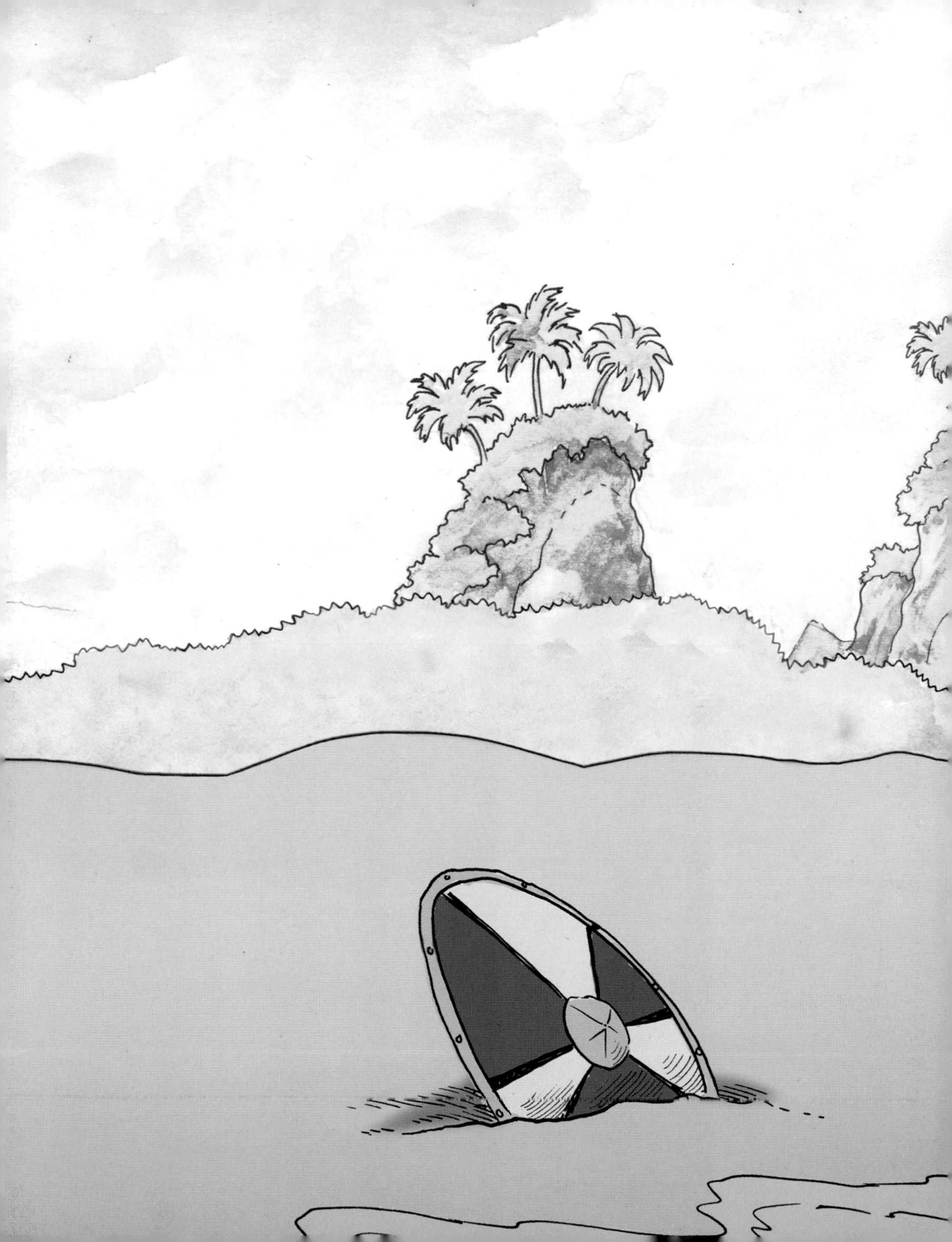

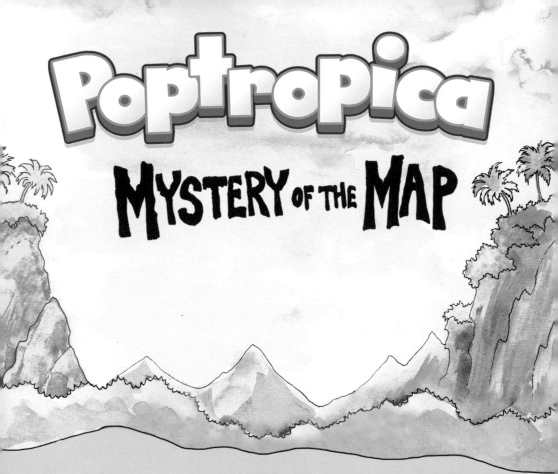

# Poptropica

## MYSTERY OF THE MAP

BY
**JACK CHABERT**
BASED ON A CONCEPT
BY **JEFF KINNEY**

ILLUSTRATED BY
**KORY MERRITT**

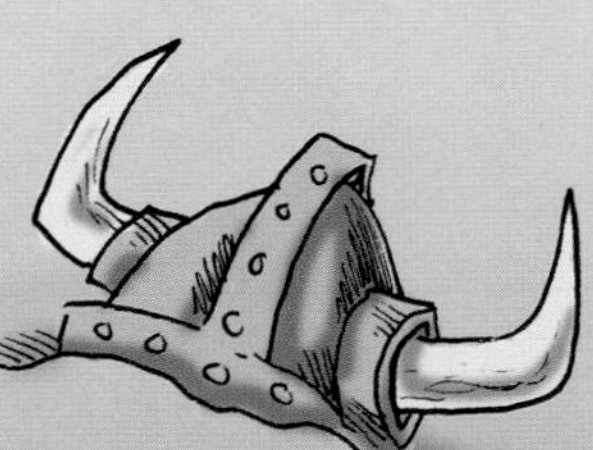

**AMULET BOOKS**
**NEW YORK**

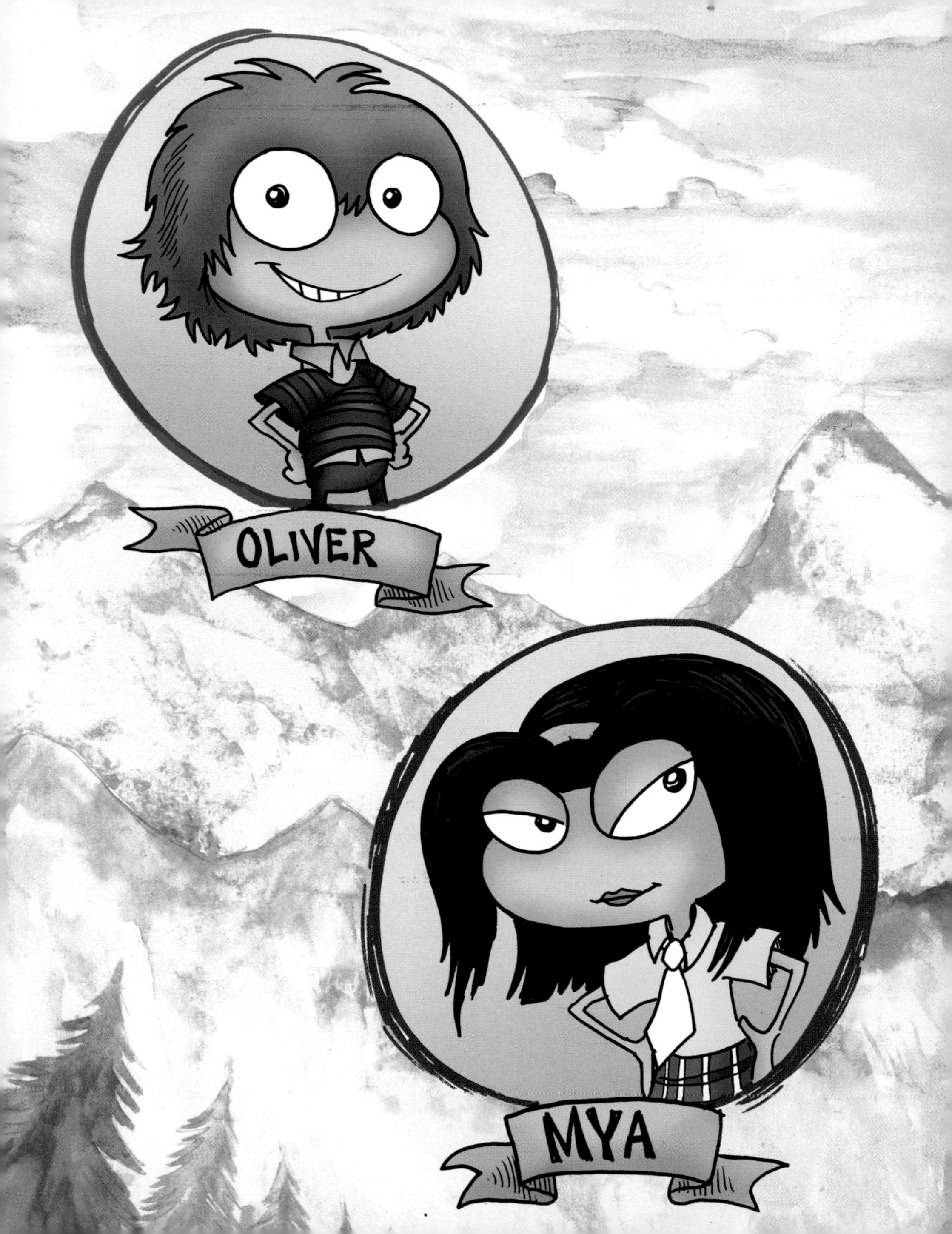
OLIVER
MYA

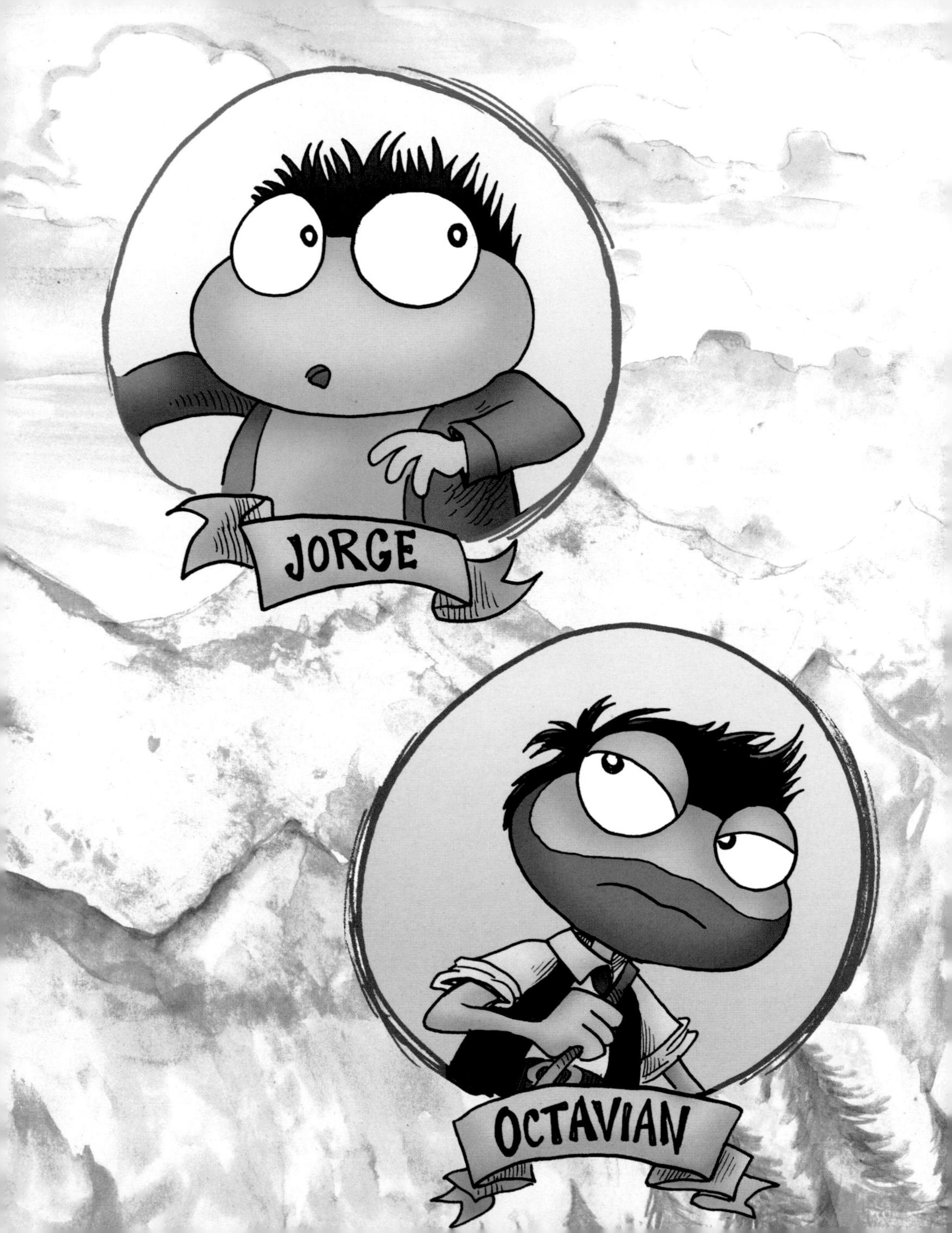
JORGE
OCTAVIAN

# Prologue

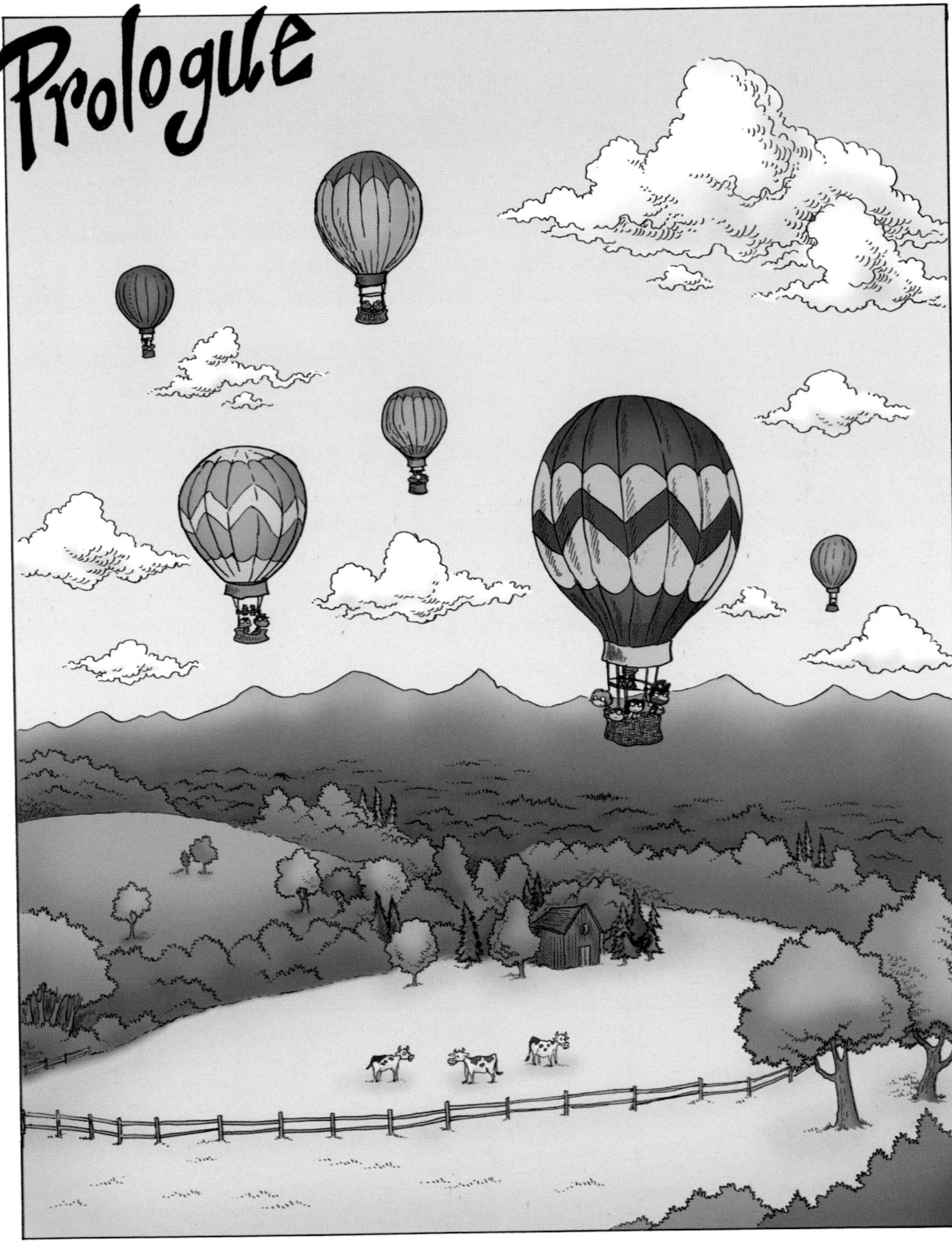

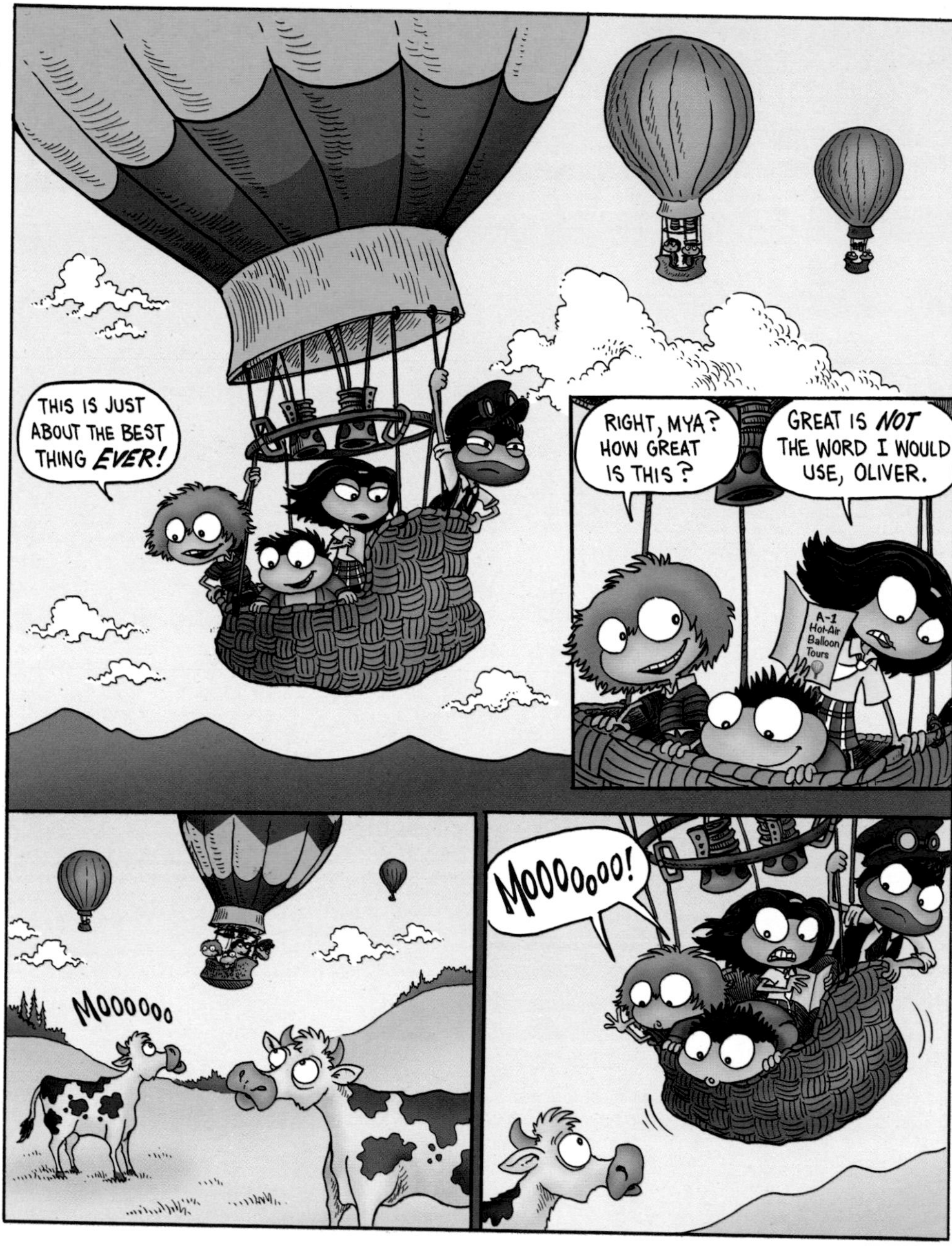

THIS IS JUST ABOUT THE BEST THING EVER!
RIGHT, MYA? HOW GREAT IS THIS?
GREAT IS NOT THE WORD I WOULD USE, OLIVER.
A-1 Hot-Air Balloon Tours
MOOOOOO
MOOOooo!

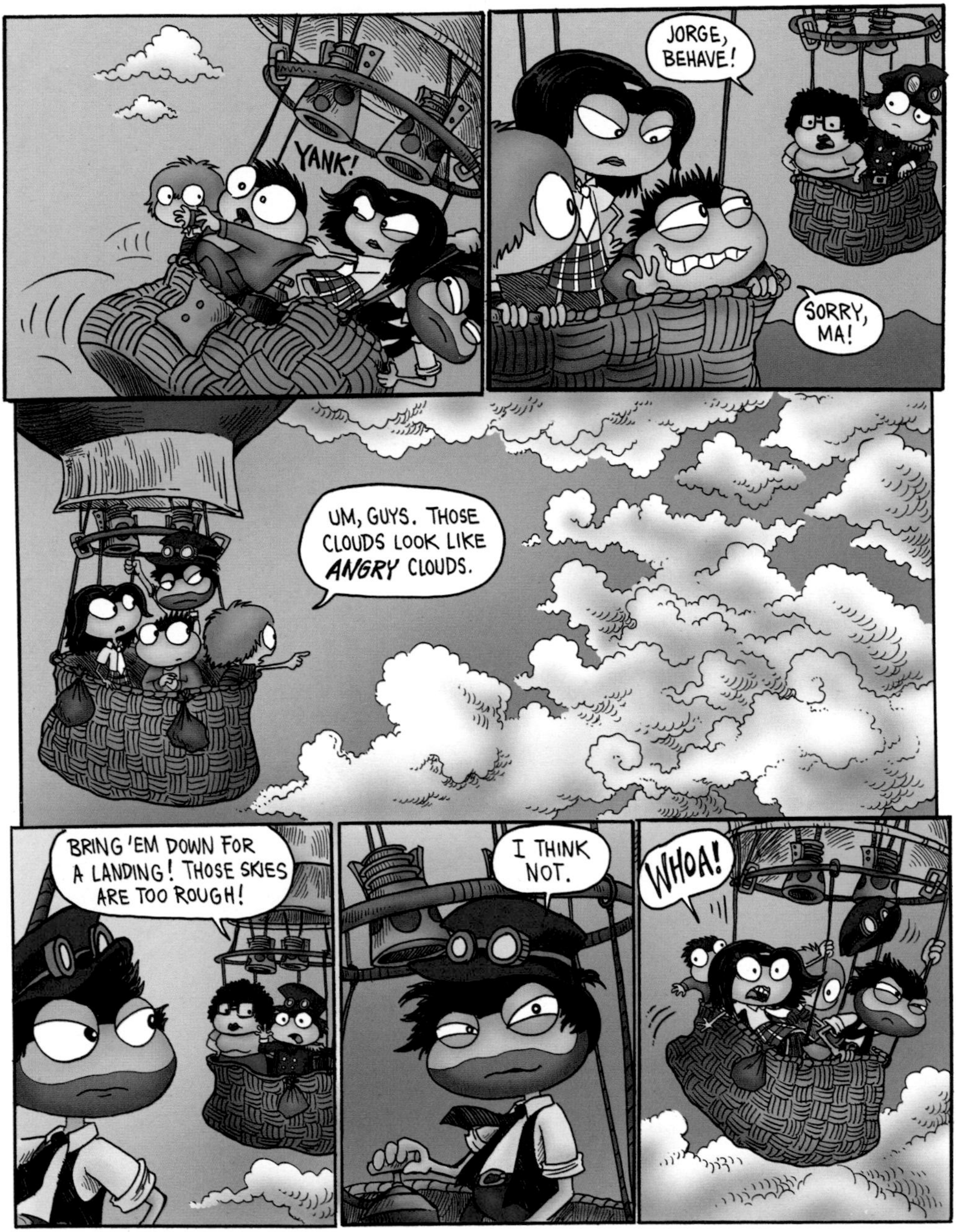
YANK!
JORGE, BEHAVE!
SORRY, MA!
UM, GUYS. THOSE CLOUDS LOOK LIKE ANGRY CLOUDS.
BRING 'EM DOWN FOR A LANDING! THOSE SKIES ARE TOO ROUGH!
I THINK NOT.
WHOA!

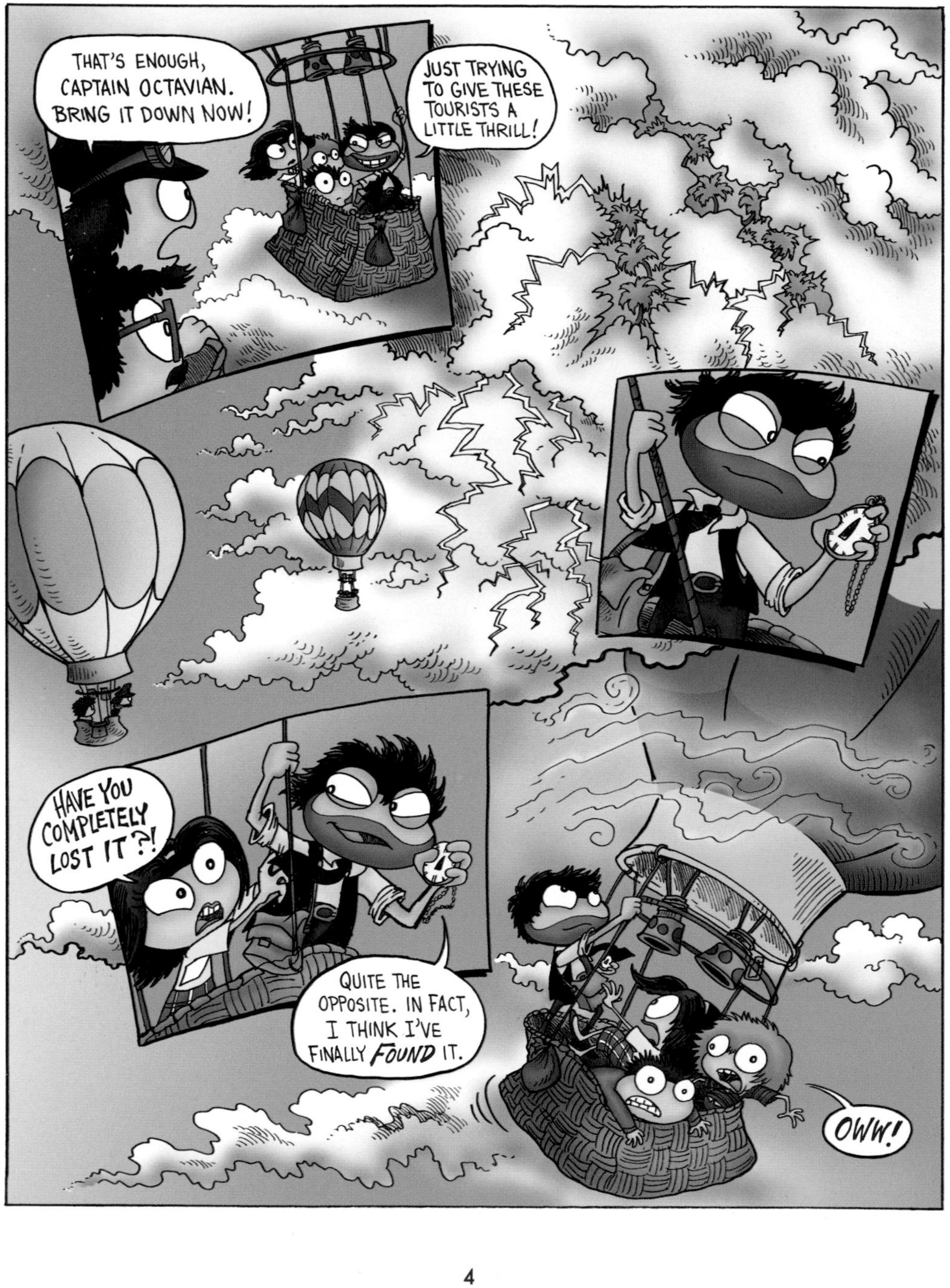
THAT'S ENOUGH, CAPTAIN OCTAVIAN. BRING IT DOWN NOW!
JUST TRYING TO GIVE THESE TOURISTS A LITTLE THRILL!
HAVE YOU COMPLETELY LOST IT?!
QUITE THE OPPOSITE. IN FACT, I THINK I'VE FINALLY FOUND IT.
OWW!

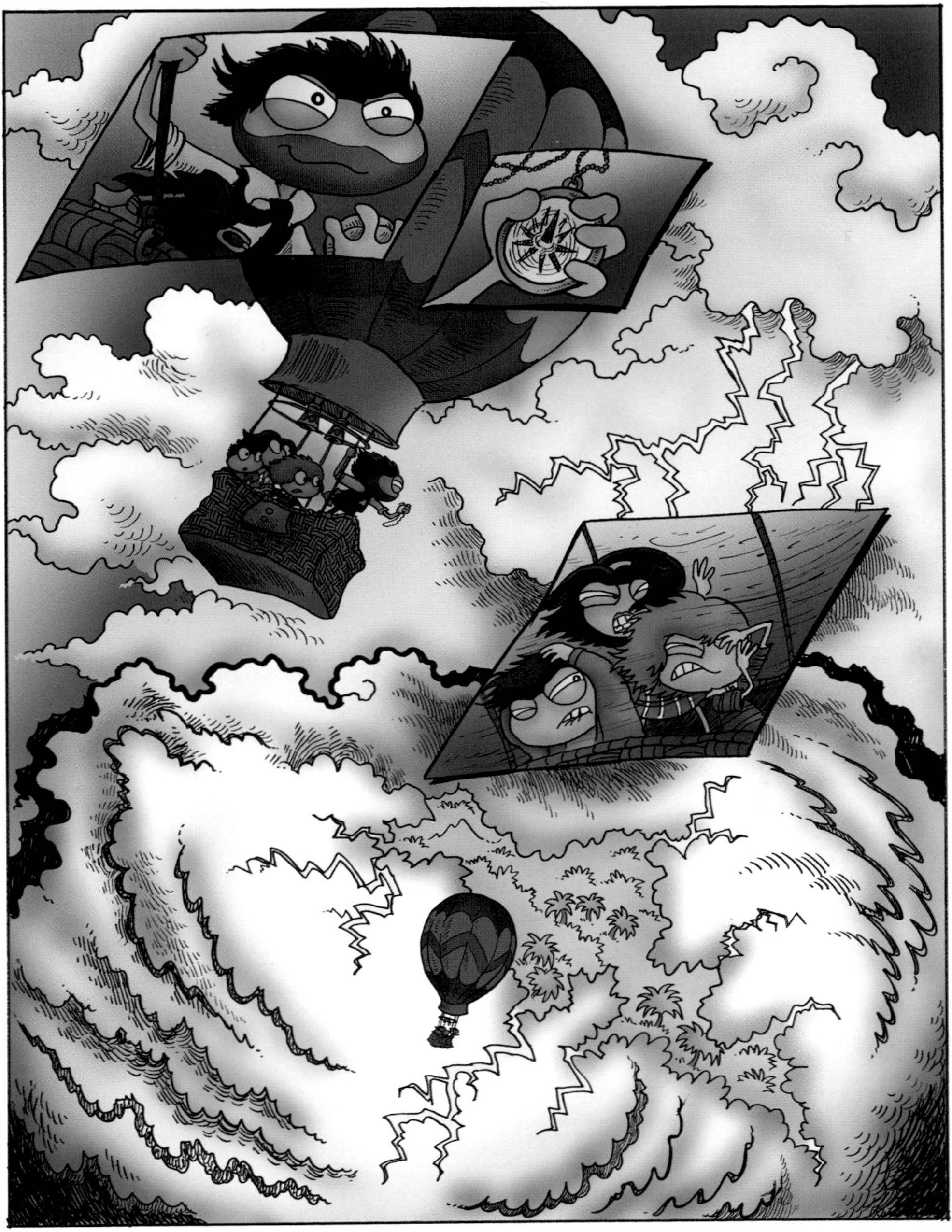

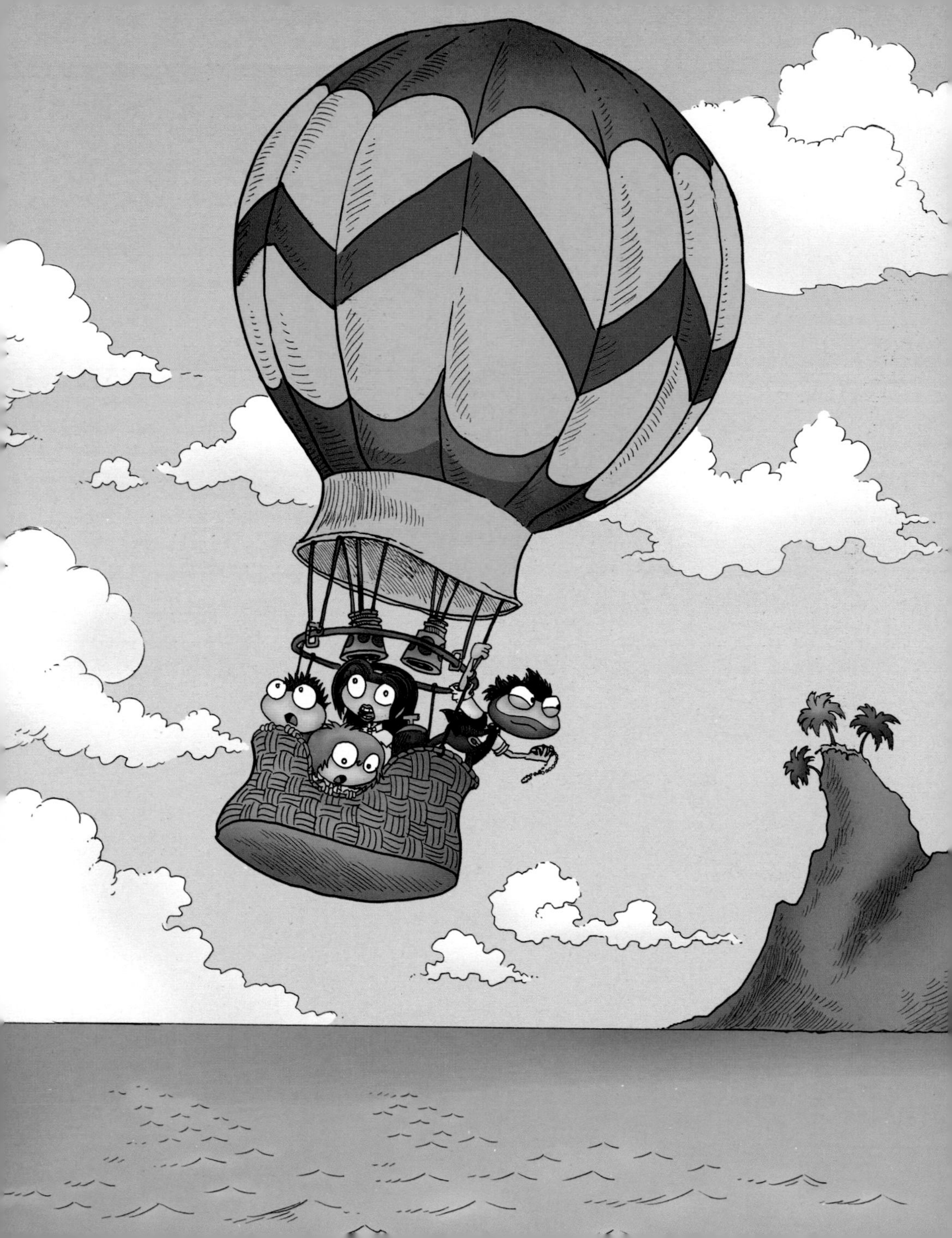

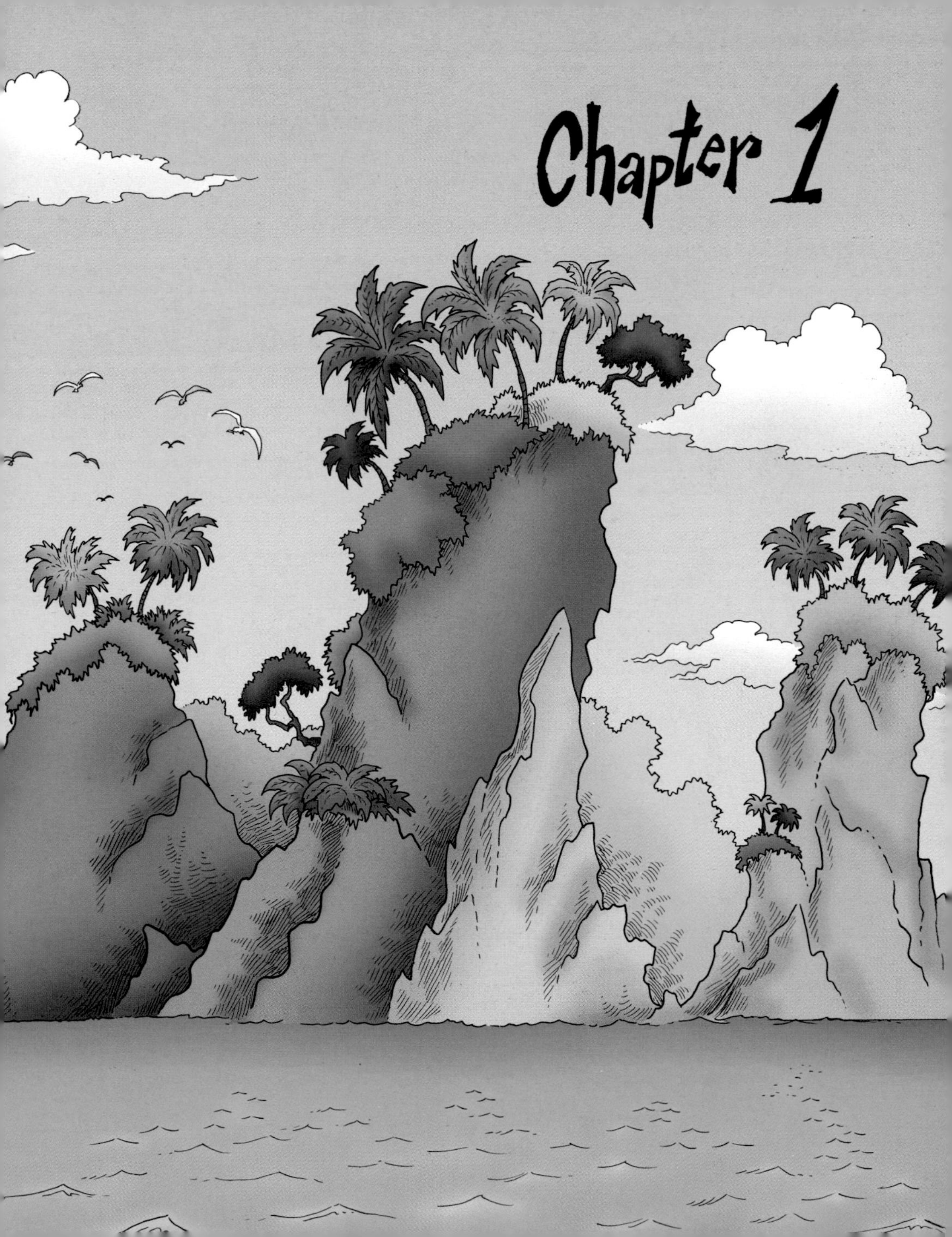
Chapter 1

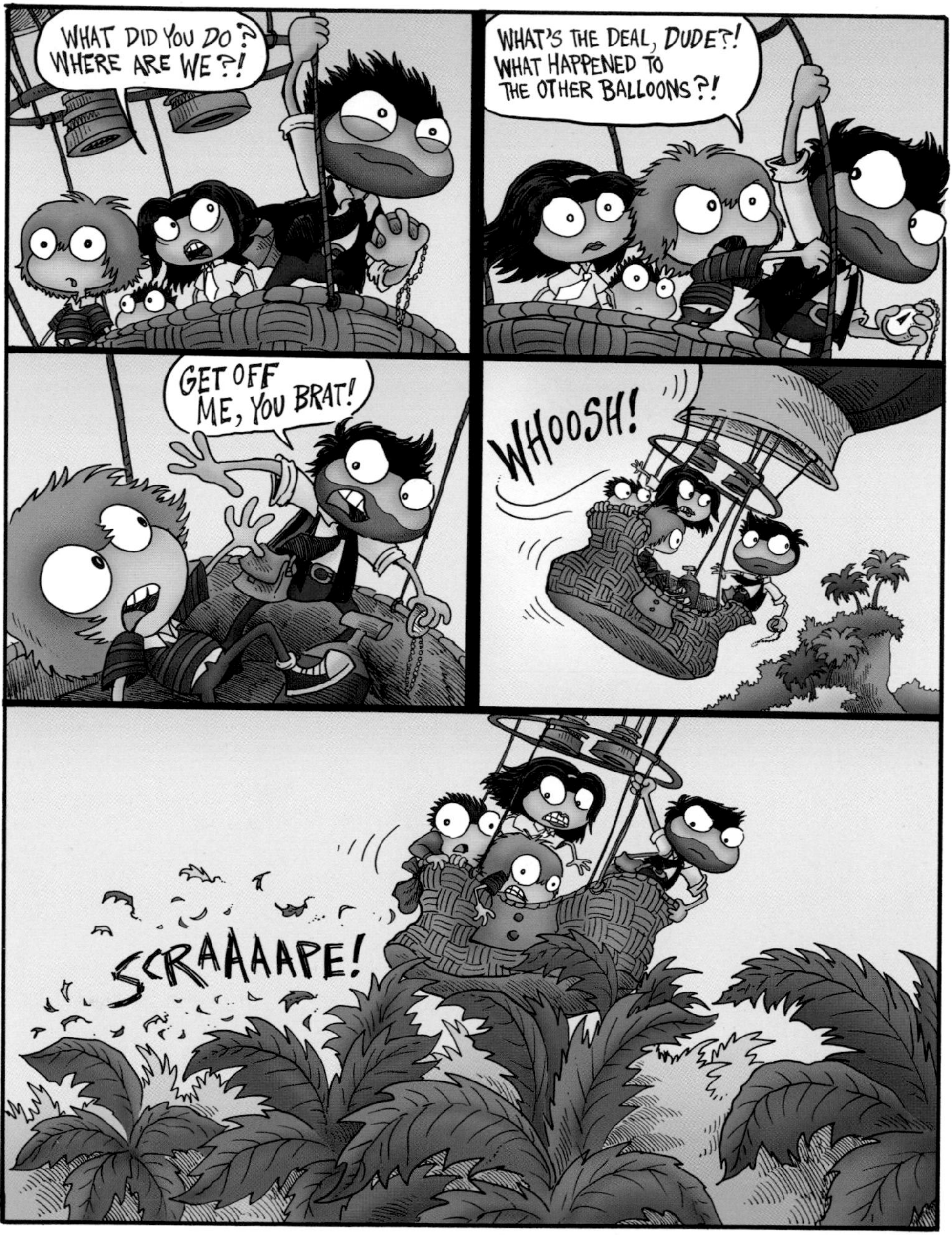
WHAT DID YOU DO?
WHERE ARE WE?!
WHAT'S THE DEAL, DUDE?!
WHAT HAPPENED TO
THE OTHER BALLOONS?!
GET OFF
ME, YOU BRAT!
WHOOSH!
SCRAAAAPE!

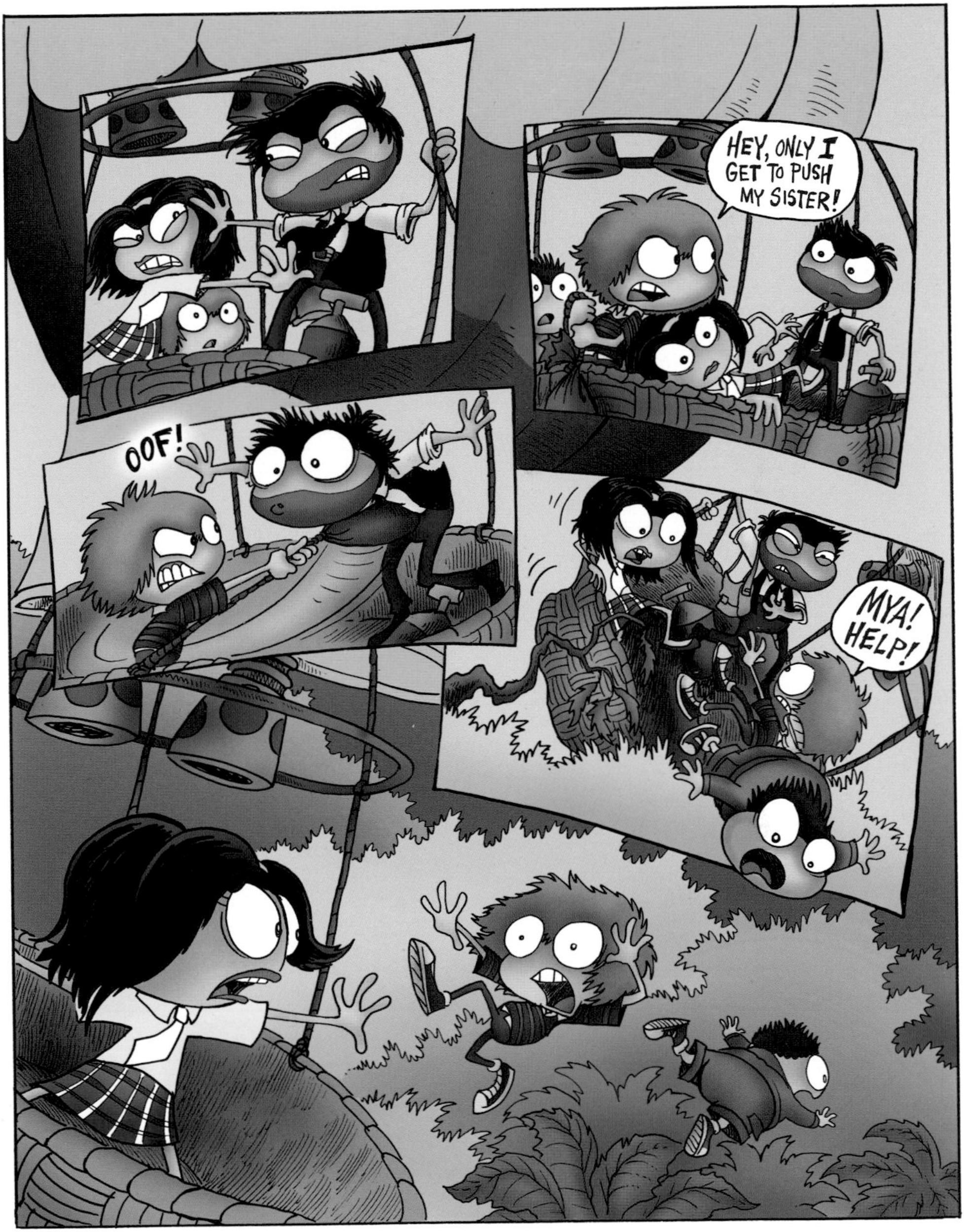
HEY, ONLY I GET TO PUSH MY SISTER!
OOF!
MYA! HELP!

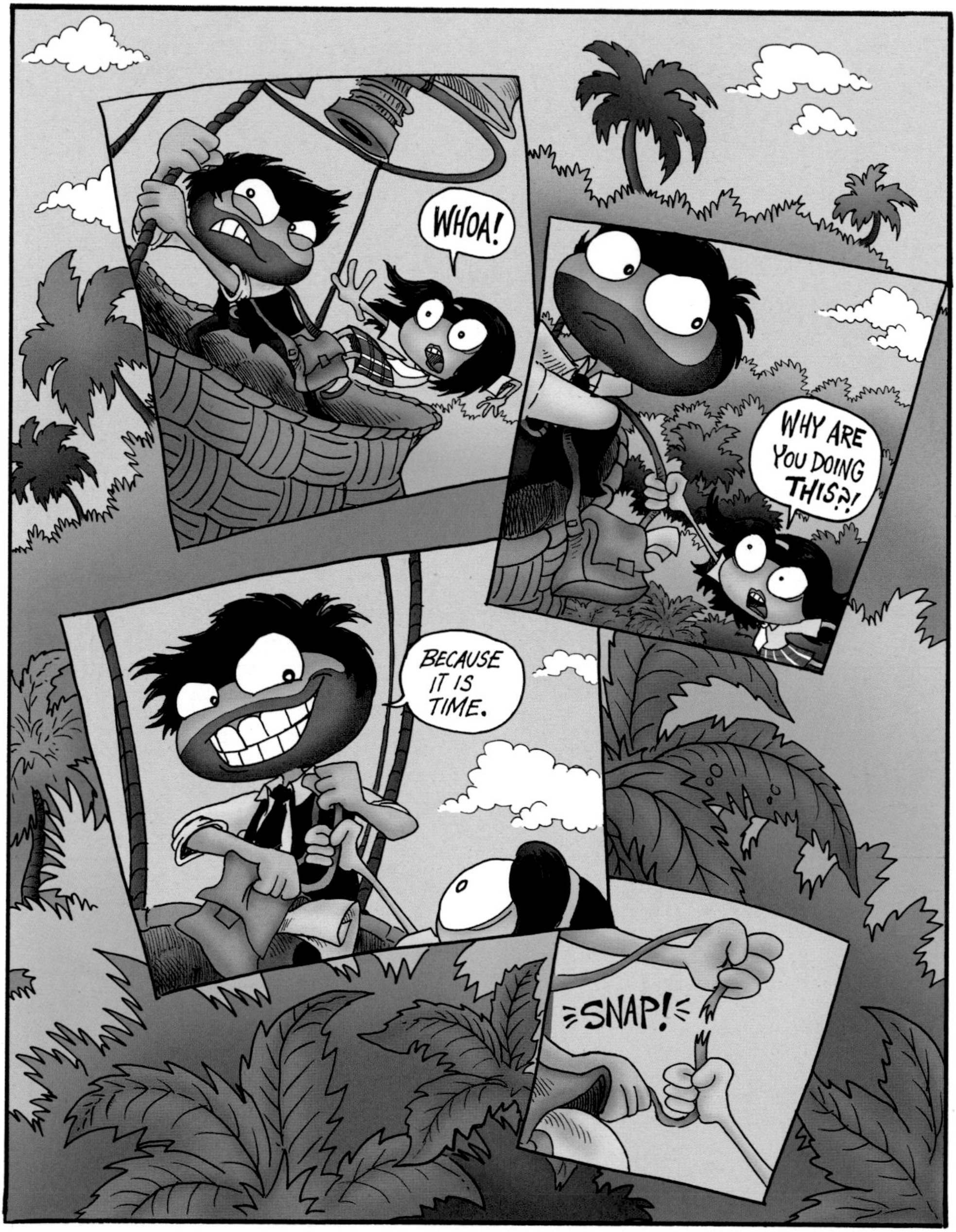
WHOA!
WHY ARE YOU DOING THIS?!
BECAUSE IT IS TIME.
SNAP!

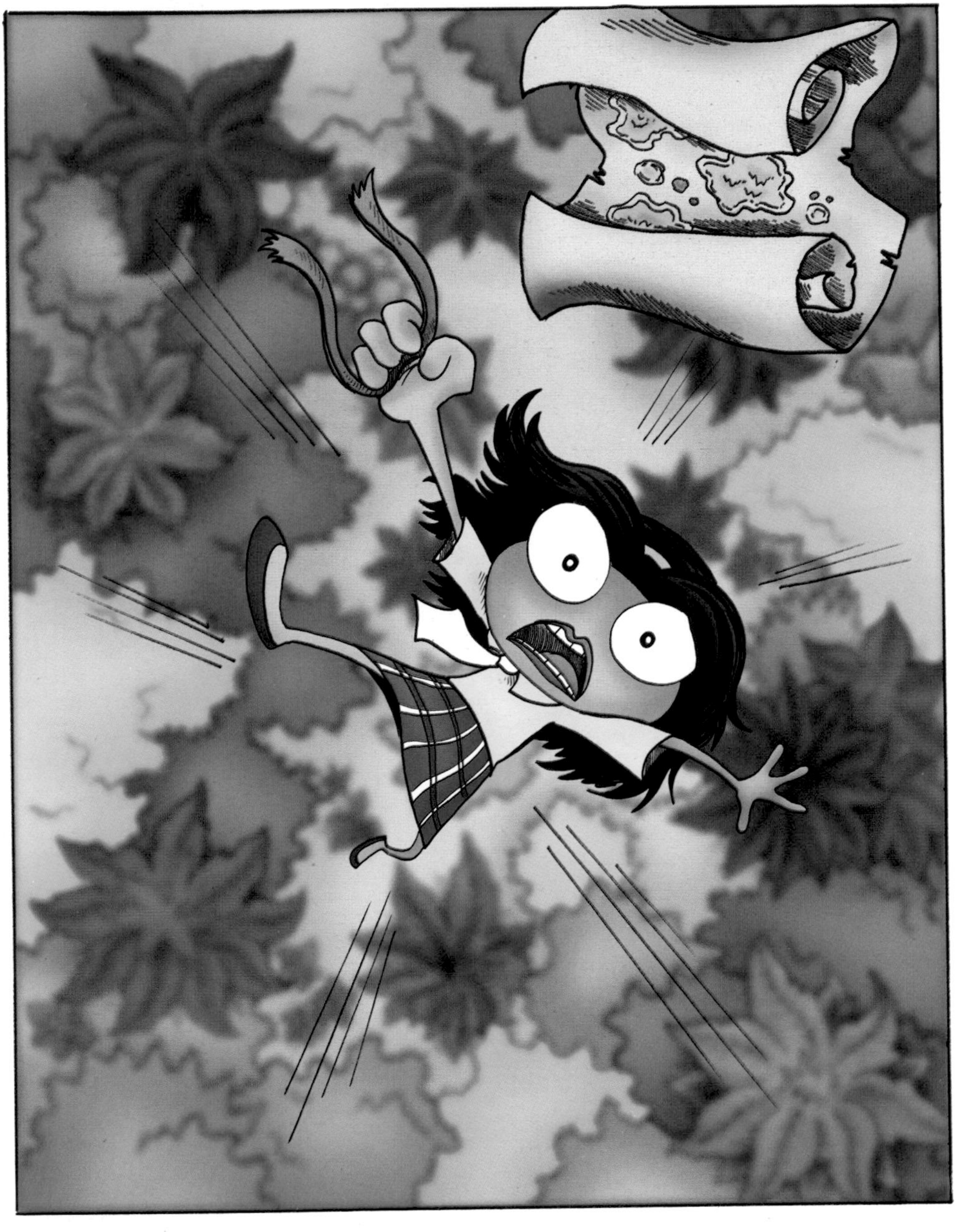

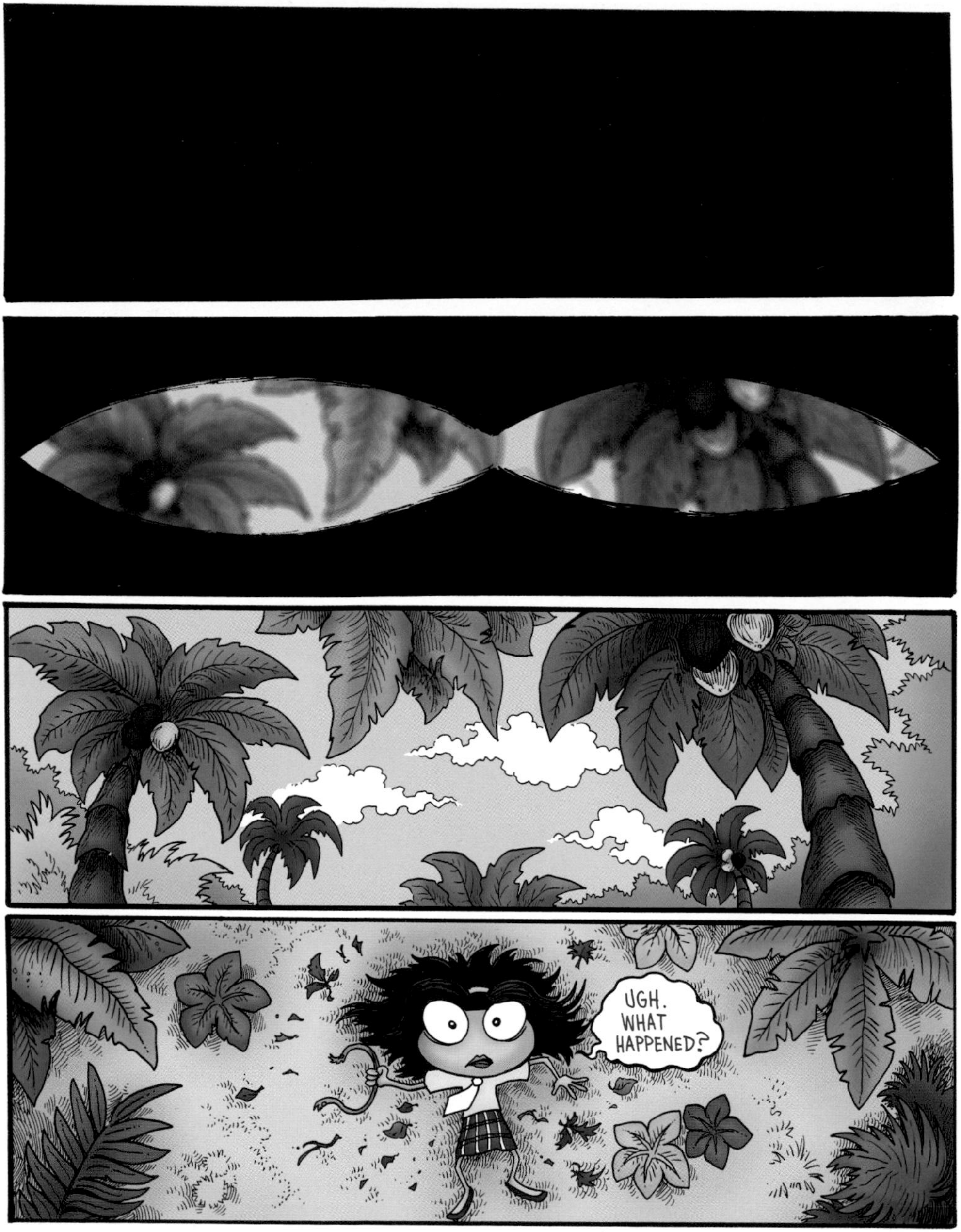
UGH. WHAT HAPPENED?

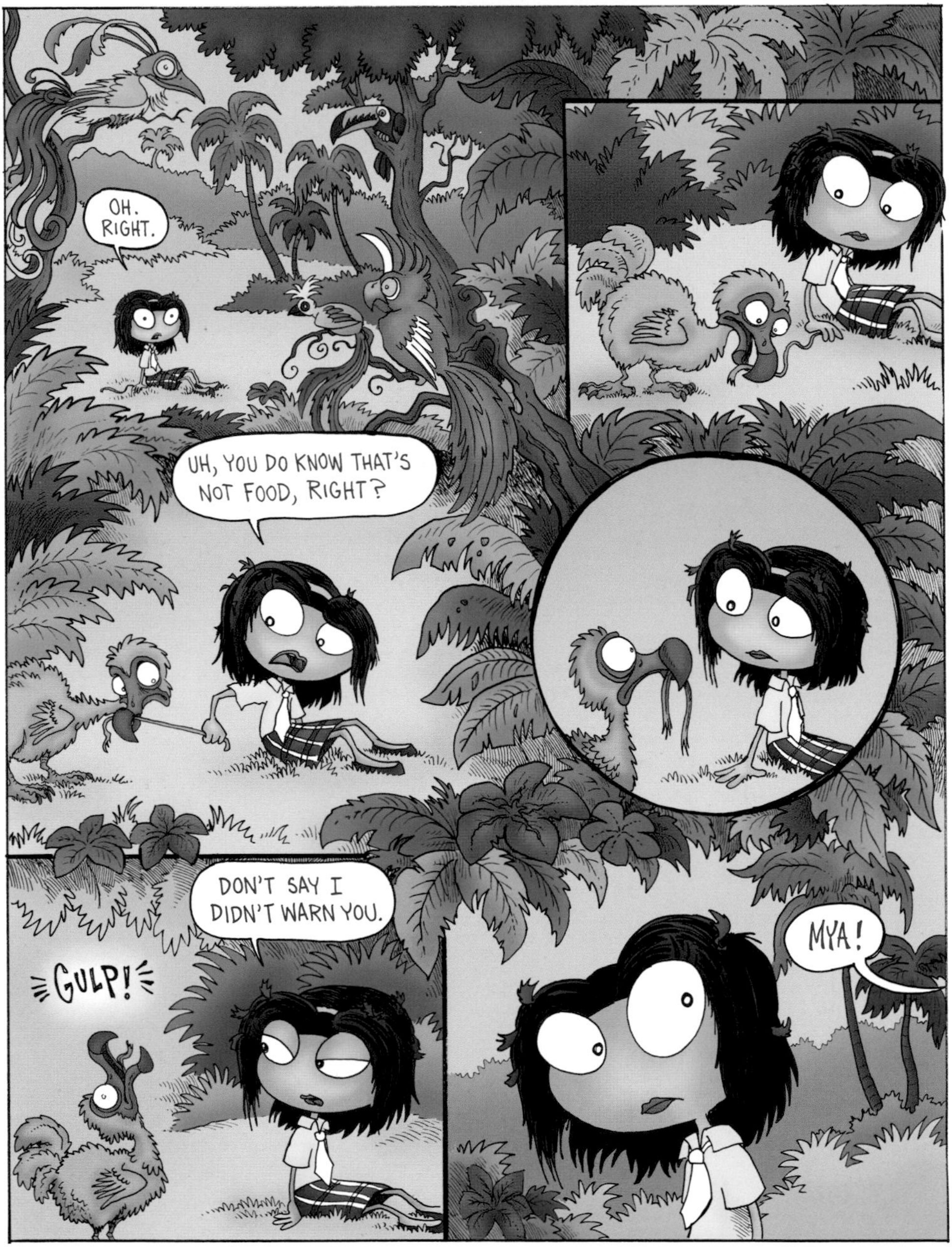
OH. RIGHT.
UH, YOU DO KNOW THAT'S NOT FOOD, RIGHT?
DON'T SAY I DIDN'T WARN YOU.
GULP!
MYA!

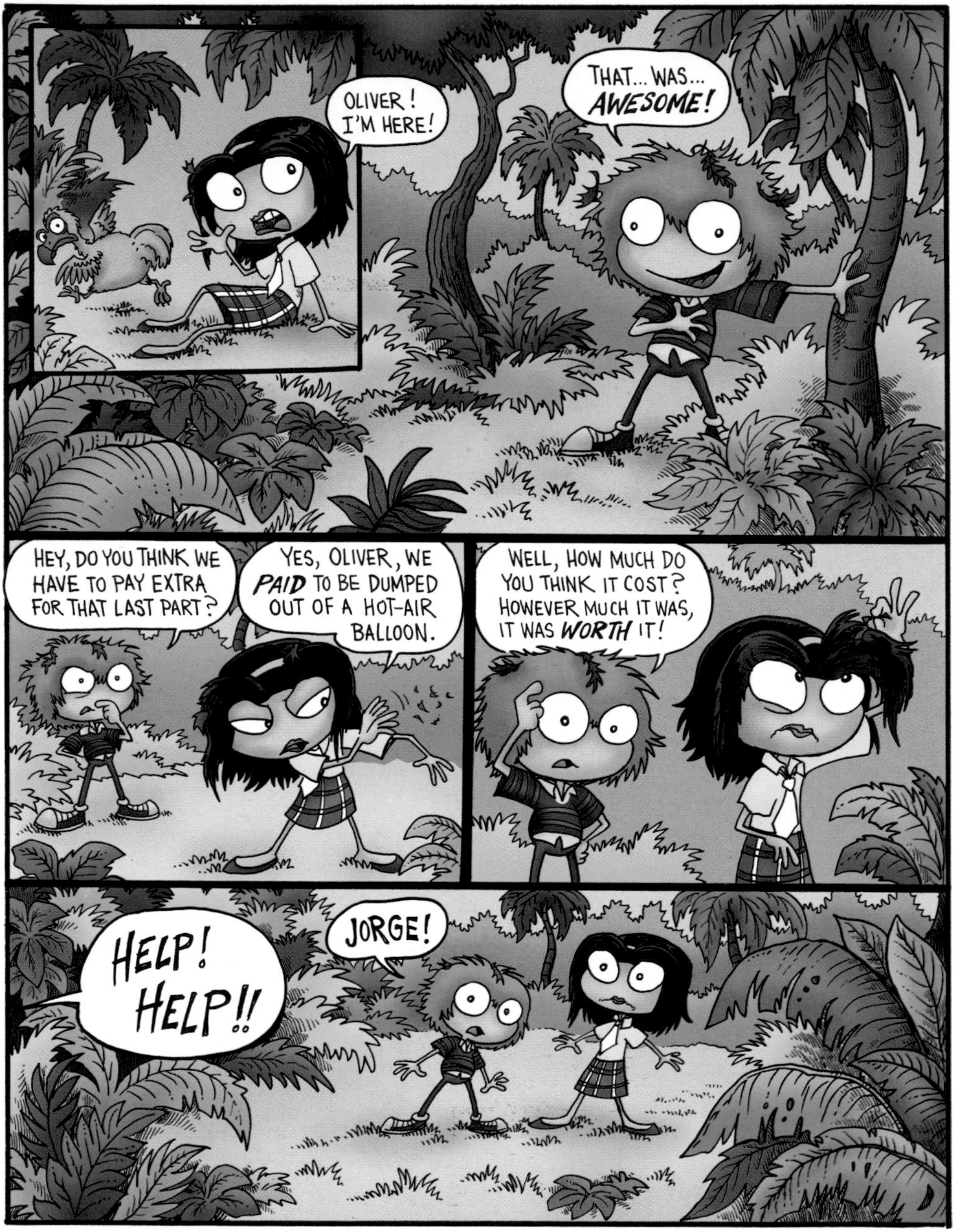
OLIVER! I'M HERE!
THAT... WAS... AWESOME!
HEY, DO YOU THINK WE HAVE TO PAY EXTRA FOR THAT LAST PART?
YES, OLIVER, WE PAID TO BE DUMPED OUT OF A HOT-AIR BALLOON.
WELL, HOW MUCH DO YOU THINK IT COST? HOWEVER MUCH IT WAS, IT WAS WORTH IT!
HELP! HELP!!
JORGE!

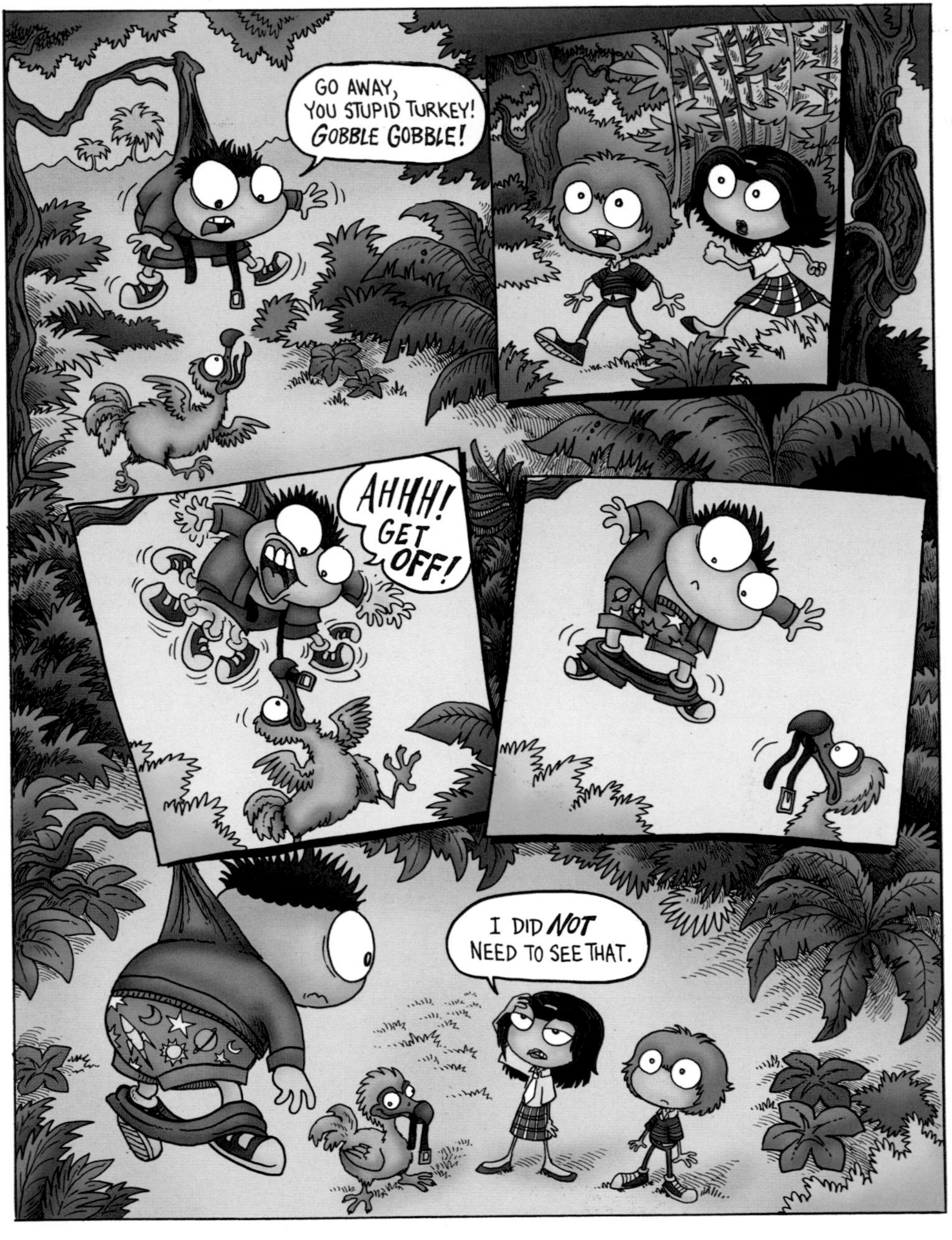
GO AWAY, YOU STUPID TURKEY! GOBBLE GOBBLE!
AHHH! GET OFF!
I DID NOT NEED TO SEE THAT.

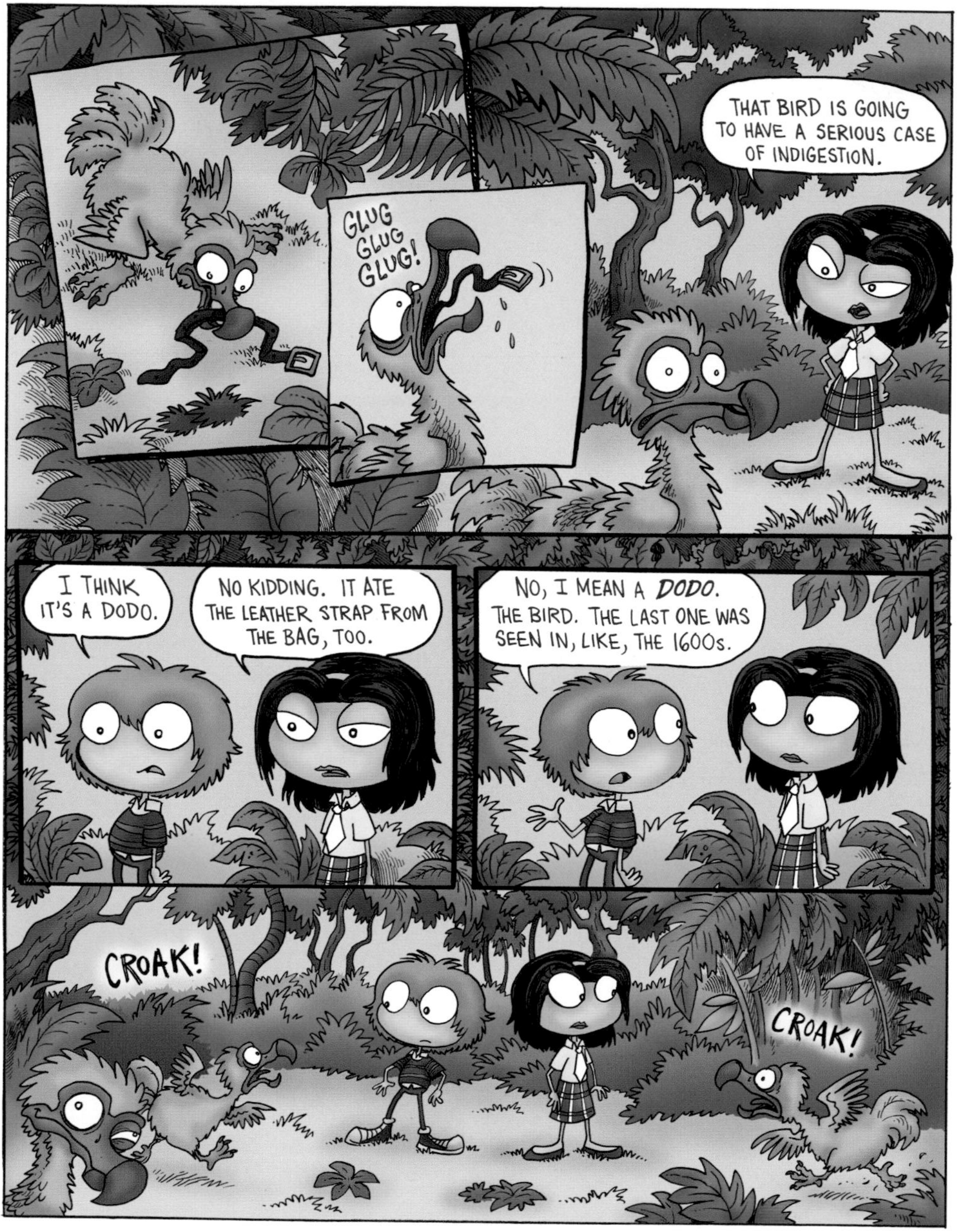
GLUG GLUG GLUG!
THAT BIRD IS GOING TO HAVE A SERIOUS CASE OF INDIGESTION.
I THINK IT'S A DODO.
NO KIDDING. IT ATE THE LEATHER STRAP FROM THE BAG, TOO.
NO, I MEAN A *DODO*. THE BIRD. THE LAST ONE WAS SEEN IN, LIKE, THE 1600s.
CROAK!
CROAK!

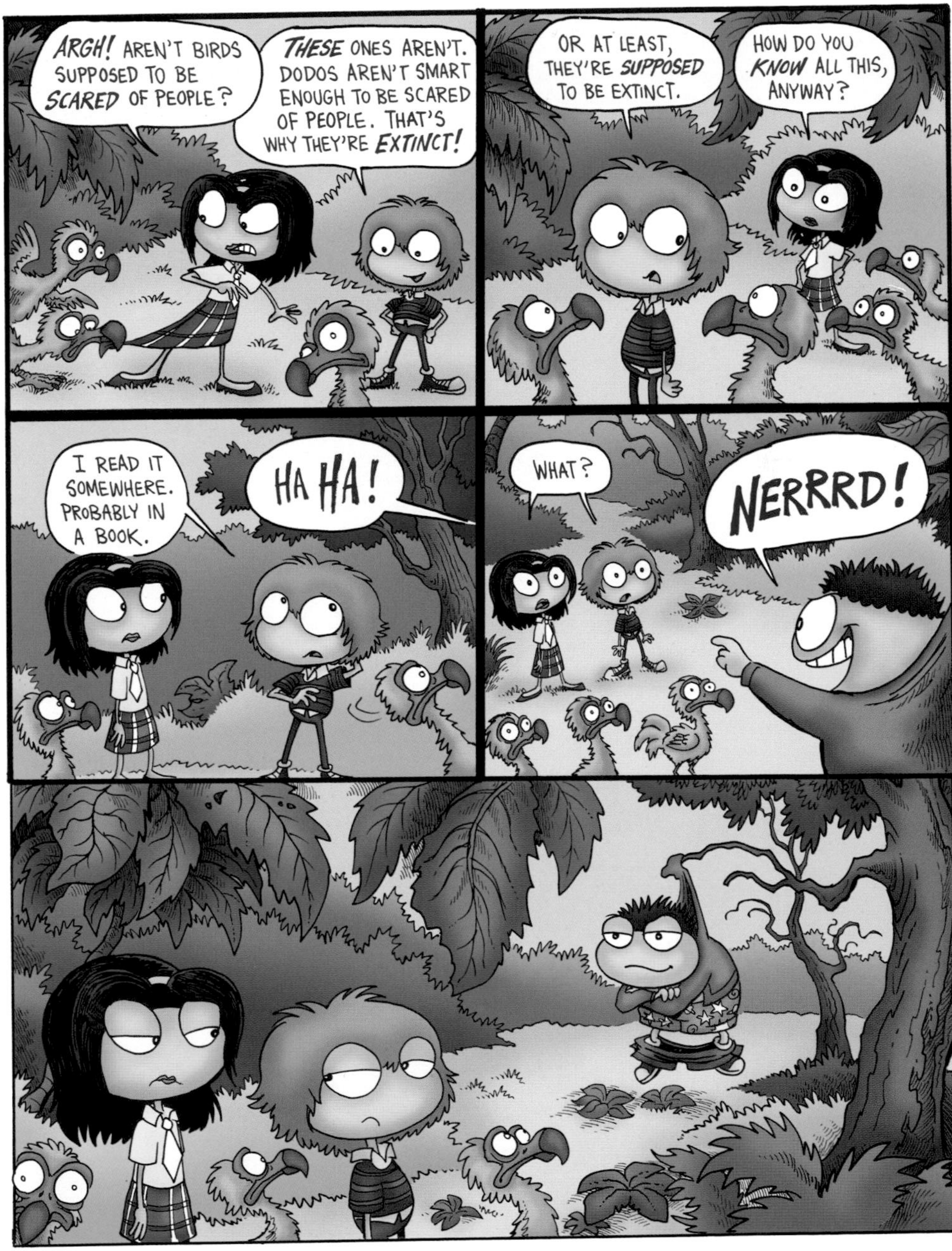
ARGH! AREN'T BIRDS SUPPOSED TO BE SCARED OF PEOPLE?
THESE ONES AREN'T. DODOS AREN'T SMART ENOUGH TO BE SCARED OF PEOPLE. THAT'S WHY THEY'RE EXTINCT!
OR AT LEAST, THEY'RE SUPPOSED TO BE EXTINCT.
HOW DO YOU KNOW ALL THIS, ANYWAY?
I READ IT SOMEWHERE. PROBABLY IN A BOOK.
HA HA!
WHAT?
NERRRD!

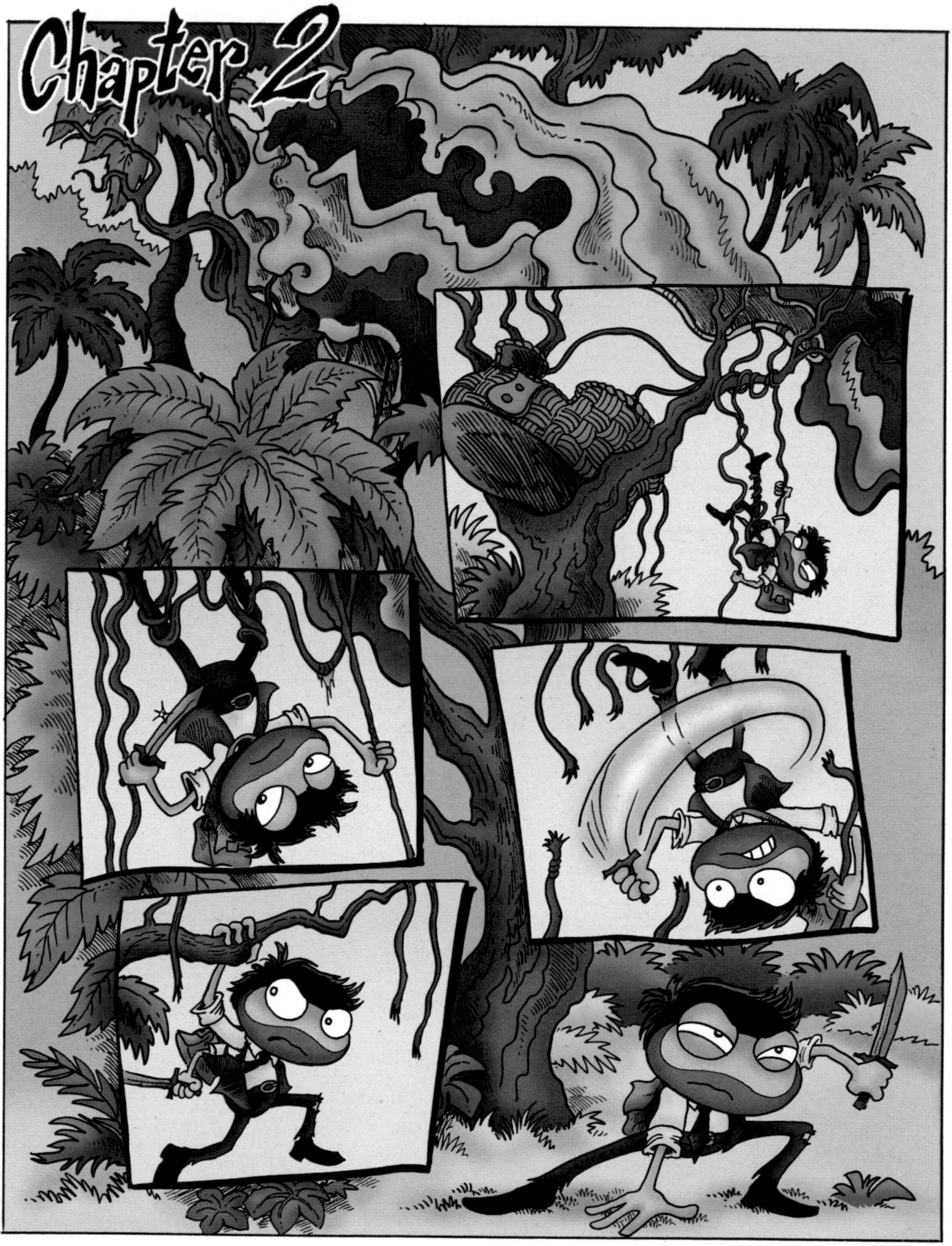
Chapter 2

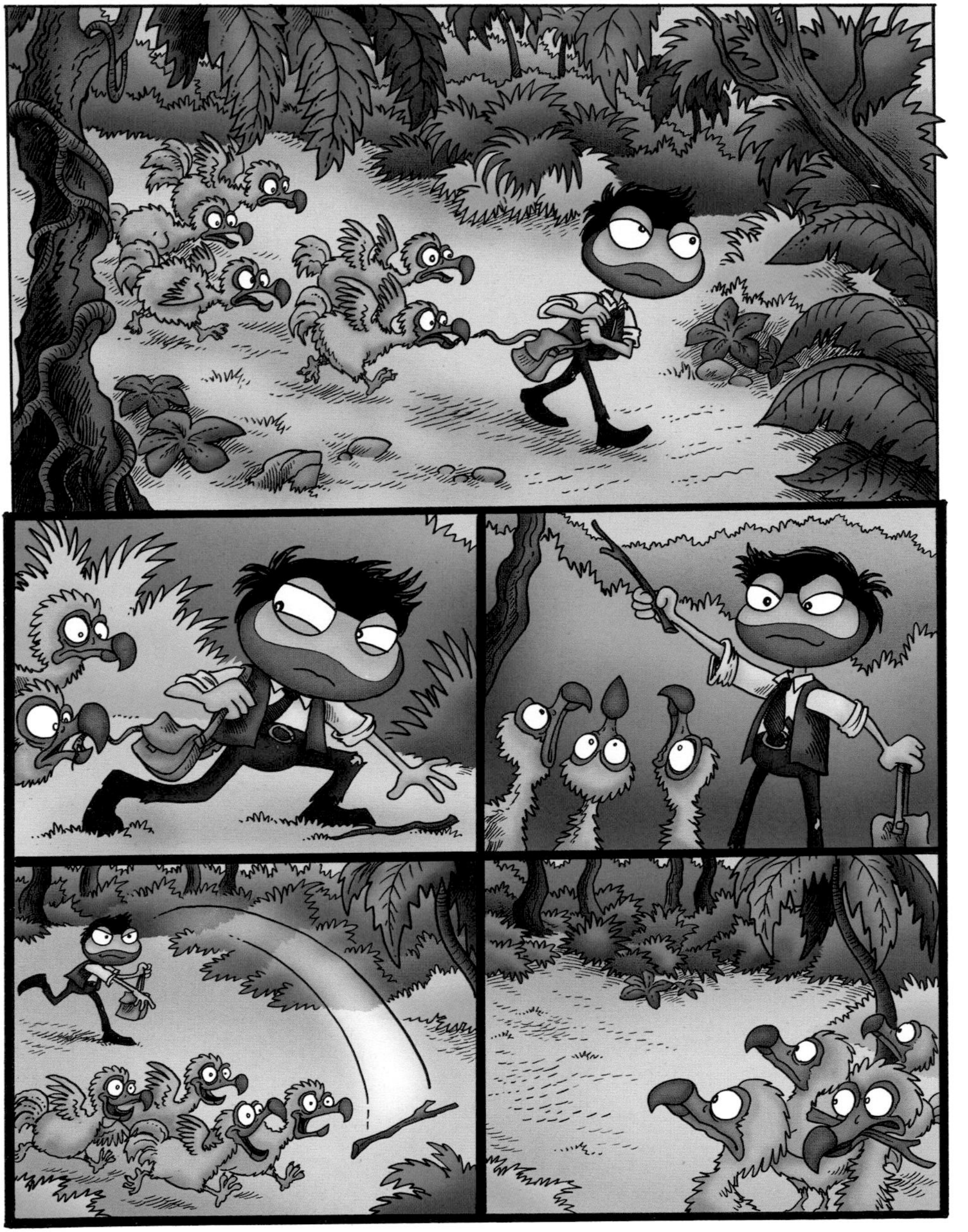

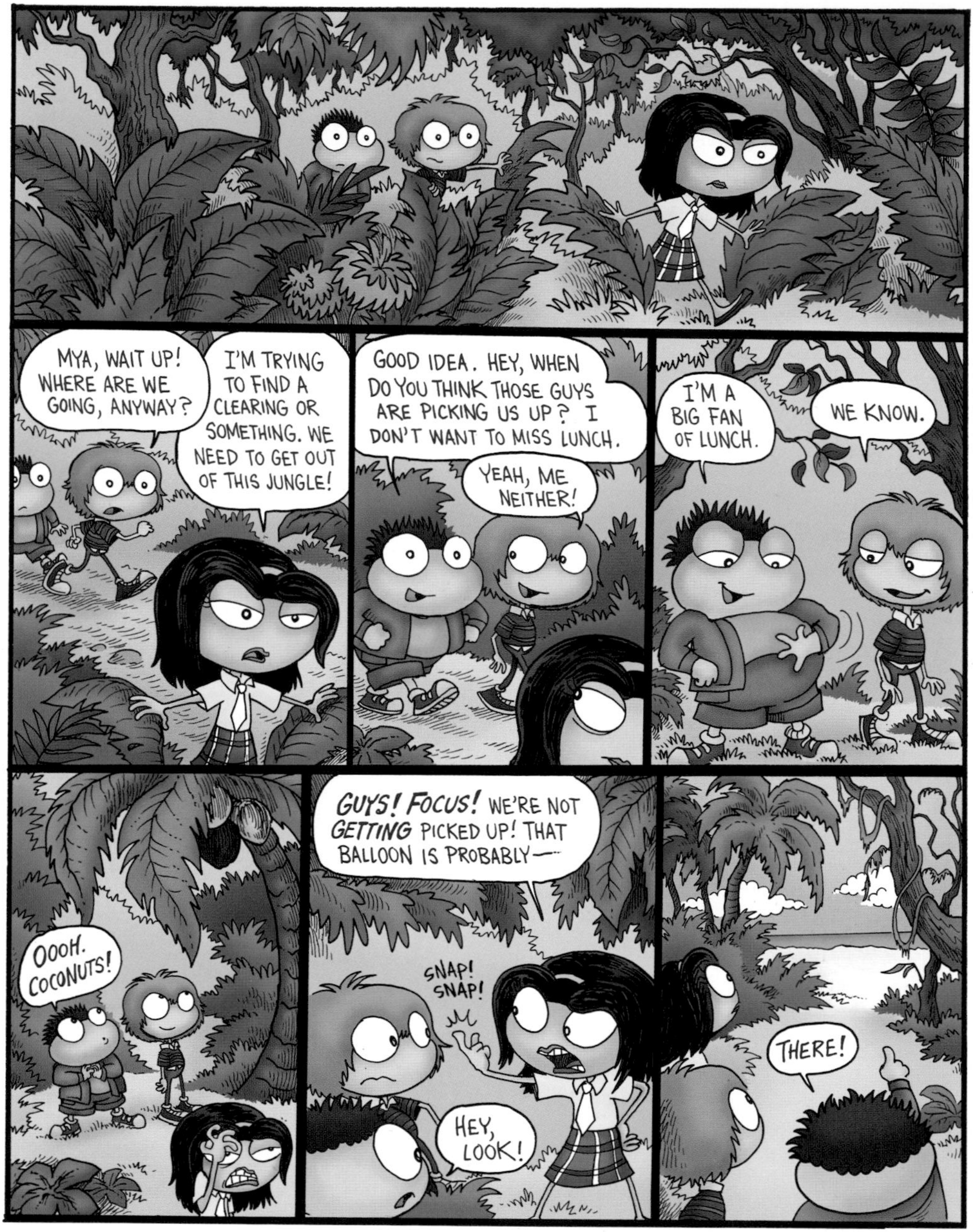
MYA, WAIT UP! WHERE ARE WE GOING, ANYWAY?
I'M TRYING TO FIND A CLEARING OR SOMETHING. WE NEED TO GET OUT OF THIS JUNGLE!
GOOD IDEA. HEY, WHEN DO YOU THINK THOSE GUYS ARE PICKING US UP? I DON'T WANT TO MISS LUNCH.
YEAH, ME NEITHER!
I'M A BIG FAN OF LUNCH.
WE KNOW.
OOOH. COCONUTS!
GUYS! FOCUS! WE'RE NOT GETTING PICKED UP! THAT BALLOON IS PROBABLY—
SNAP! SNAP!
HEY, LOOK!
THERE!

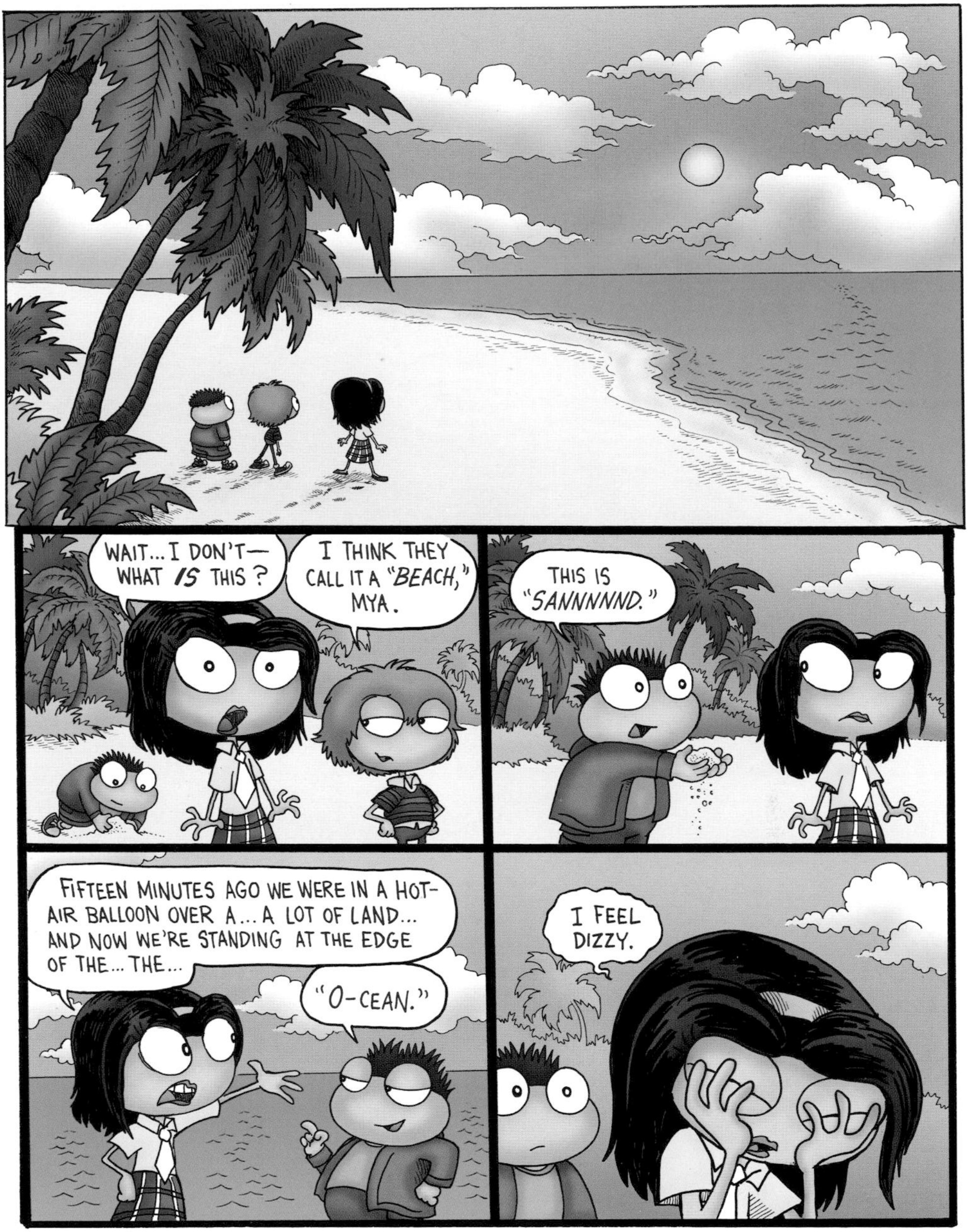
WAIT... I DON'T— WHAT *IS* THIS?
I THINK THEY CALL IT A "*BEACH*," MYA.
THIS IS "*SANNNNND.*"
FIFTEEN MINUTES AGO WE WERE IN A HOT-AIR BALLOON OVER A... A LOT OF LAND... AND NOW WE'RE STANDING AT THE EDGE OF THE... THE...
"O-CEAN."
I FEEL DIZZY.

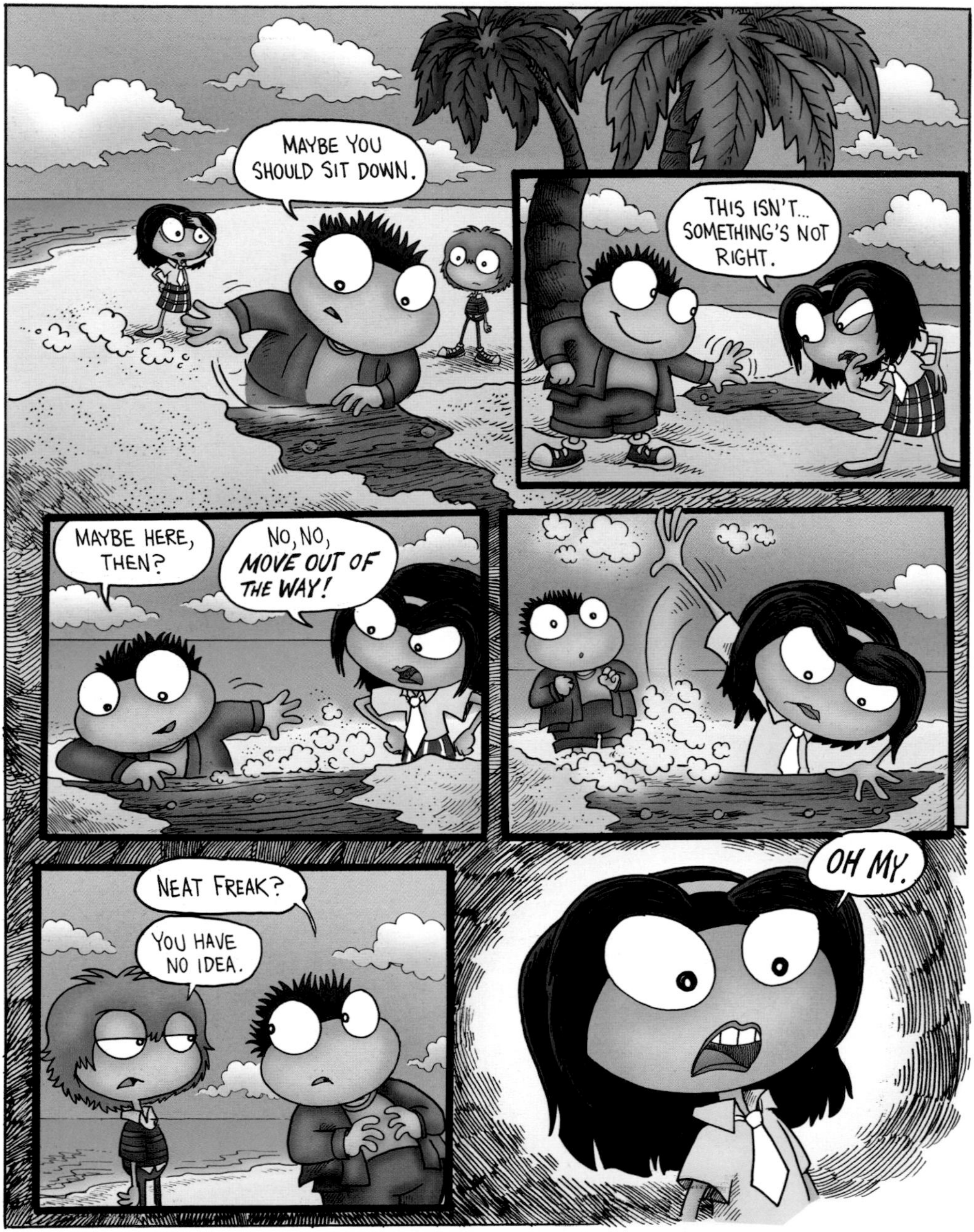
MAYBE YOU SHOULD SIT DOWN.
THIS ISN'T... SOMETHING'S NOT RIGHT.
MAYBE HERE, THEN?
NO, NO, MOVE OUT OF THE WAY!
NEAT FREAK?
YOU HAVE NO IDEA.
OH MY.

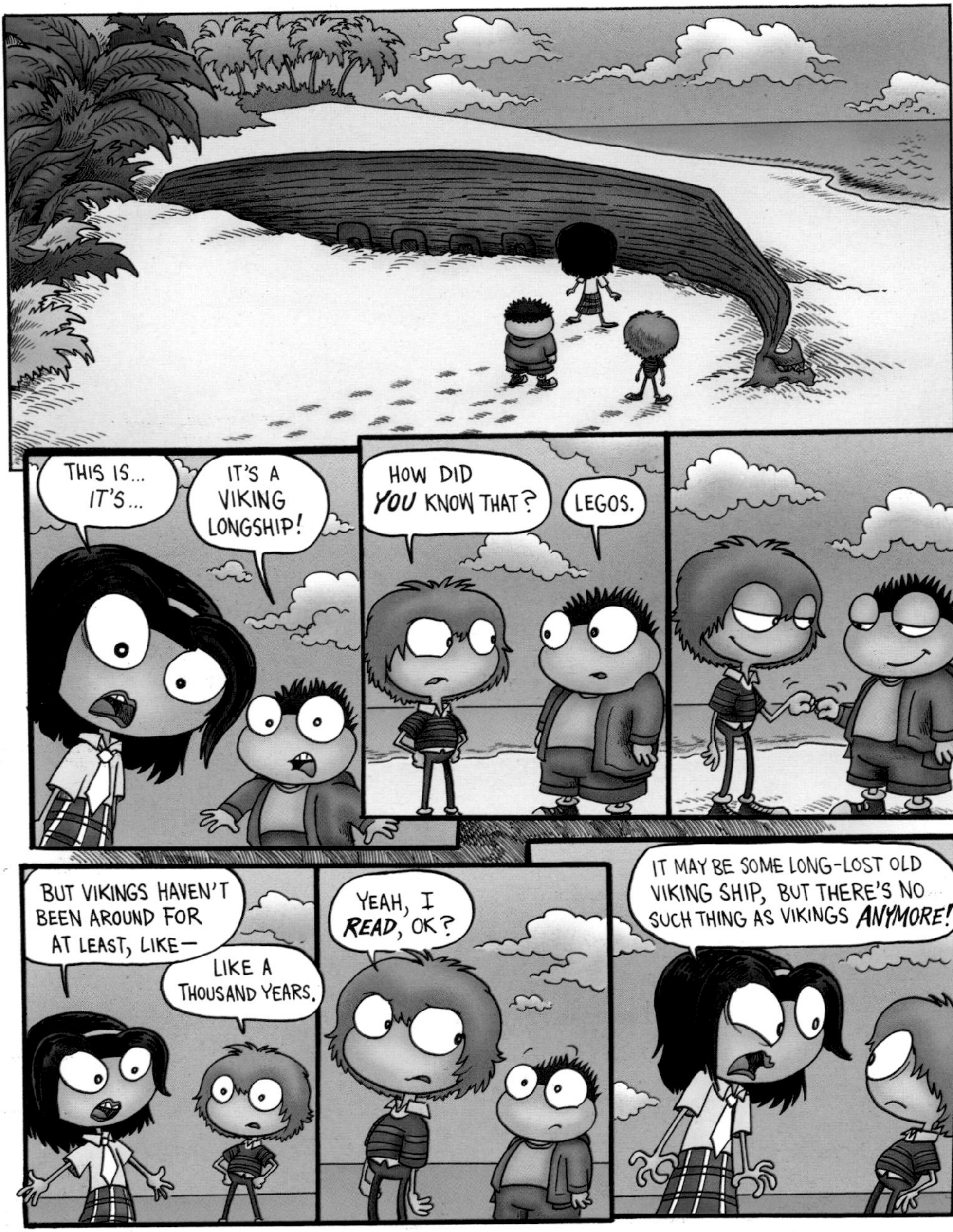
THIS IS... IT'S...
IT'S A VIKING LONGSHIP!
HOW DID YOU KNOW THAT?
LEGOS.
BUT VIKINGS HAVEN'T BEEN AROUND FOR AT LEAST, LIKE—
LIKE A THOUSAND YEARS.
YEAH, I READ, OK?
IT MAY BE SOME LONG-LOST OLD VIKING SHIP, BUT THERE'S NO SUCH THING AS VIKINGS ANYMORE!

# Chapter 3

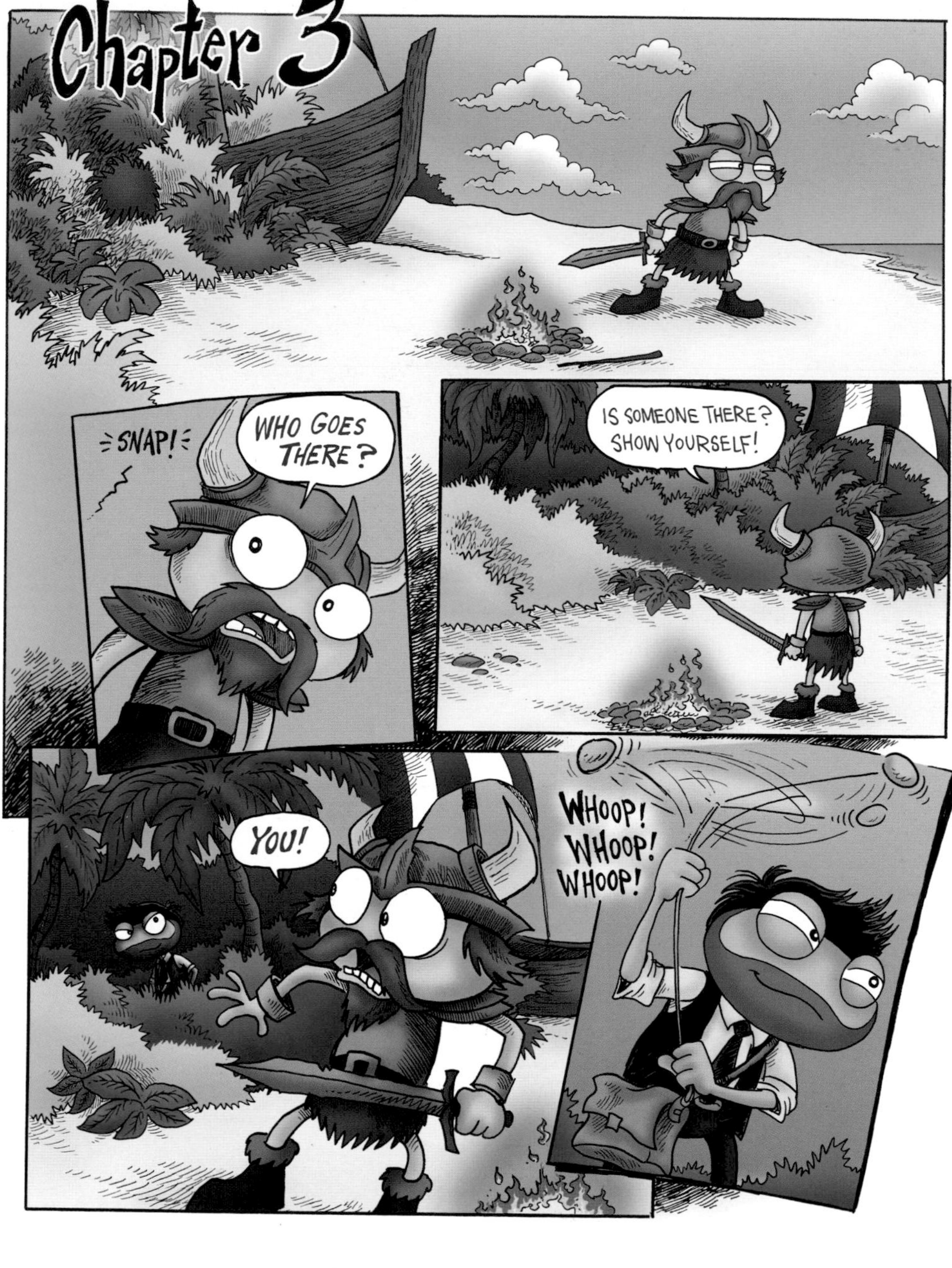

SNAP!
WHO GOES THERE?
IS SOMEONE THERE? SHOW YOURSELF!
YOU!
WHOOP! WHOOP! WHOOP!

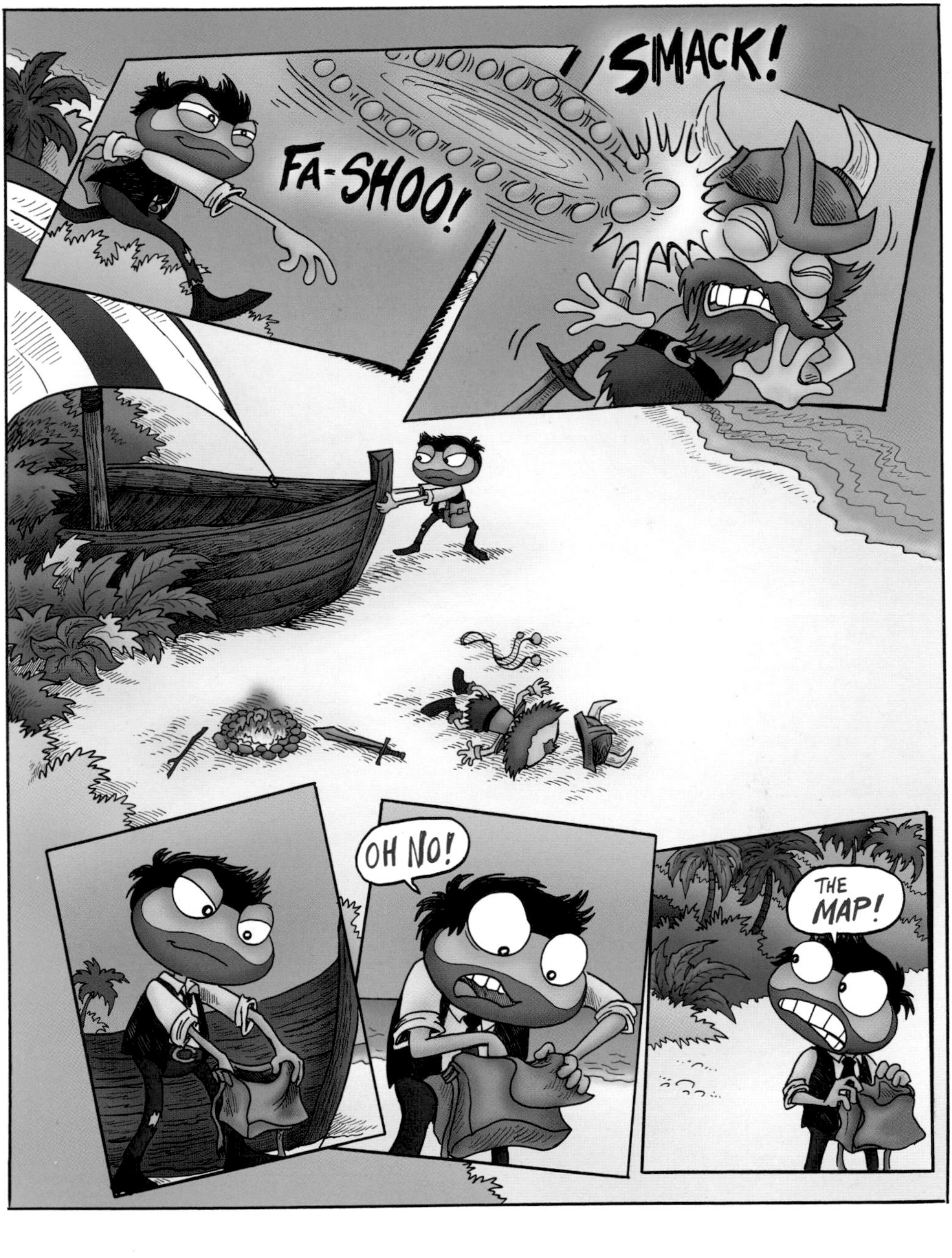
FA-SHOO!
SMACK!
OH NO!
THE MAP!

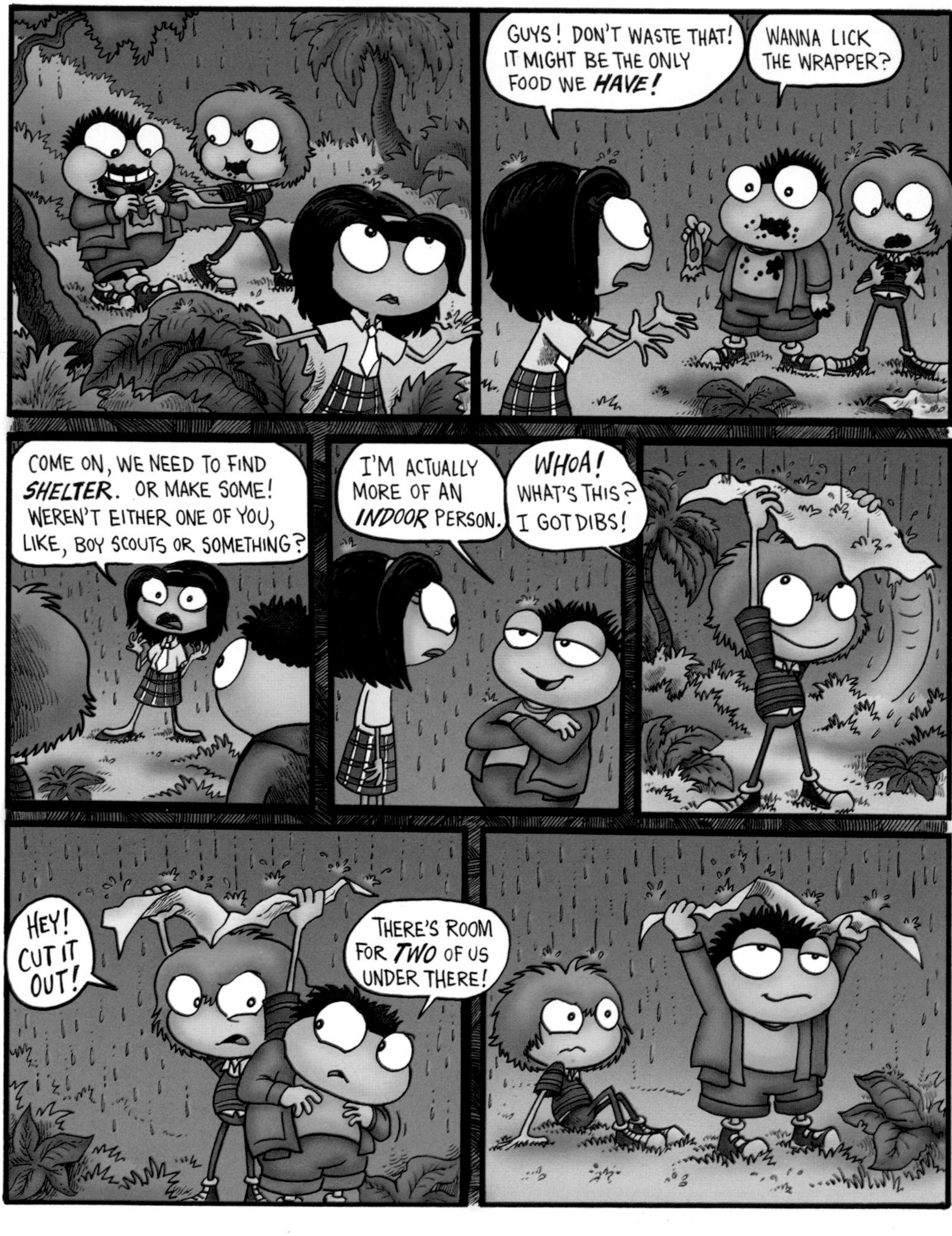
GUYS! DON'T WASTE THAT! IT MIGHT BE THE ONLY FOOD WE HAVE!
WANNA LICK THE WRAPPER?
COME ON, WE NEED TO FIND SHELTER. OR MAKE SOME! WEREN'T EITHER ONE OF YOU, LIKE, BOY SCOUTS OR SOMETHING?
I'M ACTUALLY MORE OF AN INDOOR PERSON.
WHOA! WHAT'S THIS? I GOT DIBS!
HEY! CUT IT OUT!
THERE'S ROOM FOR TWO OF US UNDER THERE!

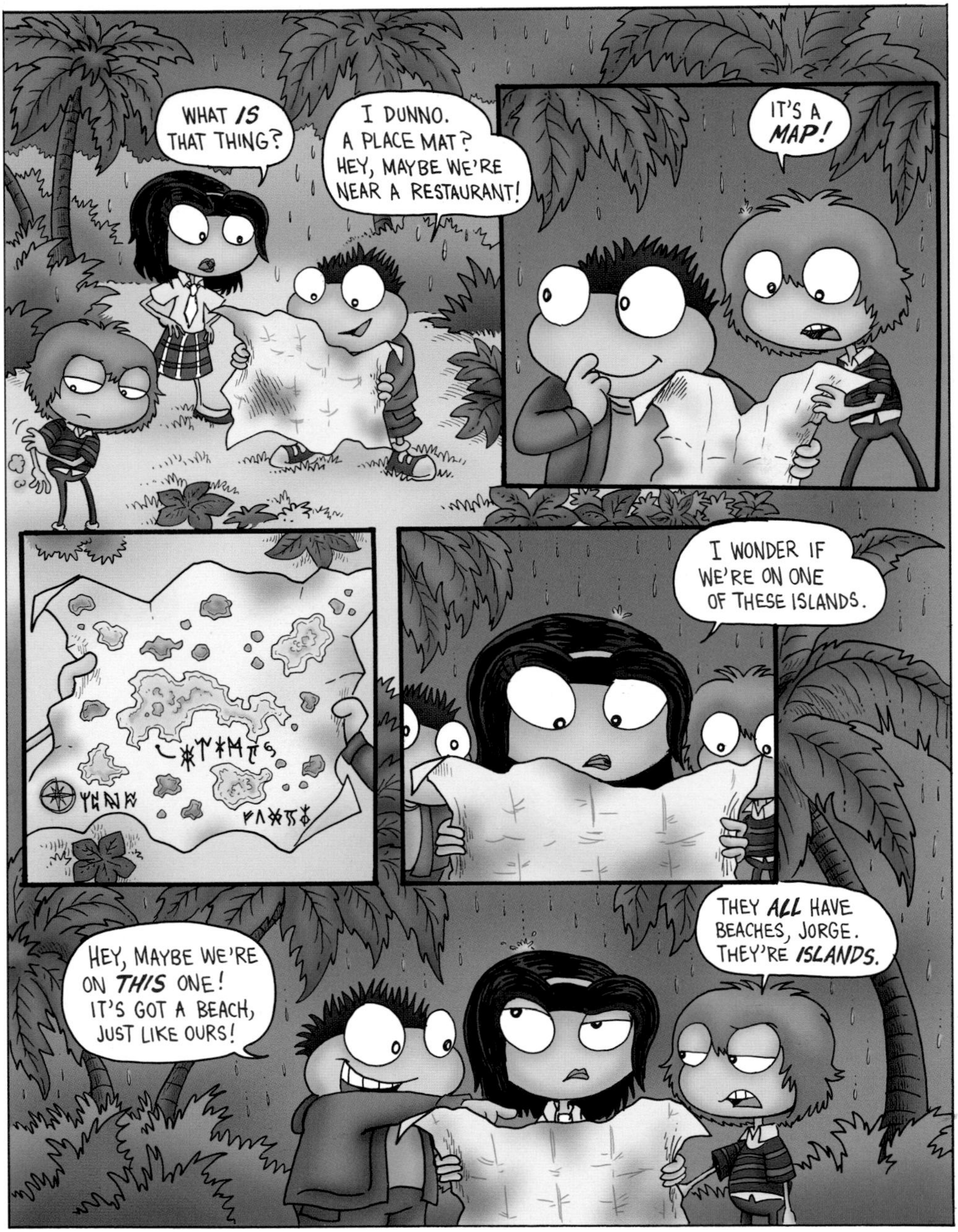

WHAT *IS* THAT THING?
I DUNNO. A PLACE MAT? HEY, MAYBE WE'RE NEAR A RESTAURANT!
IT'S A *MAP!*
I WONDER IF WE'RE ON ONE OF THESE ISLANDS.
HEY, MAYBE WE'RE ON *THIS* ONE! IT'S GOT A BEACH, JUST LIKE OURS!
THEY *ALL* HAVE BEACHES, JORGE. THEY'RE *ISLANDS.*

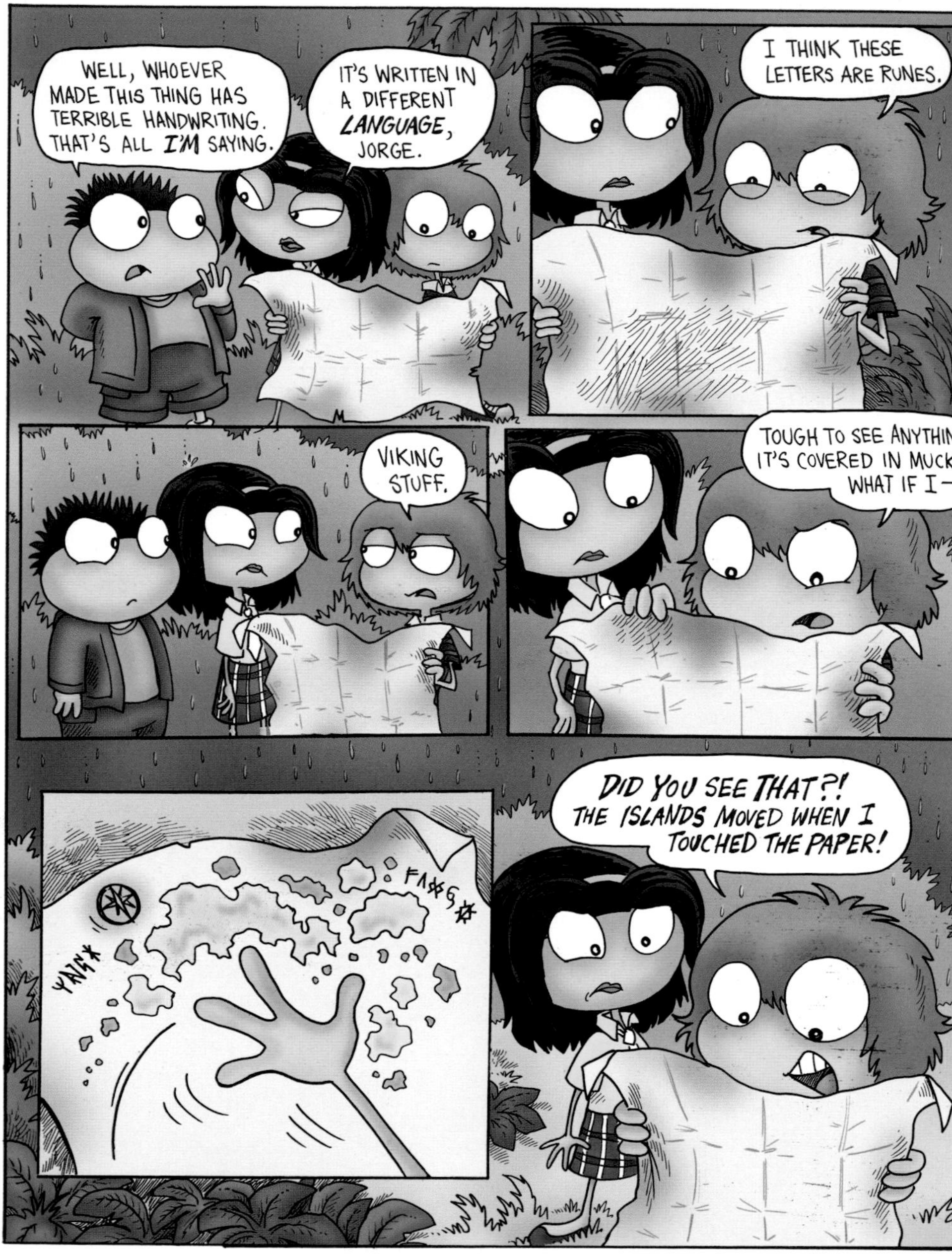
WELL, WHOEVER MADE THIS THING HAS TERRIBLE HANDWRITING. THAT'S ALL I'M SAYING.
IT'S WRITTEN IN A DIFFERENT LANGUAGE, JORGE.
I THINK THESE LETTERS ARE RUNES.
VIKING STUFF.
TOUGH TO SEE ANYTHING. IT'S COVERED IN MUCK. WHAT IF I—
DID YOU SEE THAT?! THE ISLANDS MOVED WHEN I TOUCHED THE PAPER!

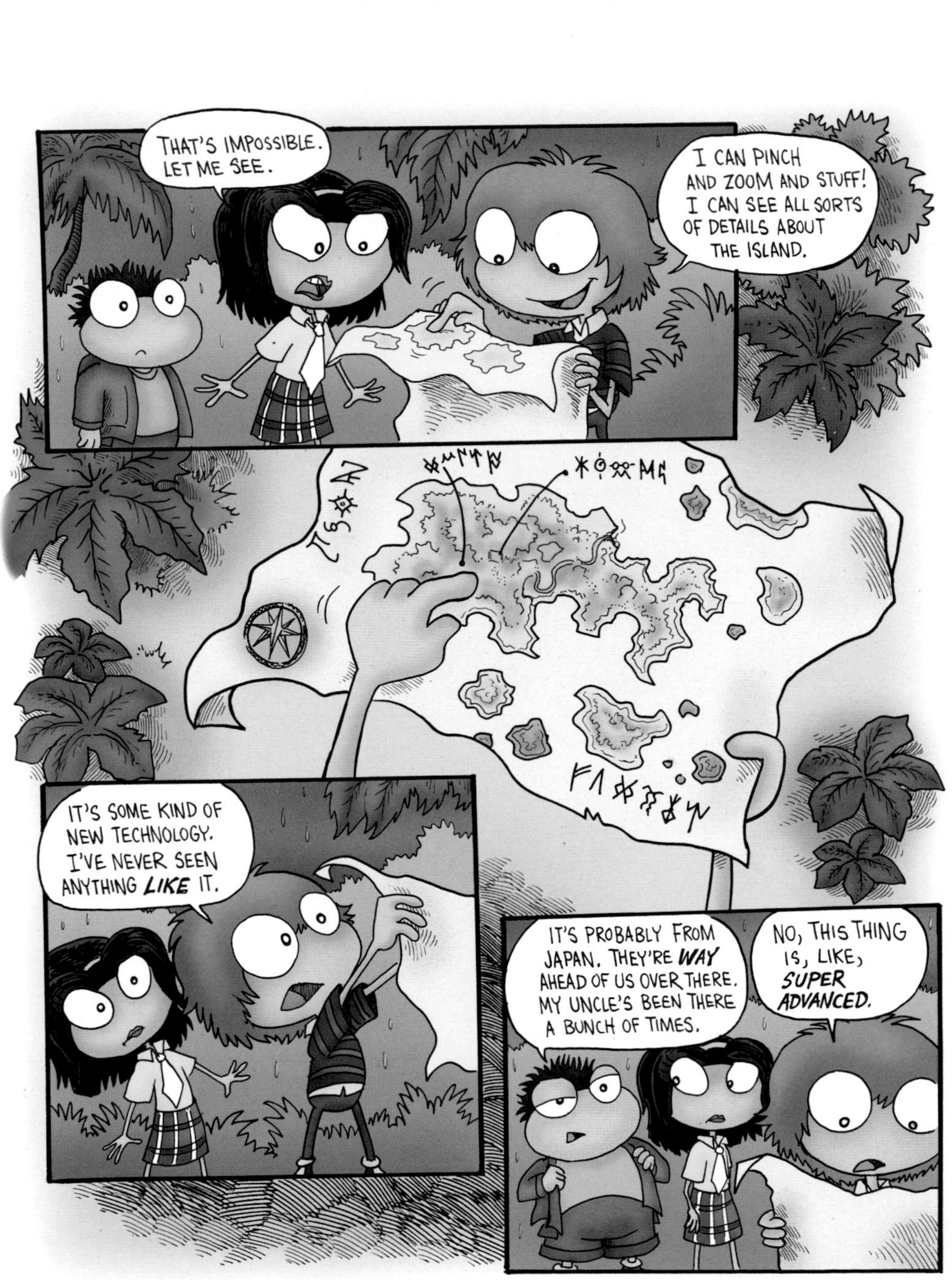
THAT'S IMPOSSIBLE. LET ME SEE.
I CAN PINCH AND ZOOM AND STUFF! I CAN SEE ALL SORTS OF DETAILS ABOUT THE ISLAND.
IT'S SOME KIND OF NEW TECHNOLOGY. I'VE NEVER SEEN ANYTHING **LIKE** IT.
IT'S PROBABLY FROM JAPAN. THEY'RE **WAY** AHEAD OF US OVER THERE. MY UNCLE'S BEEN THERE A BUNCH OF TIMES.
NO, THIS THING IS, LIKE, **SUPER ADVANCED.**

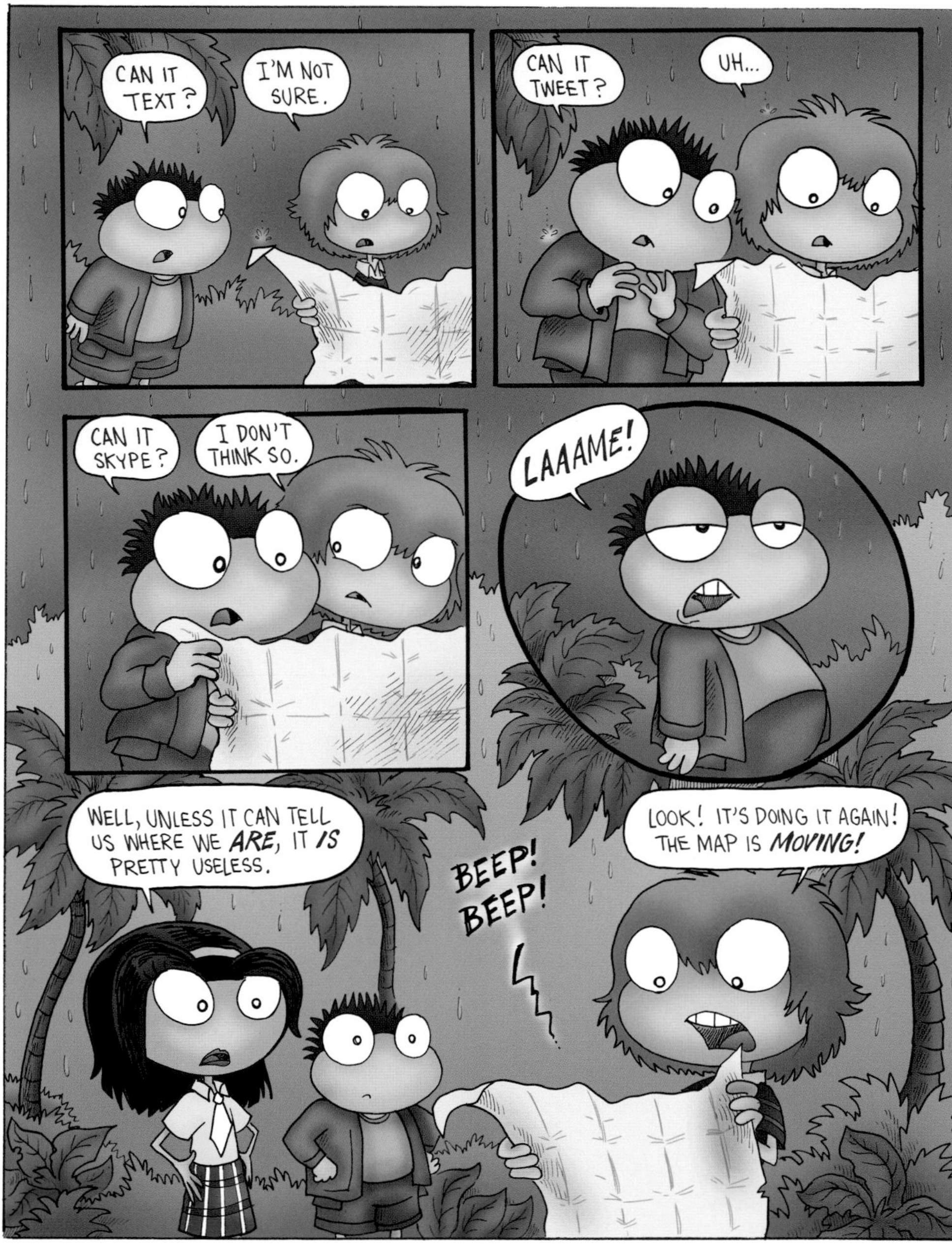
CAN IT TEXT?
I'M NOT SURE.
CAN IT TWEET?
UH...
CAN IT SKYPE?
I DON'T THINK SO.
LAAAME!
WELL, UNLESS IT CAN TELL US WHERE WE ARE, IT IS PRETTY USELESS.
BEEP! BEEP!
LOOK! IT'S DOING IT AGAIN! THE MAP IS MOVING!

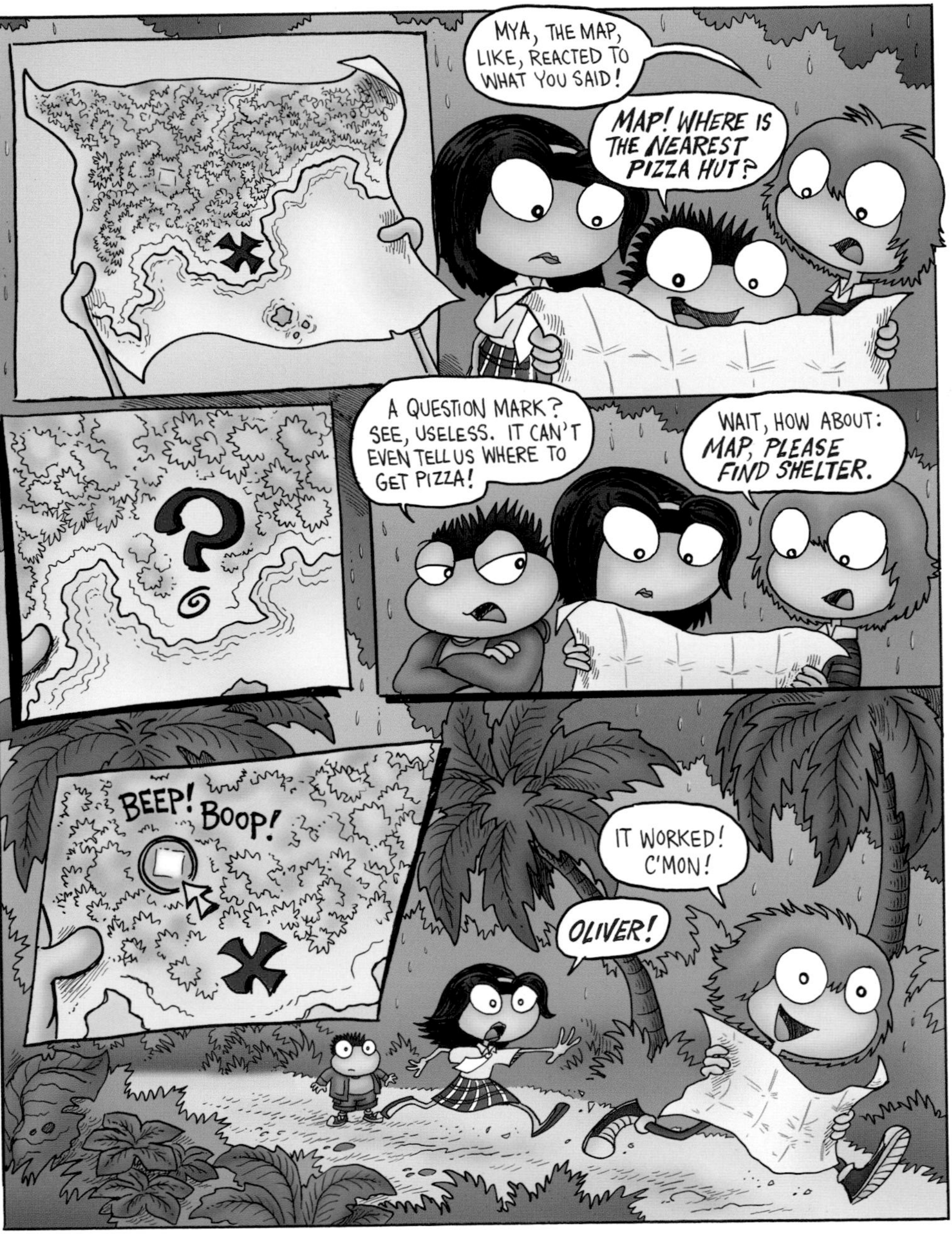
MYA, THE MAP, LIKE, REACTED TO WHAT YOU SAID!
MAP! WHERE IS THE NEAREST PIZZA HUT?
A QUESTION MARK? SEE, USELESS. IT CAN'T EVEN TELL US WHERE TO GET PIZZA!
WAIT, HOW ABOUT: MAP, PLEASE FIND SHELTER.
BEEP! BOOP!
IT WORKED! C'MON!
OLIVER!

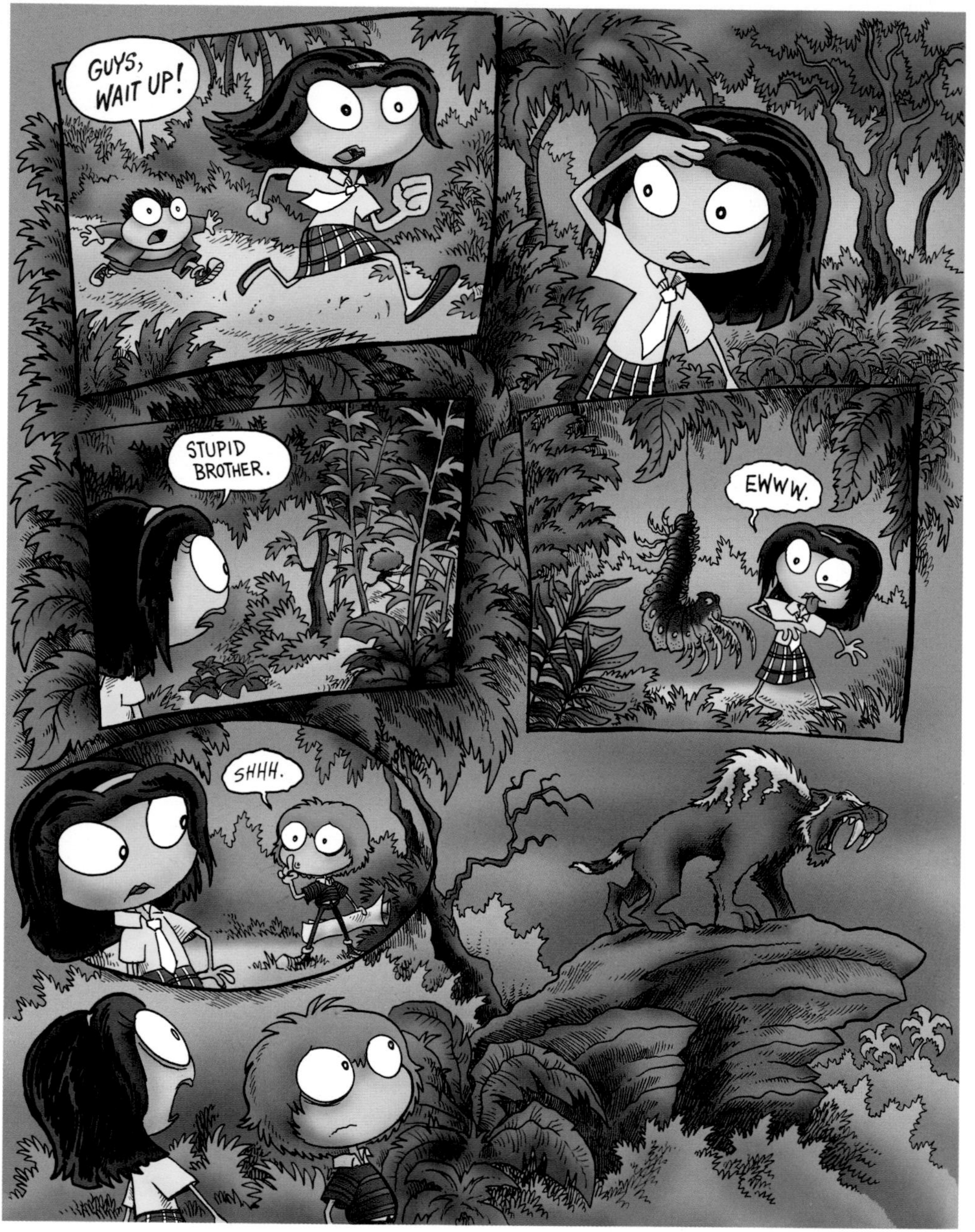
GUYS, WAIT UP!
STUPID BROTHER.
EWWW.
SHHH.

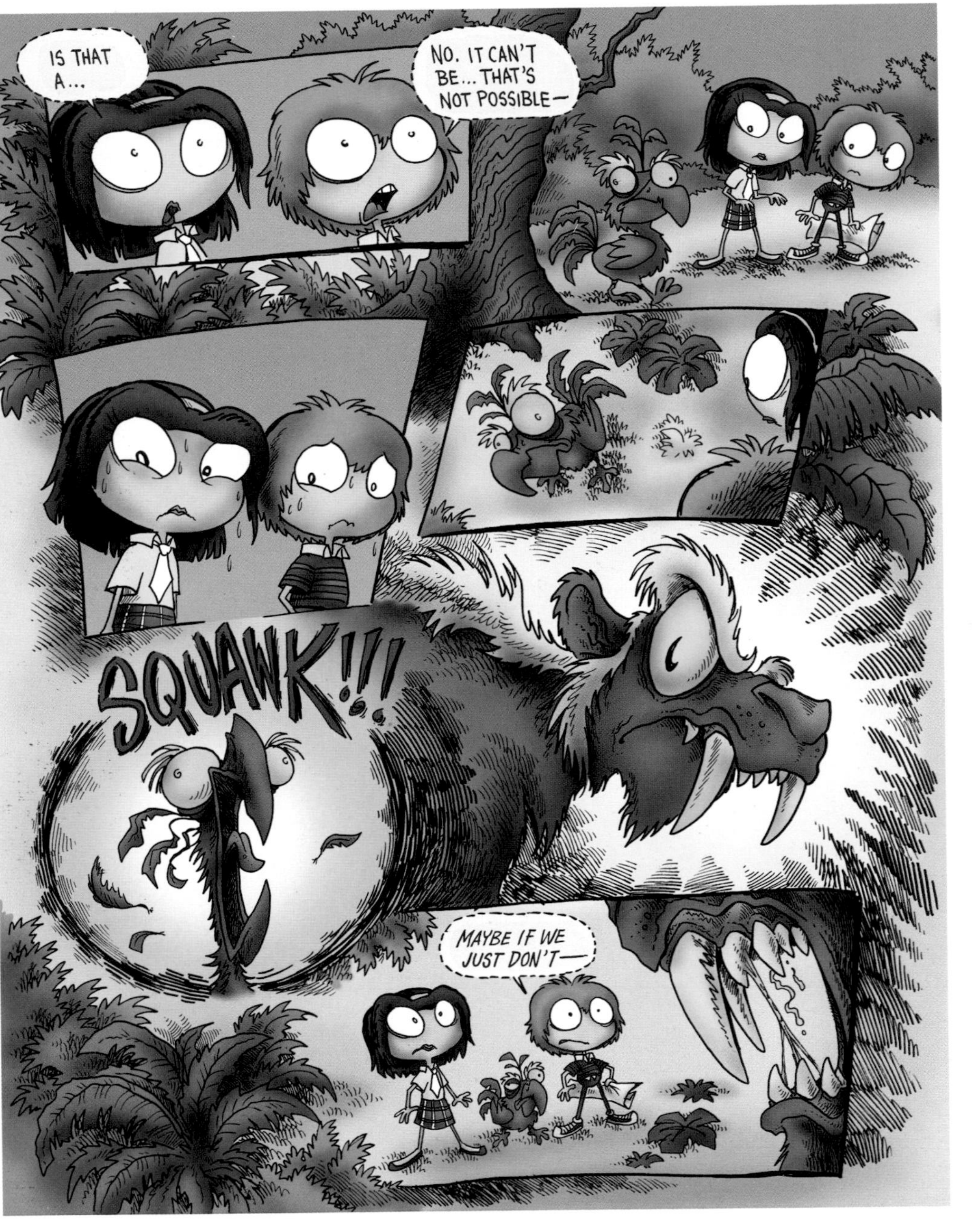
IS THAT A...
NO. IT CAN'T BE... THAT'S NOT POSSIBLE—
SQUAWK!!!
MAYBE IF WE JUST DON'T—

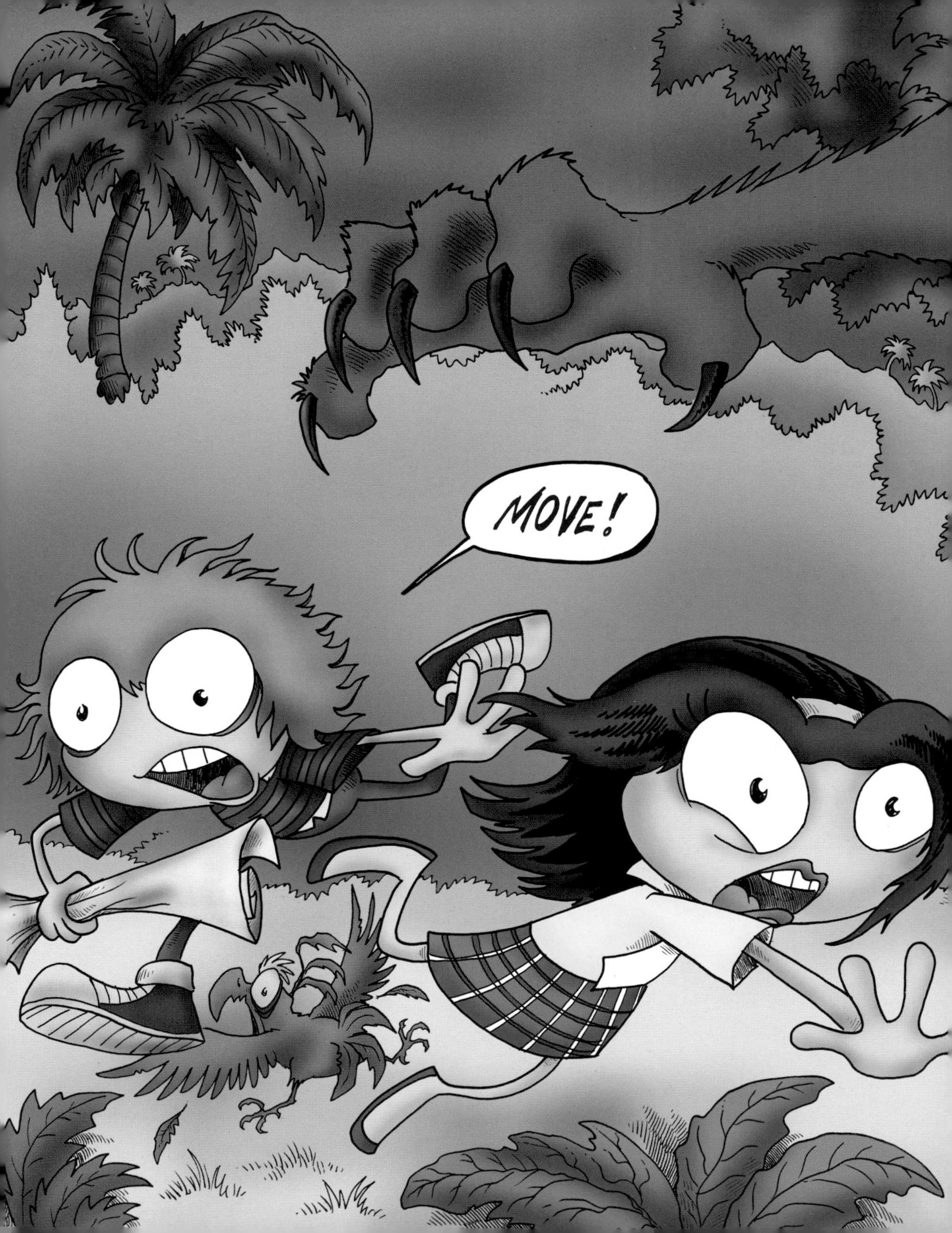
MOVE!

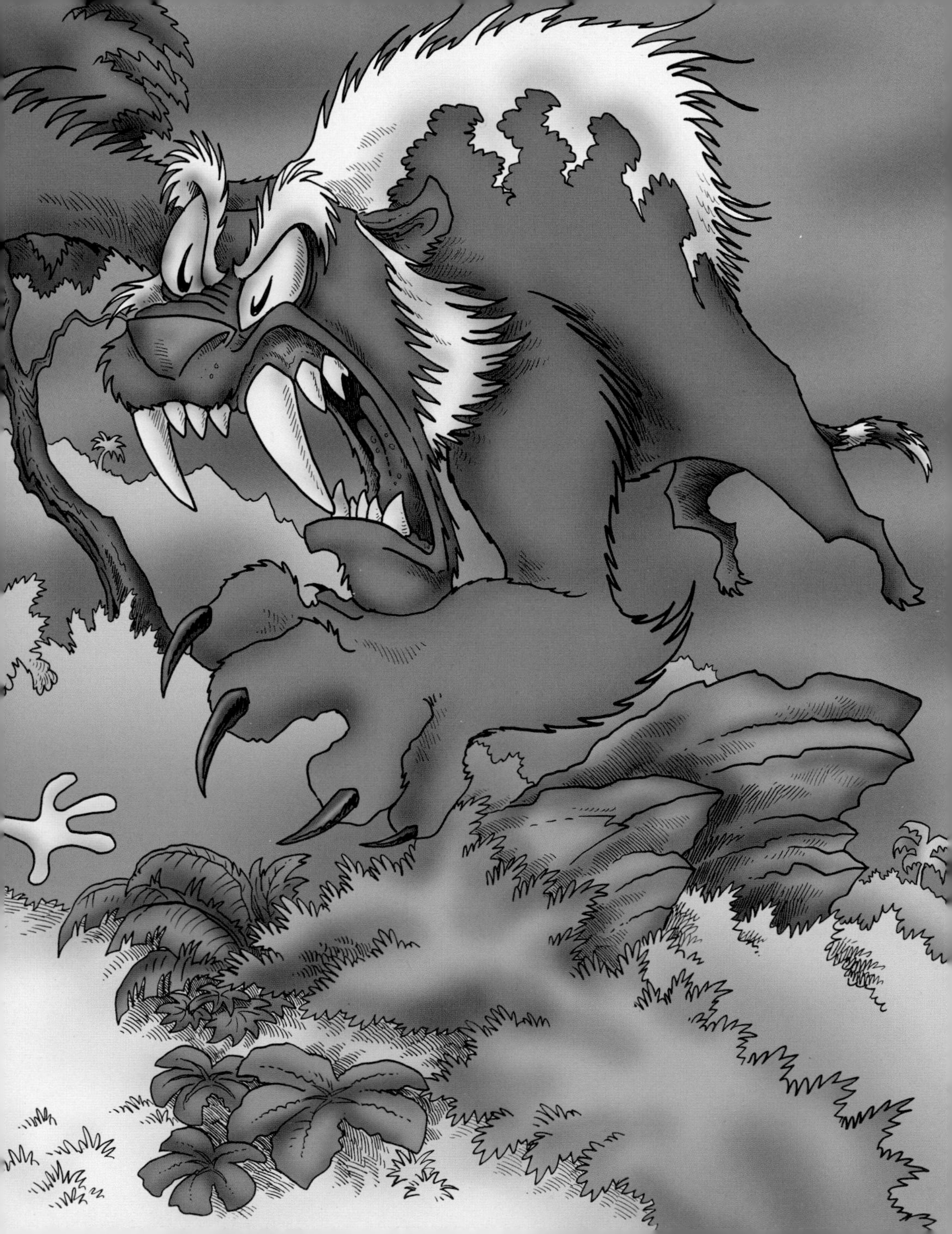

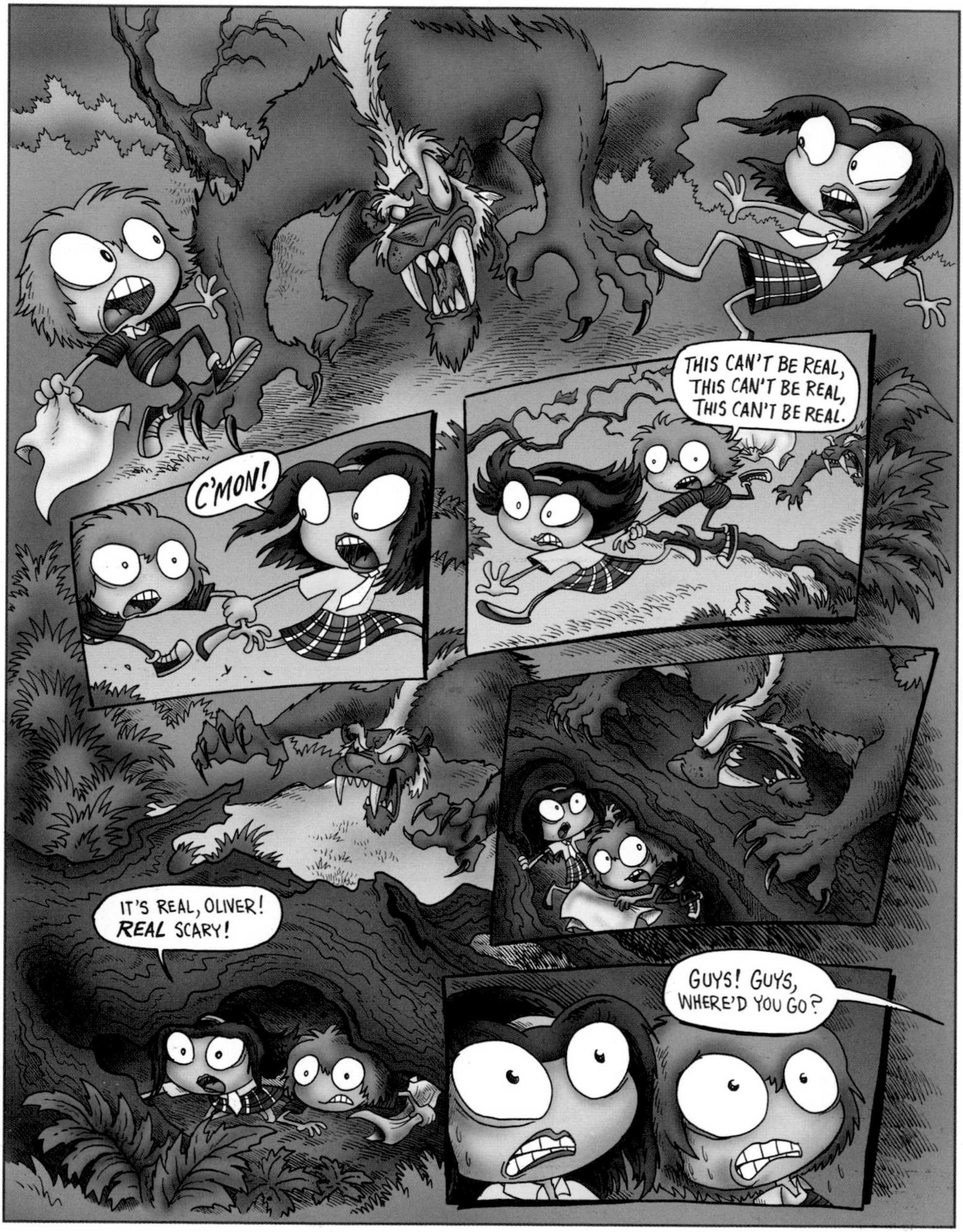
C'MON!
THIS CAN'T BE REAL, THIS CAN'T BE REAL, THIS CAN'T BE REAL.
IT'S REAL, OLIVER! REAL SCARY!
GUYS! GUYS, WHERE'D YOU GO?

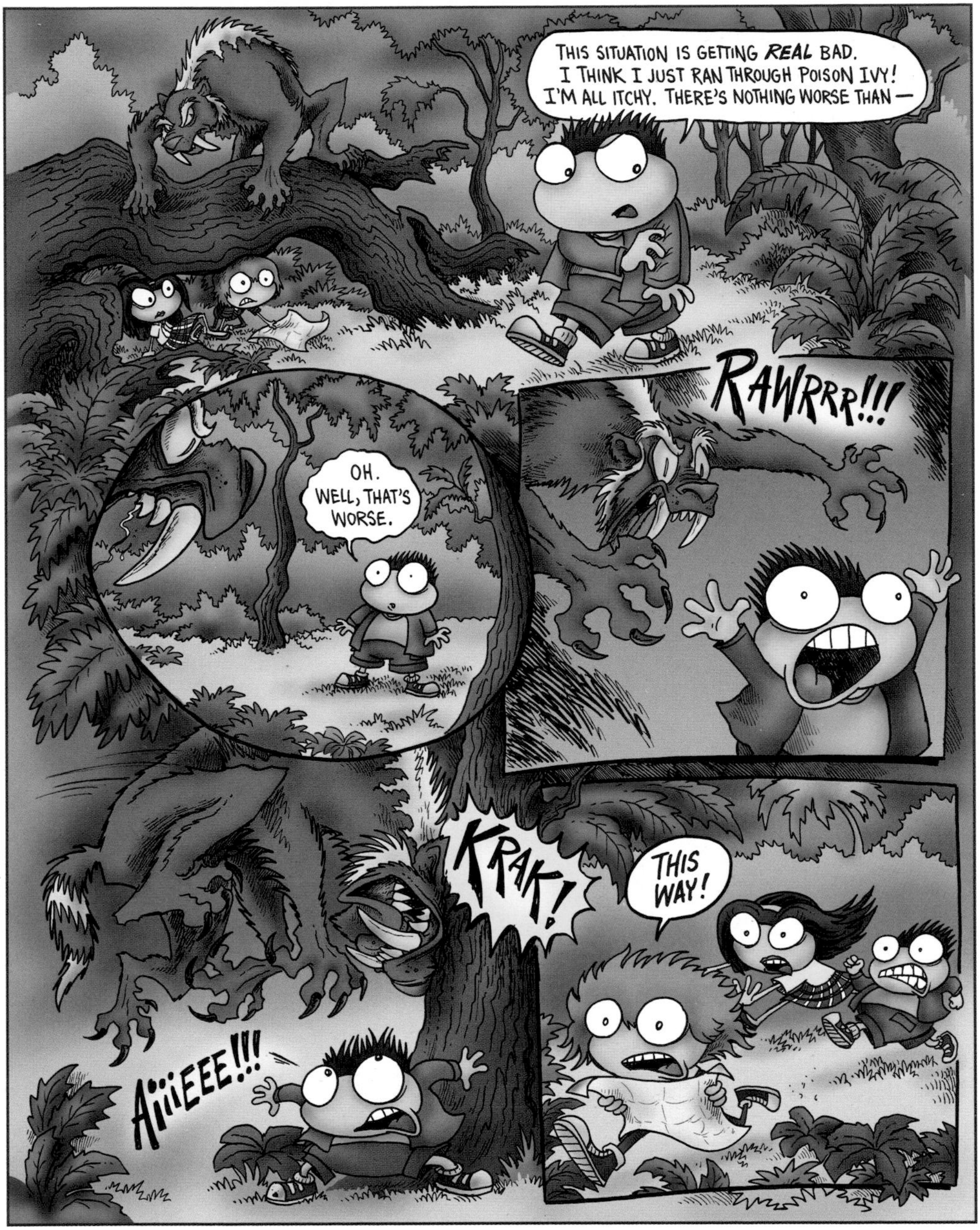

THIS SITUATION IS GETTING *REAL* BAD. I THINK I JUST RAN THROUGH POISON IVY! I'M ALL ITCHY. THERE'S NOTHING WORSE THAN—
OH. WELL, THAT'S WORSE.
RAWRRR!!!
KRAK!
AiiiEEE!!!
THIS WAY!

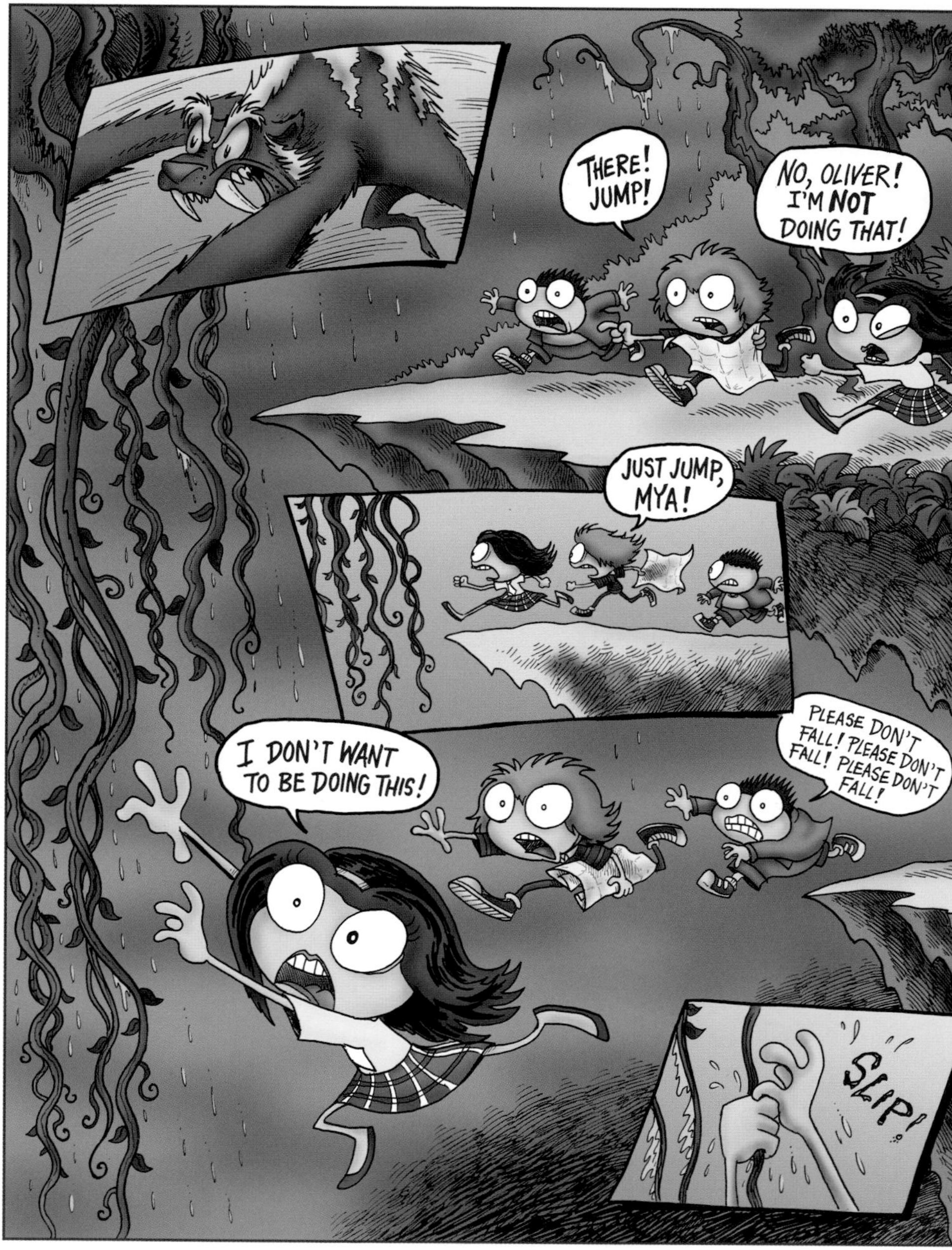
THERE! JUMP!
NO, OLIVER! I'M **NOT** DOING THAT!
JUST JUMP, MYA!
I DON'T WANT TO BE DOING THIS!
PLEASE DON'T FALL! PLEASE DON'T FALL! PLEASE DON'T FALL!
SLIP!

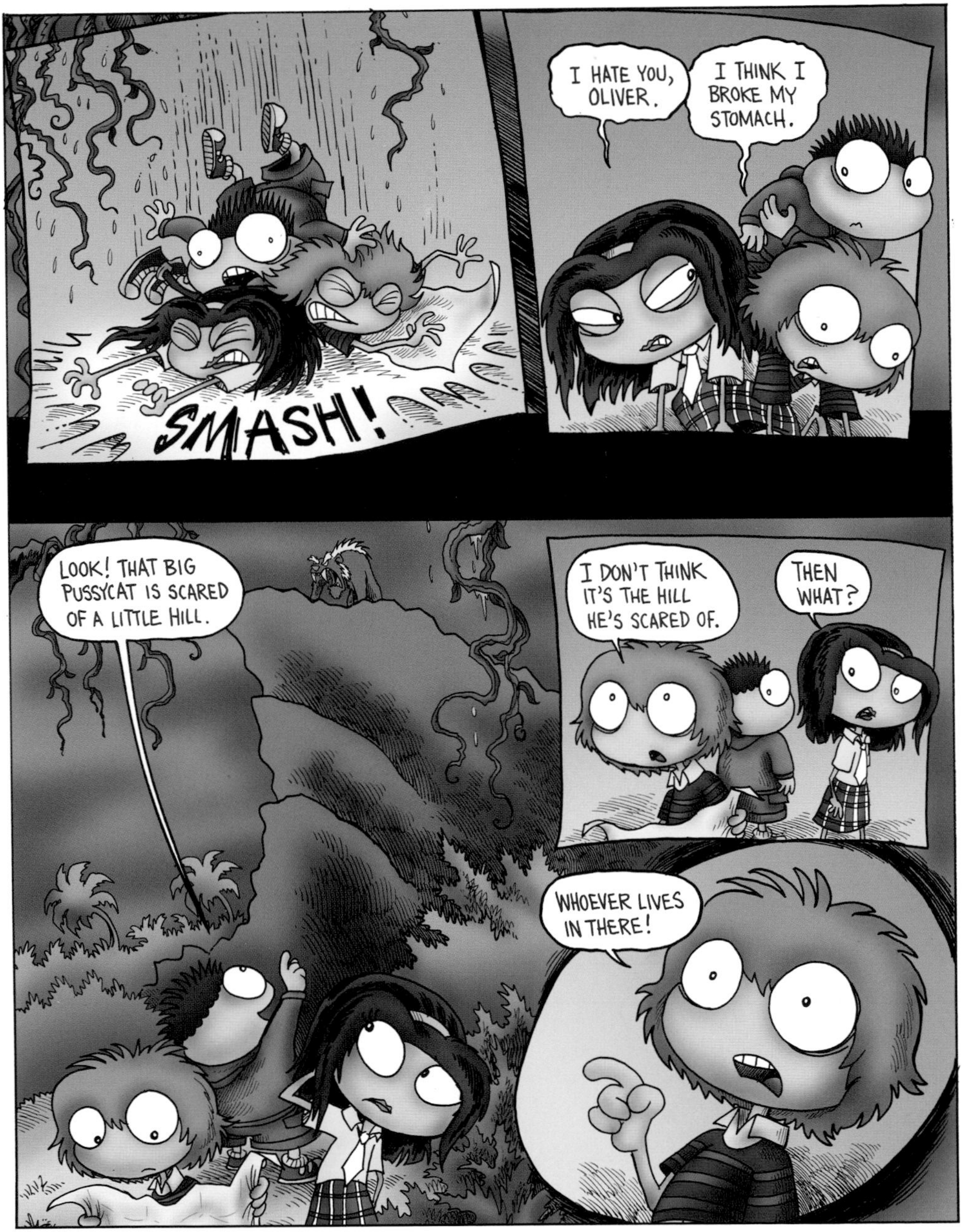
SMASH!
I HATE YOU, OLIVER.
I THINK I BROKE MY STOMACH.
LOOK! THAT BIG PUSSYCAT IS SCARED OF A LITTLE HILL.
I DON'T THINK IT'S THE HILL HE'S SCARED OF.
THEN WHAT?
WHOEVER LIVES IN THERE!

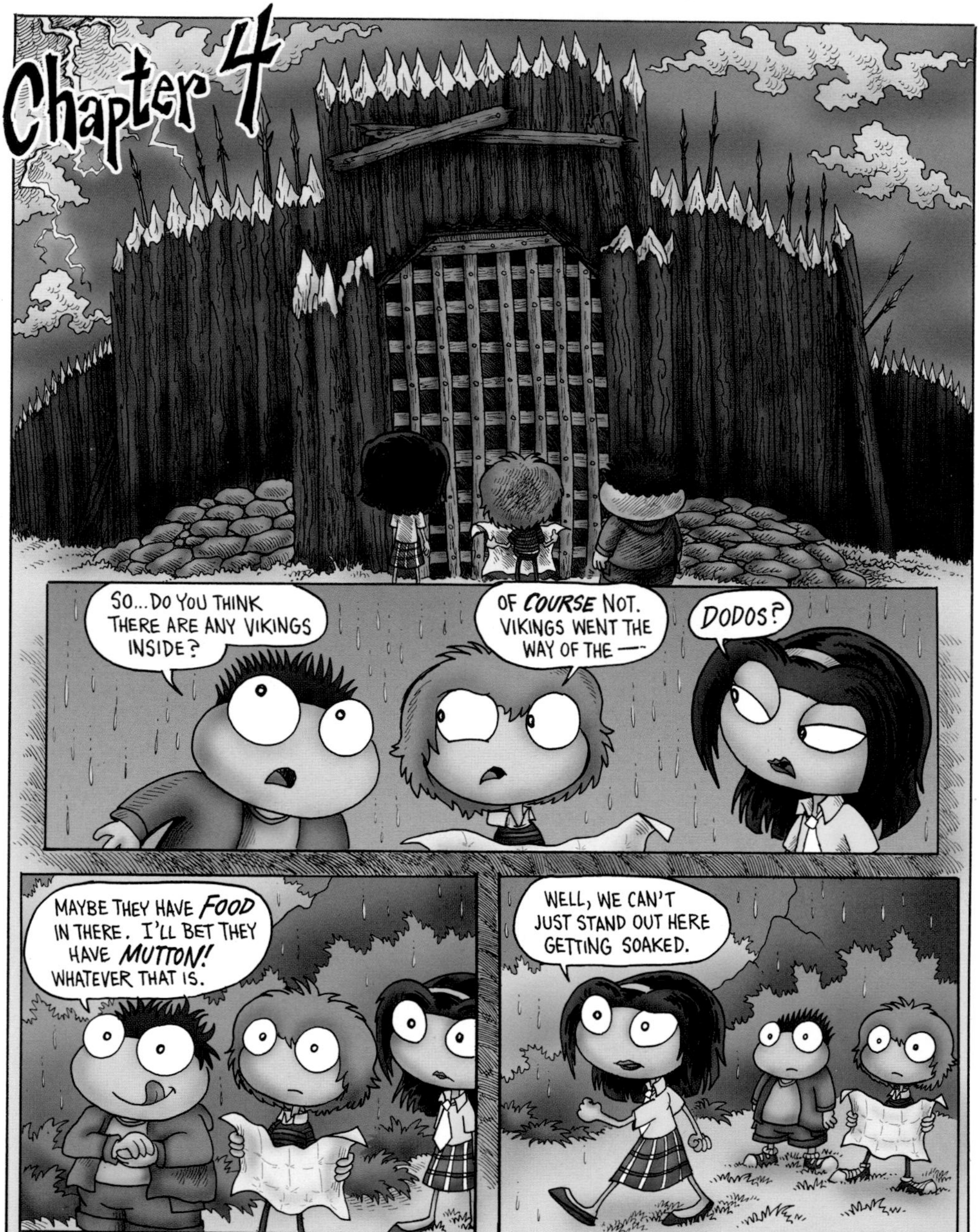
Chapter 4
SO... DO YOU THINK THERE ARE ANY VIKINGS INSIDE?
OF COURSE NOT. VIKINGS WENT THE WAY OF THE —
DODOS?
MAYBE THEY HAVE FOOD IN THERE. I'LL BET THEY HAVE MUTTON! WHATEVER THAT IS.
WELL, WE CAN'T JUST STAND OUT HERE GETTING SOAKED.

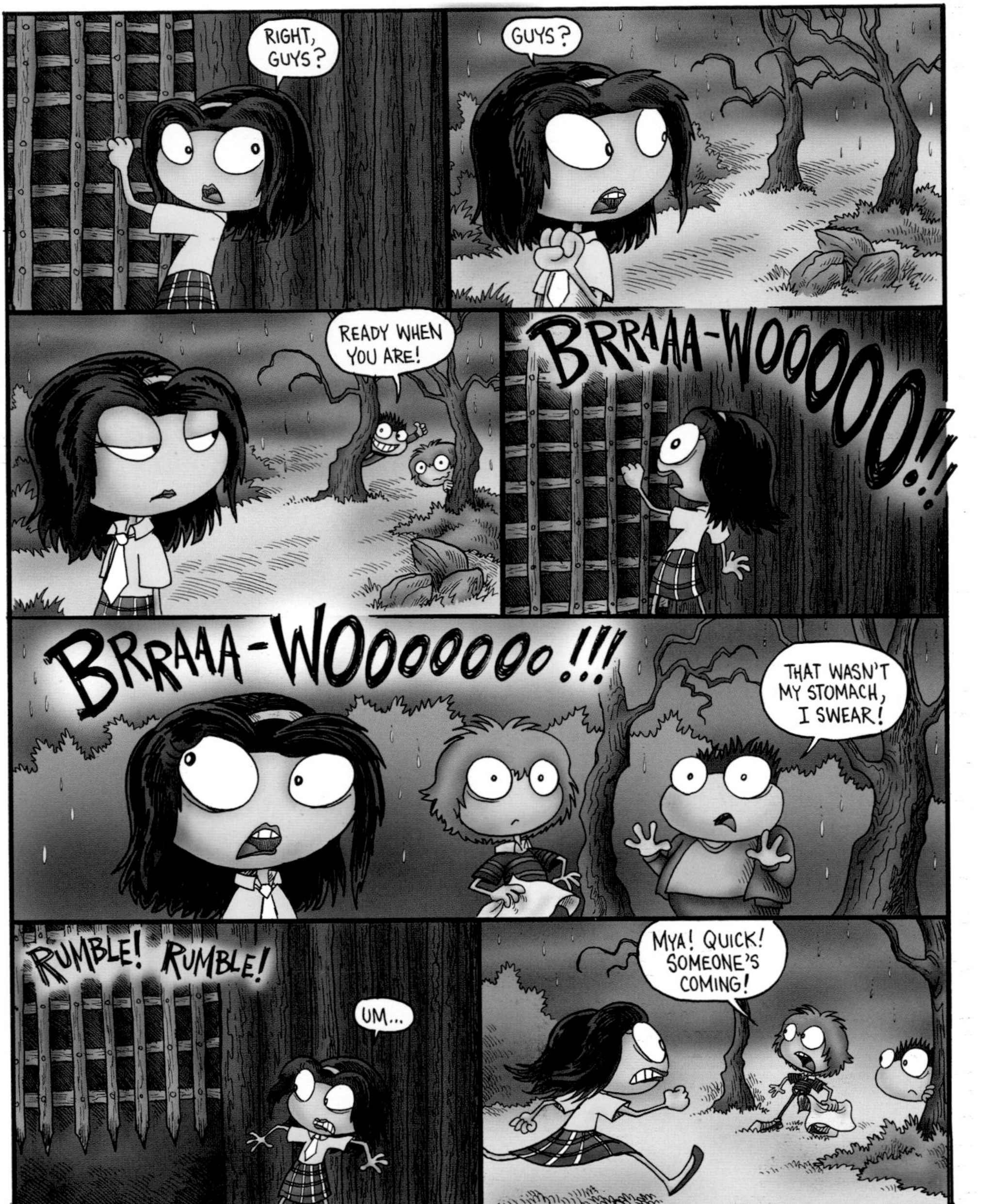
RIGHT, GUYS?
GUYS?
READY WHEN YOU ARE!
BRRAAA-WOOOOOO!!!
BRRAAA-WOOOOOOO!!!
THAT WASN'T MY STOMACH, I SWEAR!
RUMBLE! RUMBLE!
UM...
MYA! QUICK! SOMEONE'S COMING!

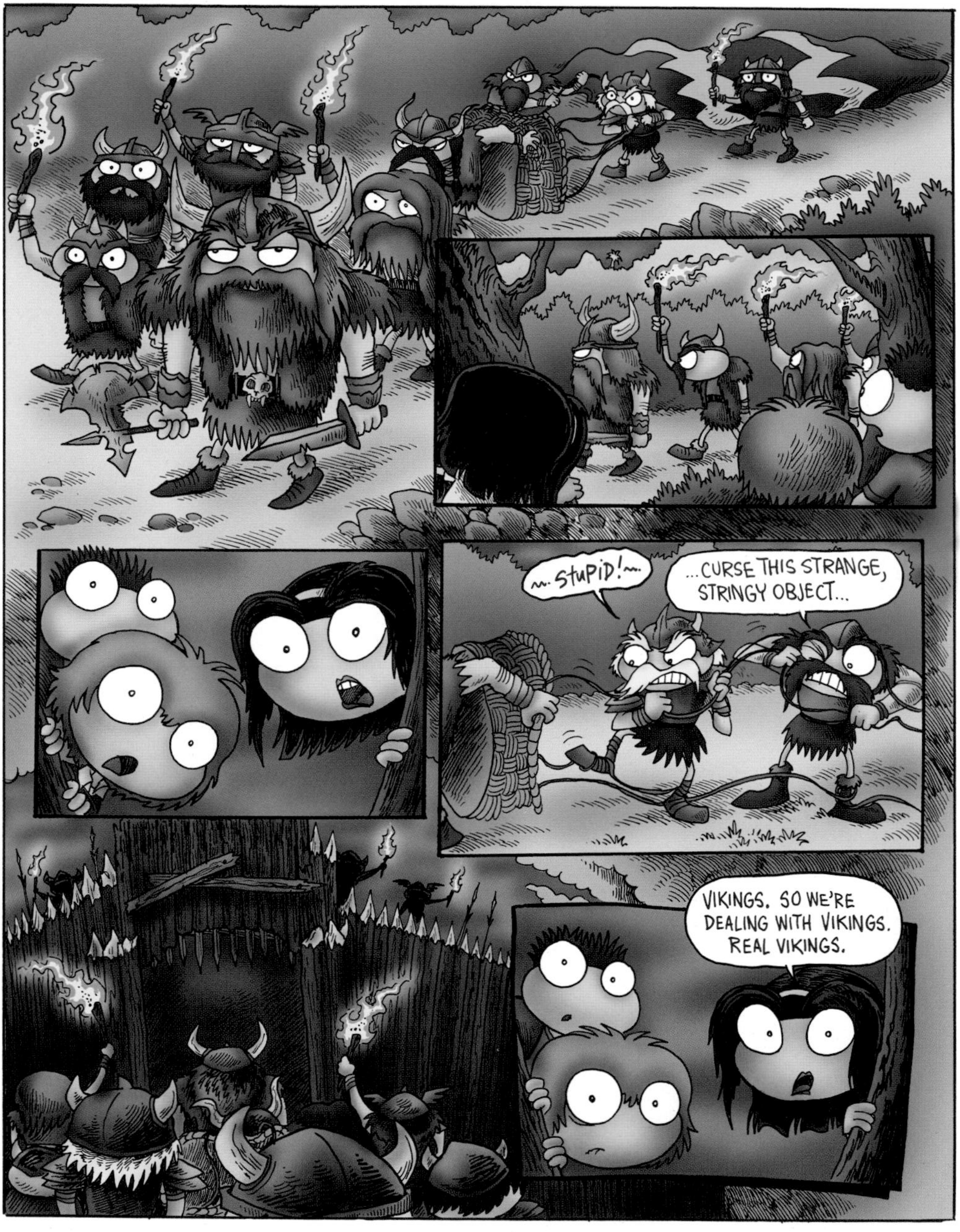
~STUPID!~
...CURSE THIS STRANGE, STRINGY OBJECT...
VIKINGS. SO WE'RE DEALING WITH VIKINGS. REAL VIKINGS.

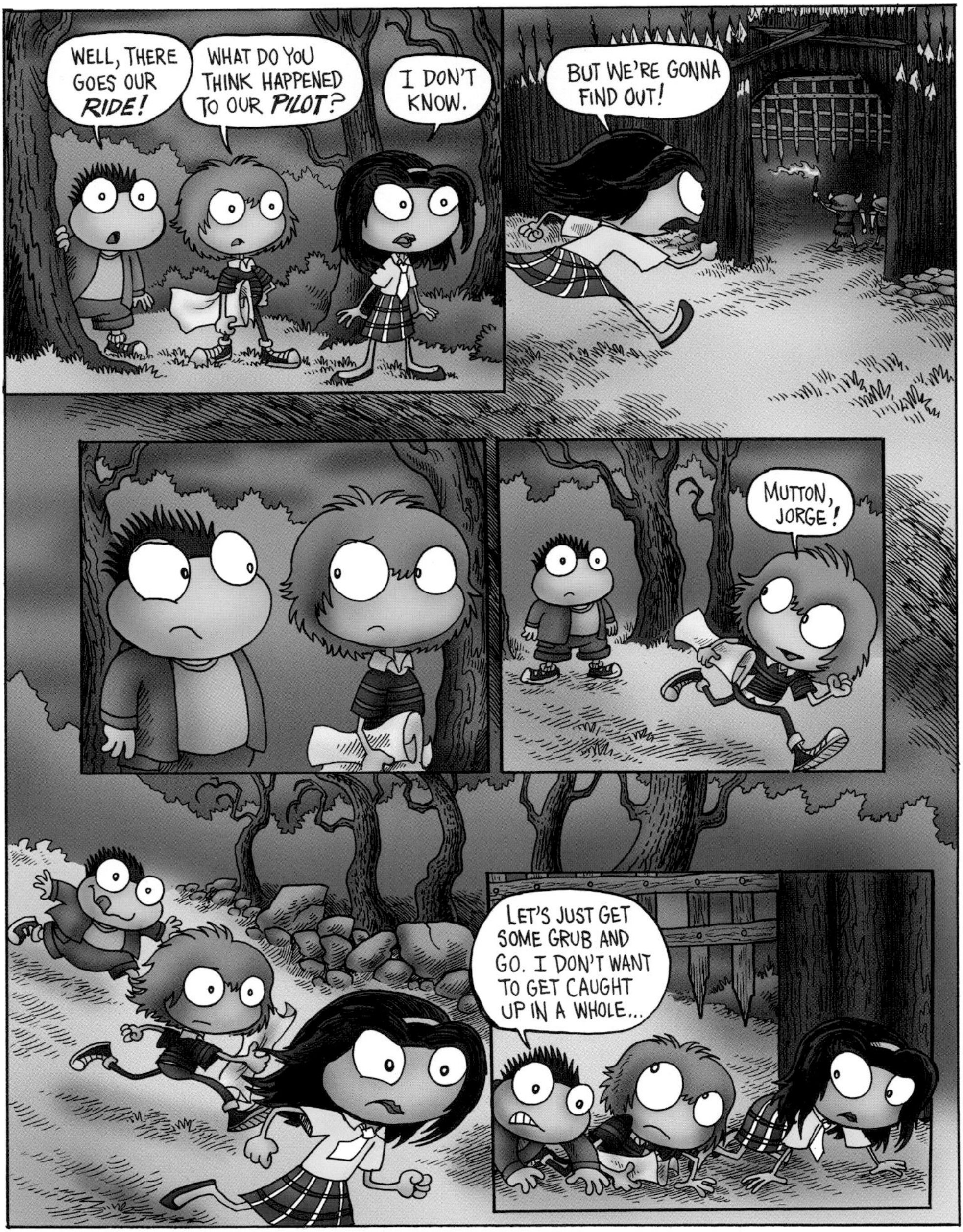
WELL, THERE GOES OUR RIDE!
WHAT DO YOU THINK HAPPENED TO OUR PILOT?
I DON'T KNOW.
BUT WE'RE GONNA FIND OUT!
MUTTON, JORGE!
LET'S JUST GET SOME GRUB AND GO. I DON'T WANT TO GET CAUGHT UP IN A WHOLE...

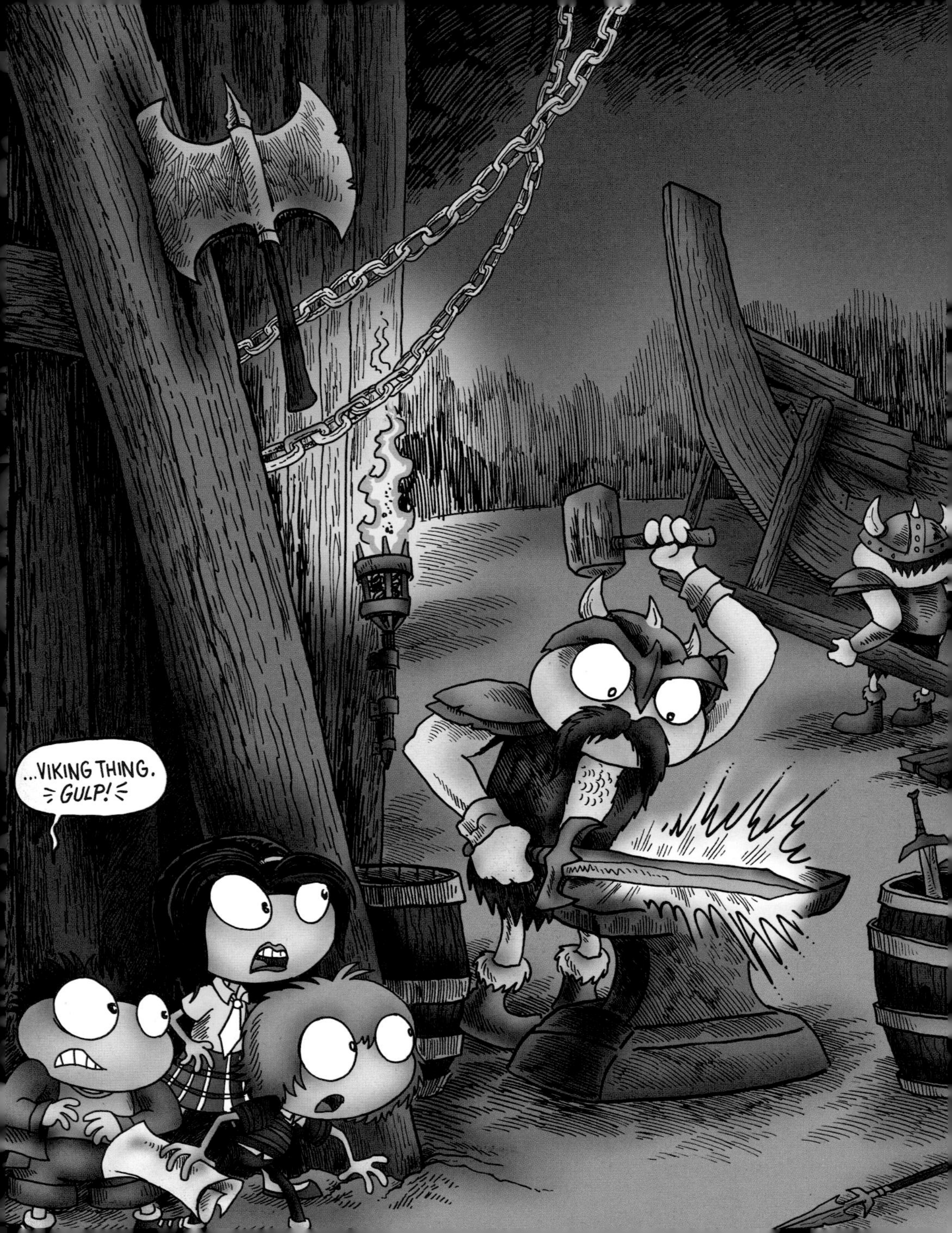
...VIKING THING.
GULP!

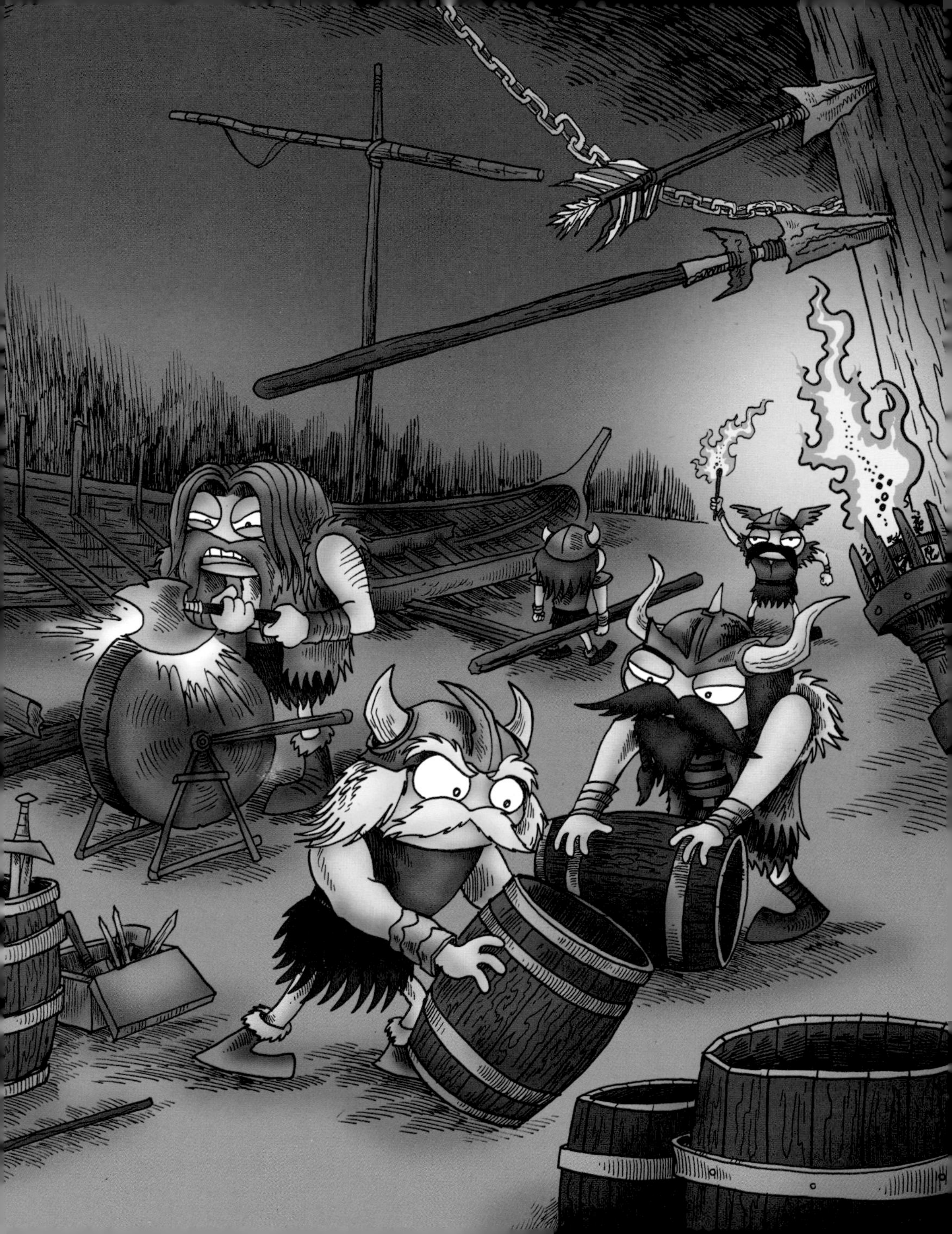

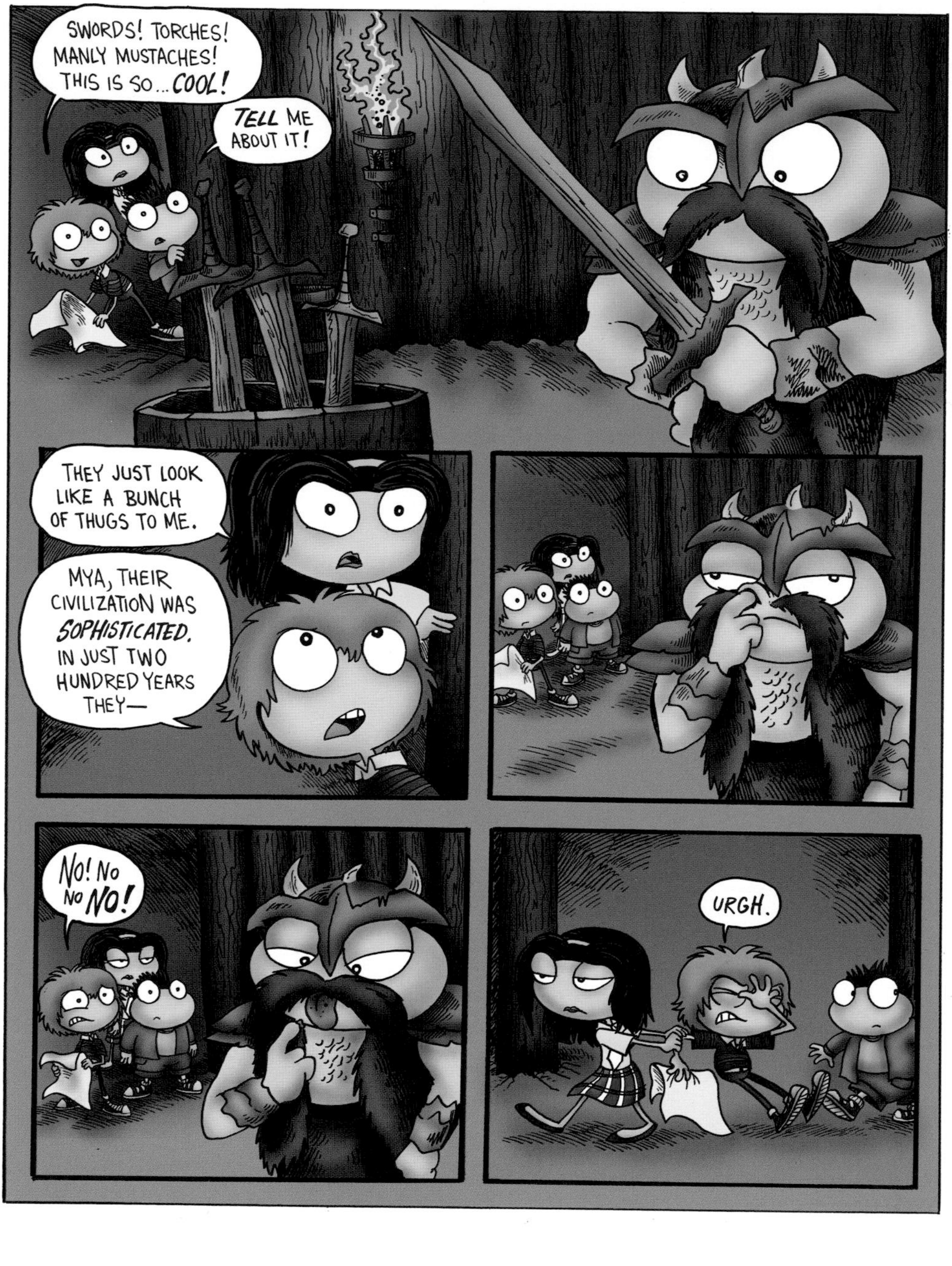
SWORDS! TORCHES! MANLY MUSTACHES! THIS IS SO... COOL!
TELL ME ABOUT IT!
THEY JUST LOOK LIKE A BUNCH OF THUGS TO ME.
MYA, THEIR CIVILIZATION WAS SOPHISTICATED. IN JUST TWO HUNDRED YEARS THEY—
NO! NO NO NO!
URGH.

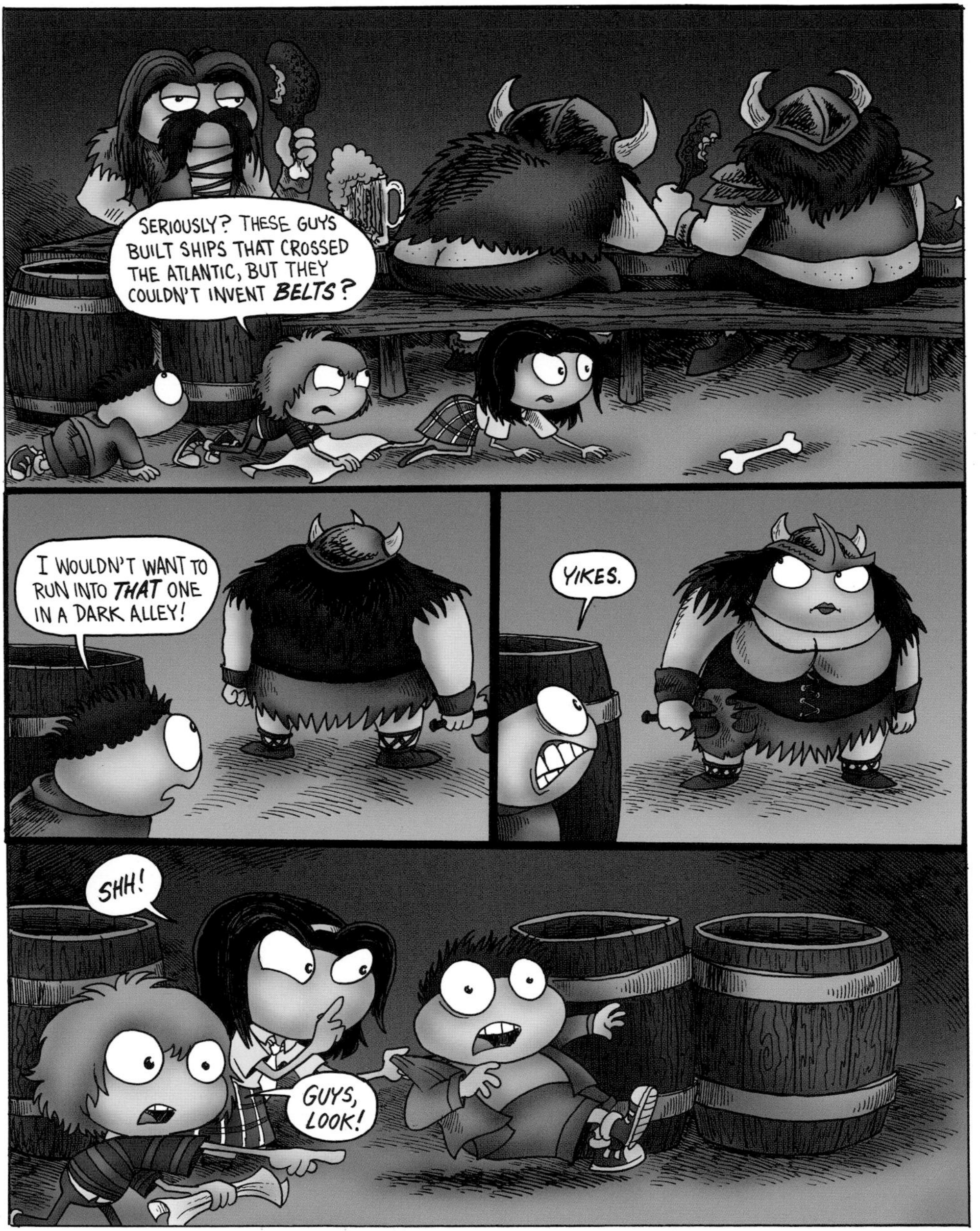
SERIOUSLY? THESE GUYS BUILT SHIPS THAT CROSSED THE ATLANTIC, BUT THEY COULDN'T INVENT BELTS?
I WOULDN'T WANT TO RUN INTO THAT ONE IN A DARK ALLEY!
YIKES.
SHH!
GUYS, LOOK!

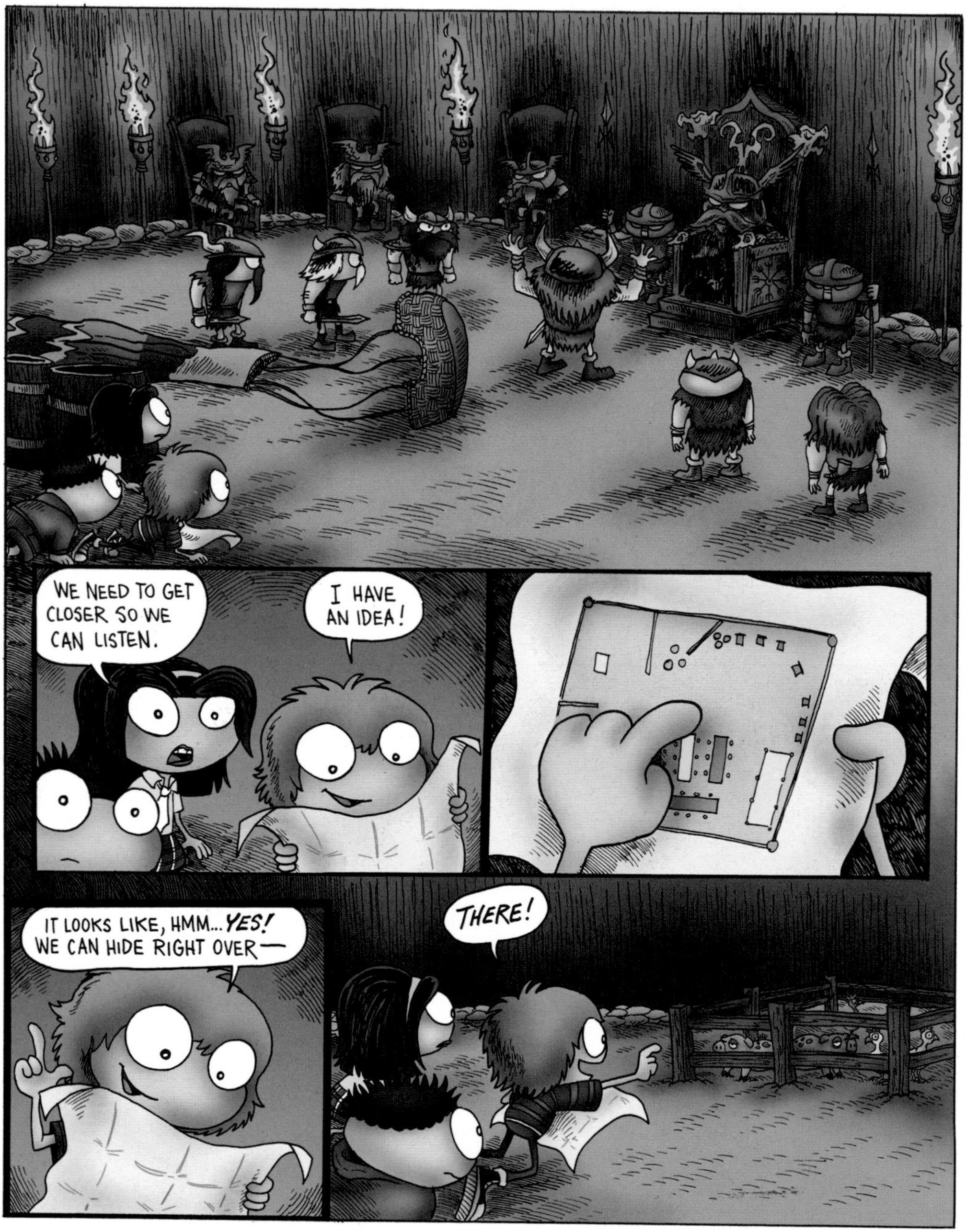
WE NEED TO GET CLOSER SO WE CAN LISTEN.
I HAVE AN IDEA!
IT LOOKS LIKE, HMM... *YES!* WE CAN HIDE RIGHT OVER—
THERE!

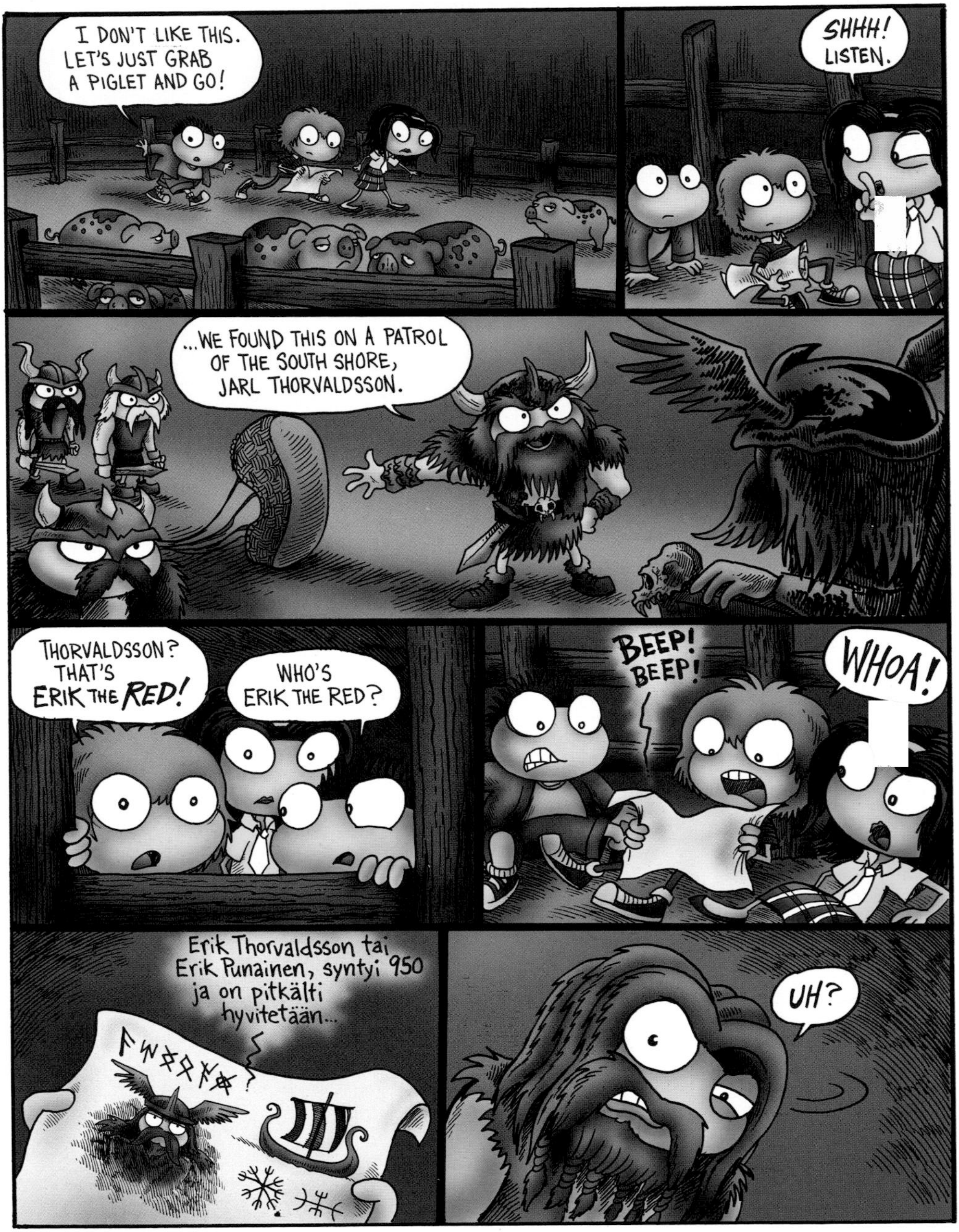
I DON'T LIKE THIS. LET'S JUST GRAB A PIGLET AND GO!
SHHH! LISTEN.
...WE FOUND THIS ON A PATROL OF THE SOUTH SHORE, JARL THORVALDSSON.
THORVALDSSON? THAT'S ERIK THE RED!
WHO'S ERIK THE RED?
BEEP! BEEP!
WHOA!
Erik Thorvaldsson tai Erik Punainen, syntyi 950 ja on pitkälti hyvitetään...
UH?

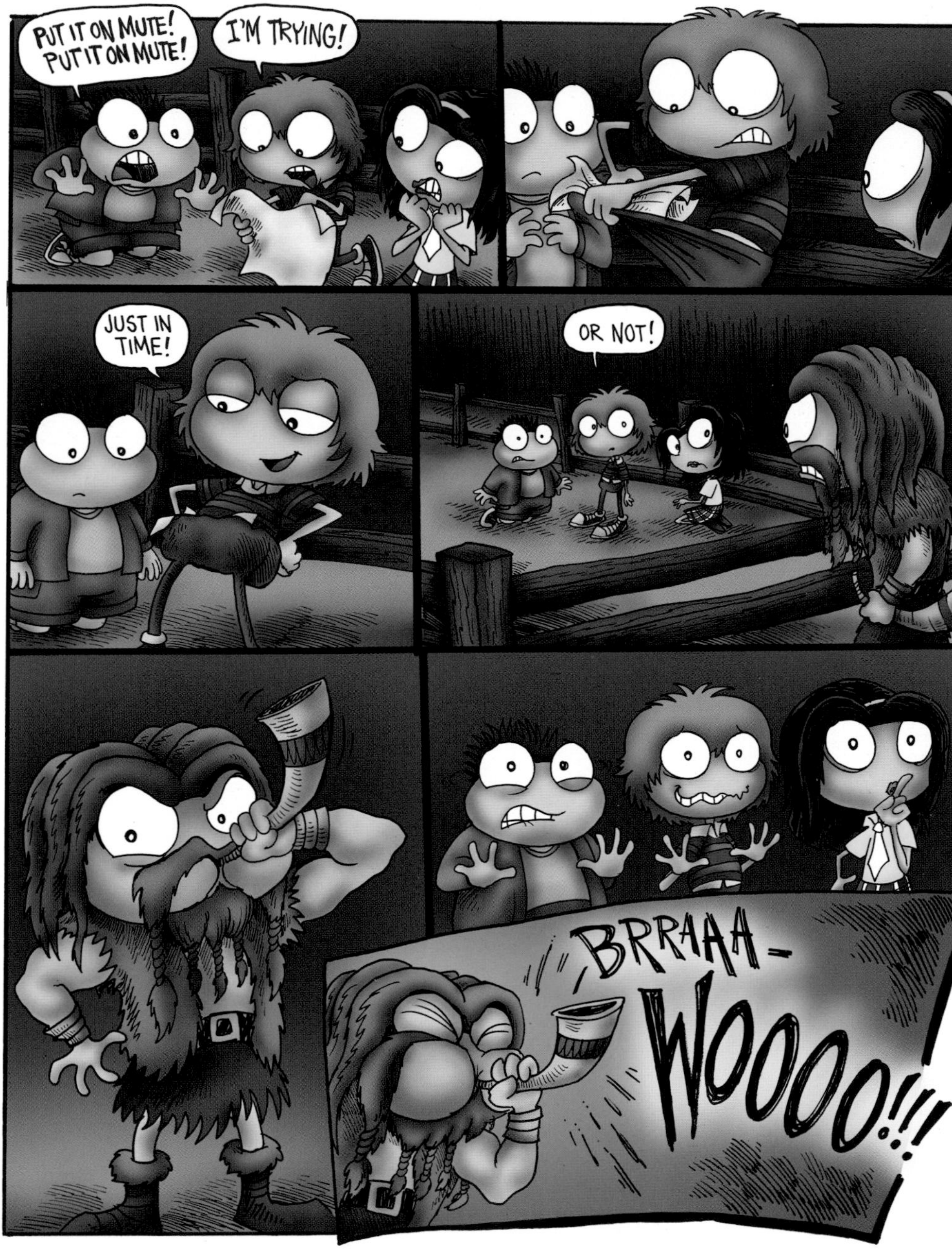
PUT IT ON MUTE! PUT IT ON MUTE!
I'M TRYING!
JUST IN TIME!
OR NOT!
BRRAAA-WOOOO!!!

# Chapter 5

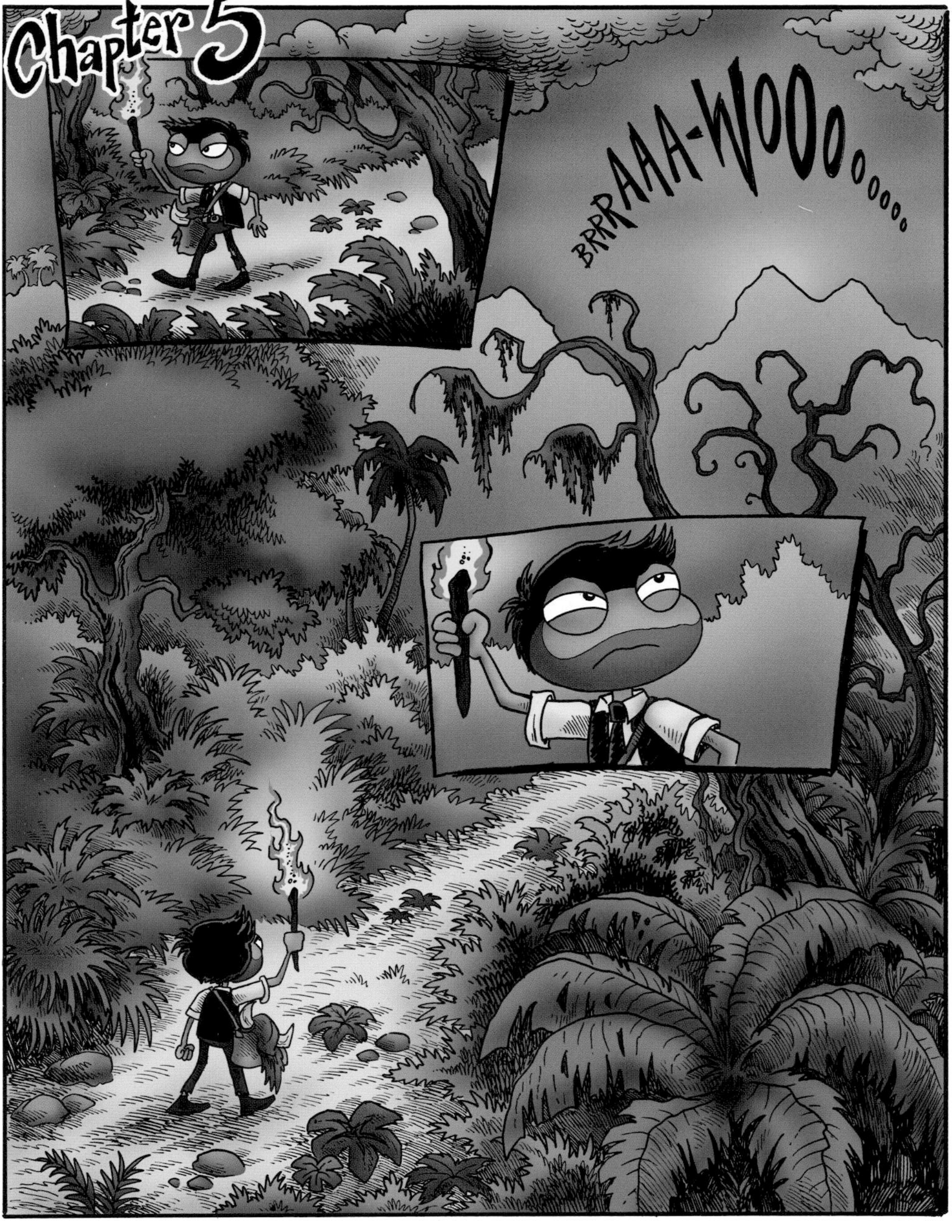
BRRRAAA-WOOOooooo

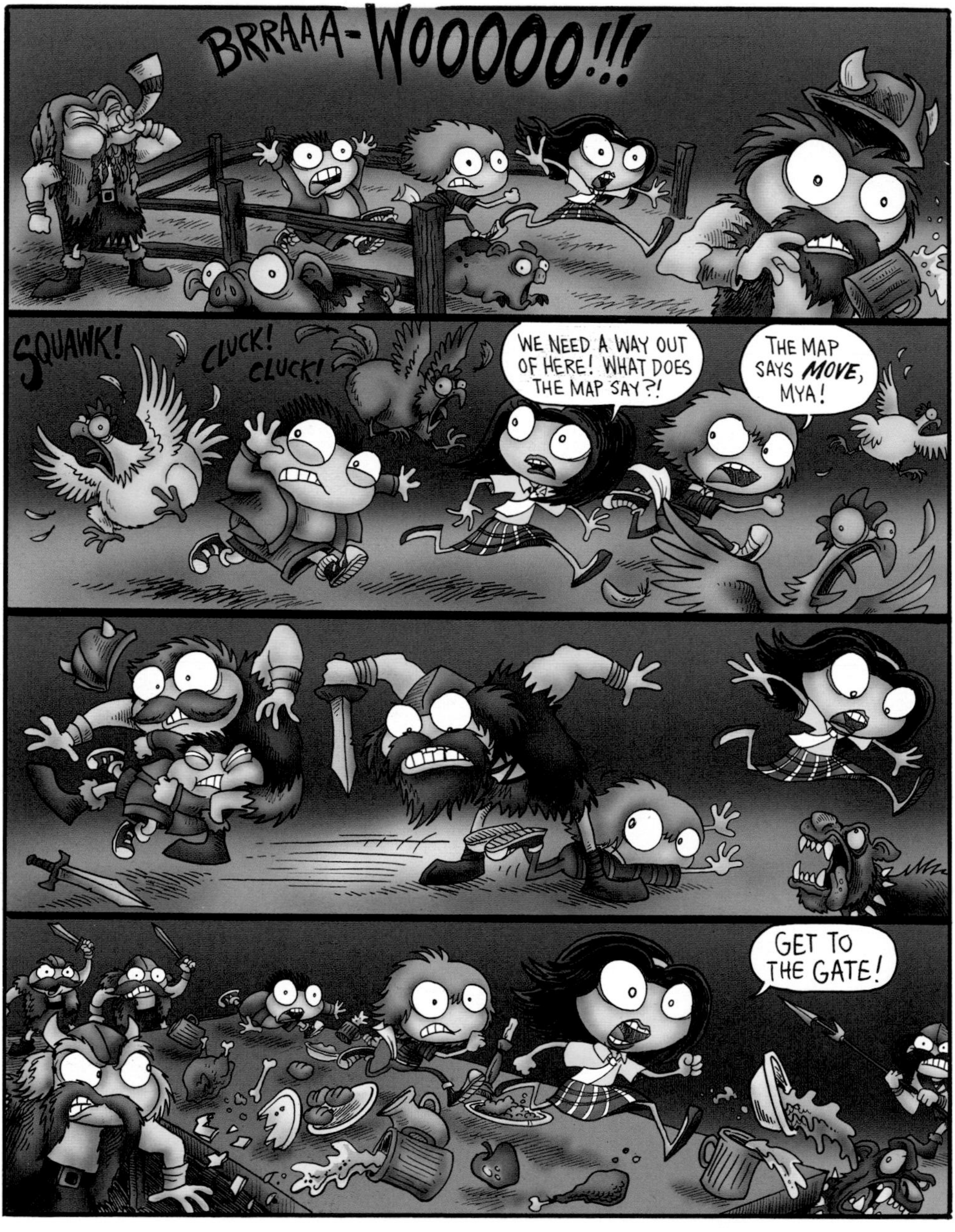
BRRAAA-WOOOOO!!!
SQUAWK!
CLUCK! CLUCK!
WE NEED A WAY OUT OF HERE! WHAT DOES THE MAP SAY?!
THE MAP SAYS MOVE, MYA!
GET TO THE GATE!

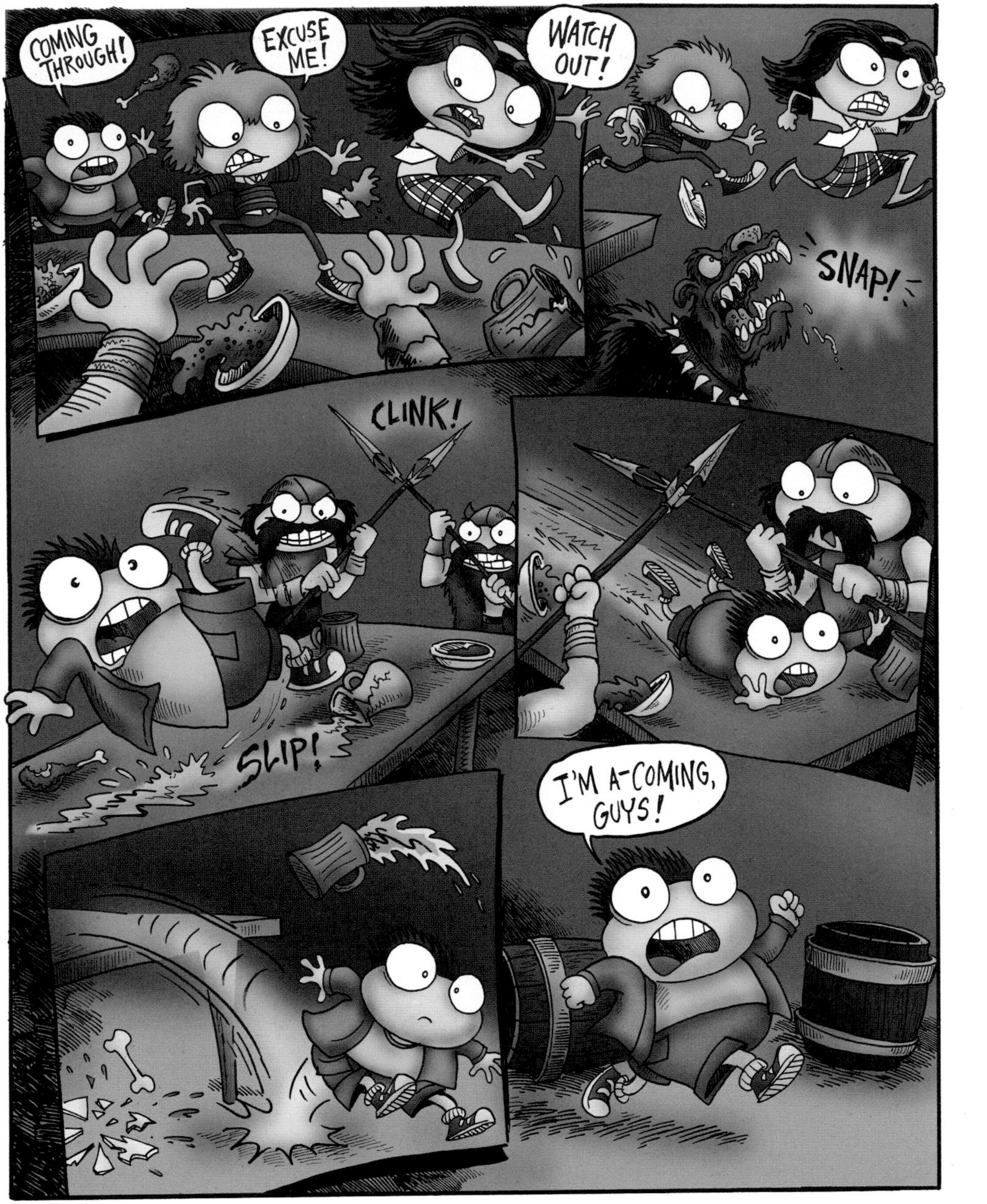
COMING THROUGH!
EXCUSE ME!
WATCH OUT!
SNAP!
CLINK!
SLIP!
I'M A-COMING, GUYS!

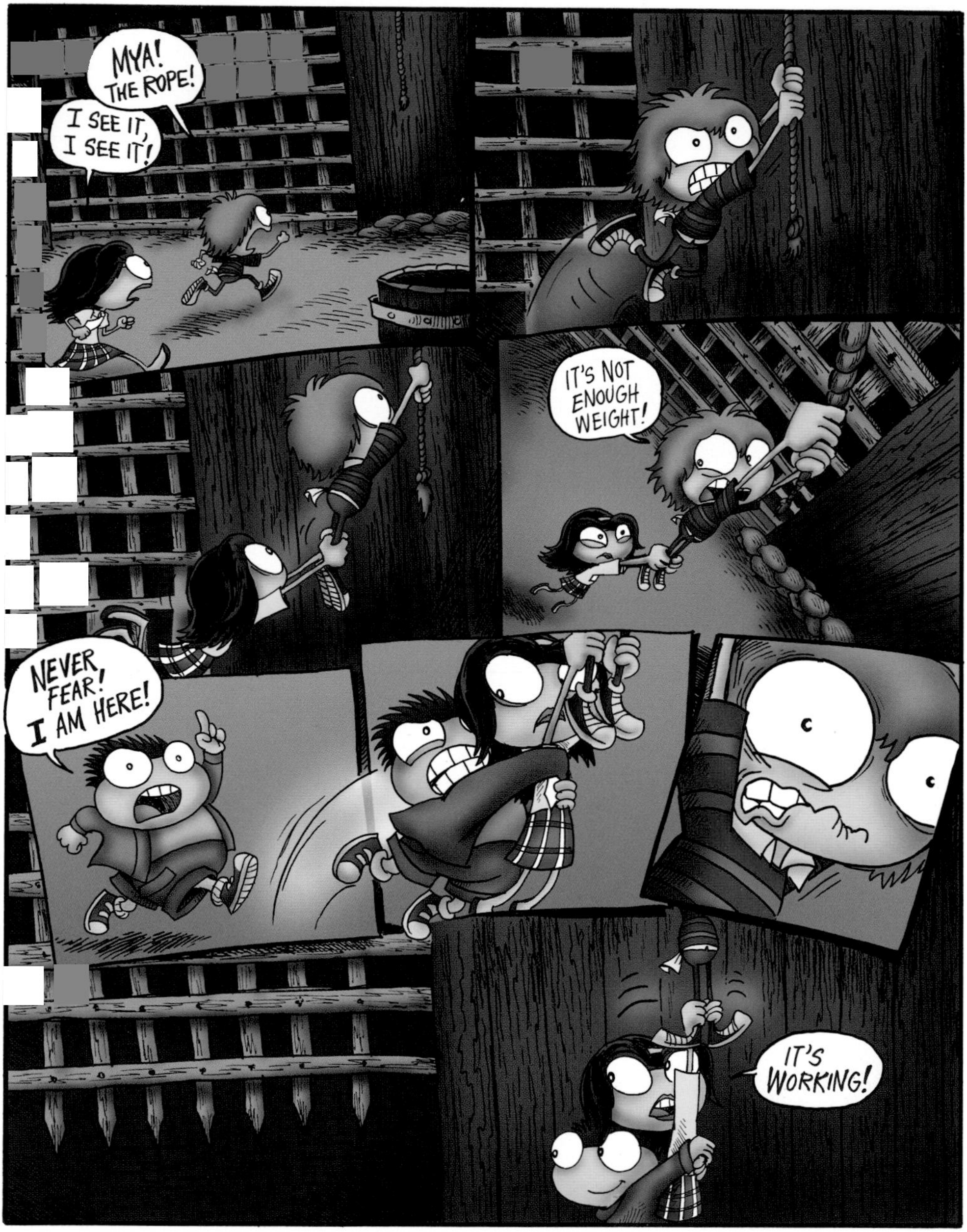
MYA! THE ROPE!
I SEE IT, I SEE IT!
IT'S NOT ENOUGH WEIGHT!
NEVER FEAR! I AM HERE!
IT'S WORKING!

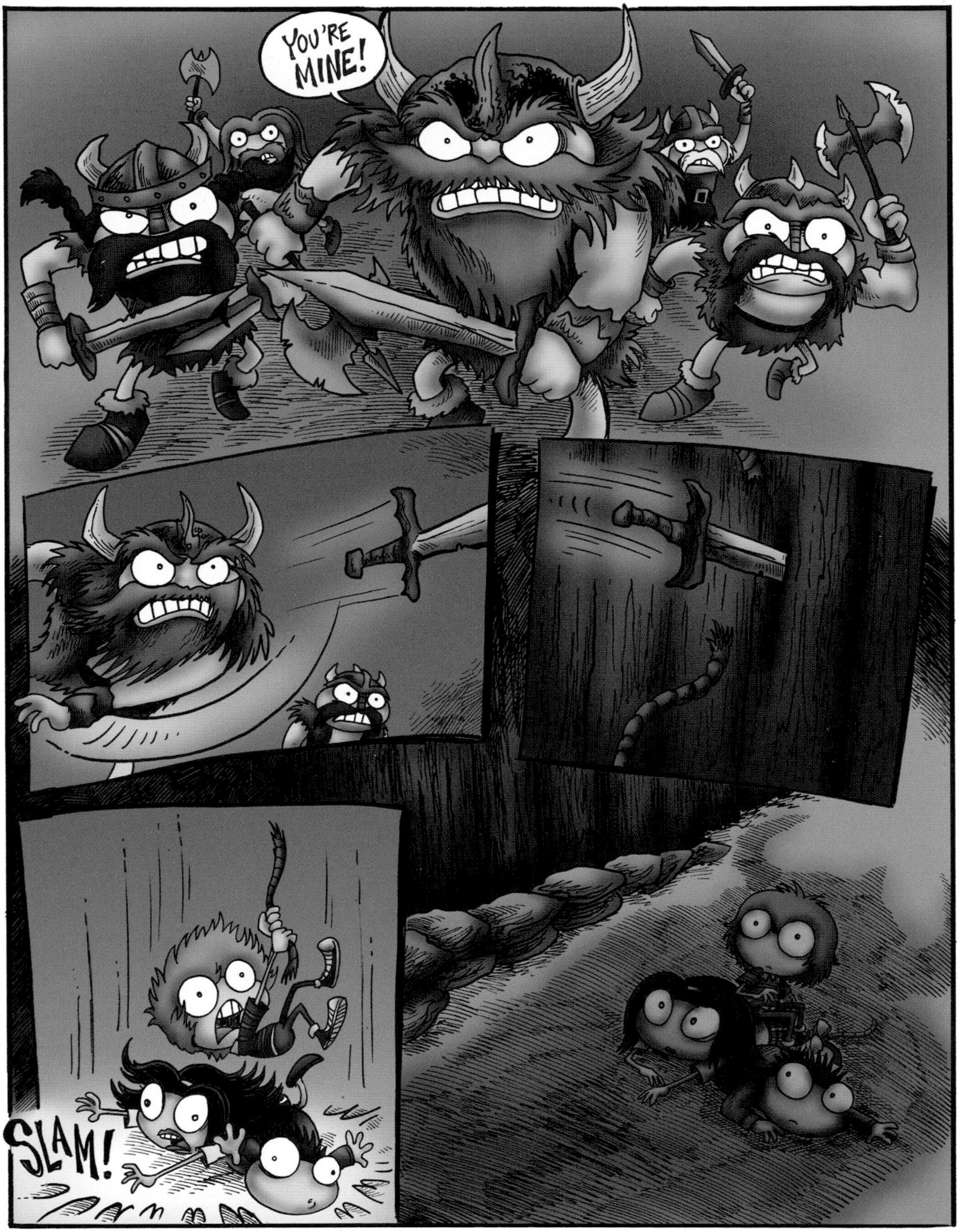
YOU'RE MINE!
SLAM!

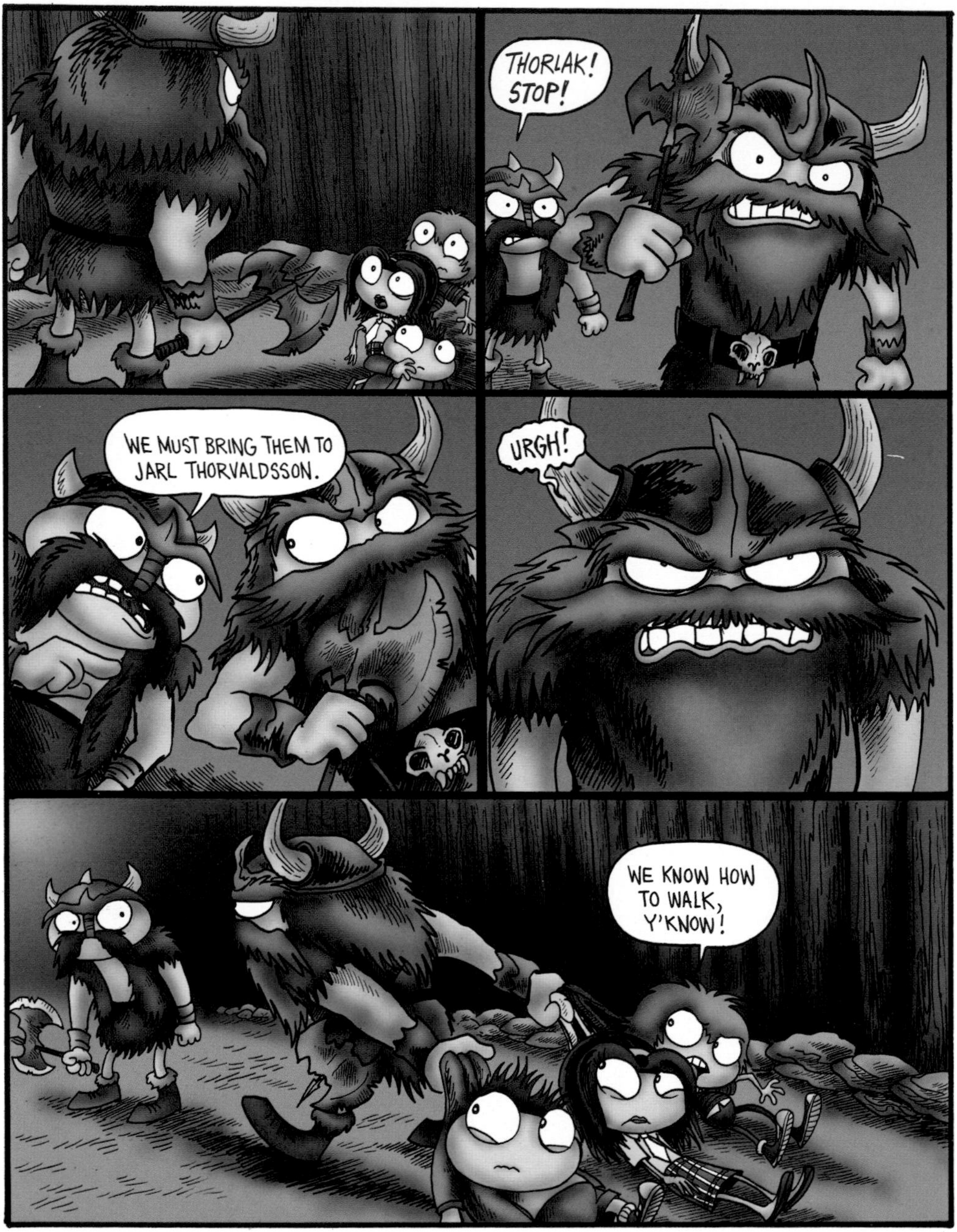
THORLAK! STOP!
WE MUST BRING THEM TO JARL THORVALDSSON.
URGH!
WE KNOW HOW TO WALK, Y'KNOW!

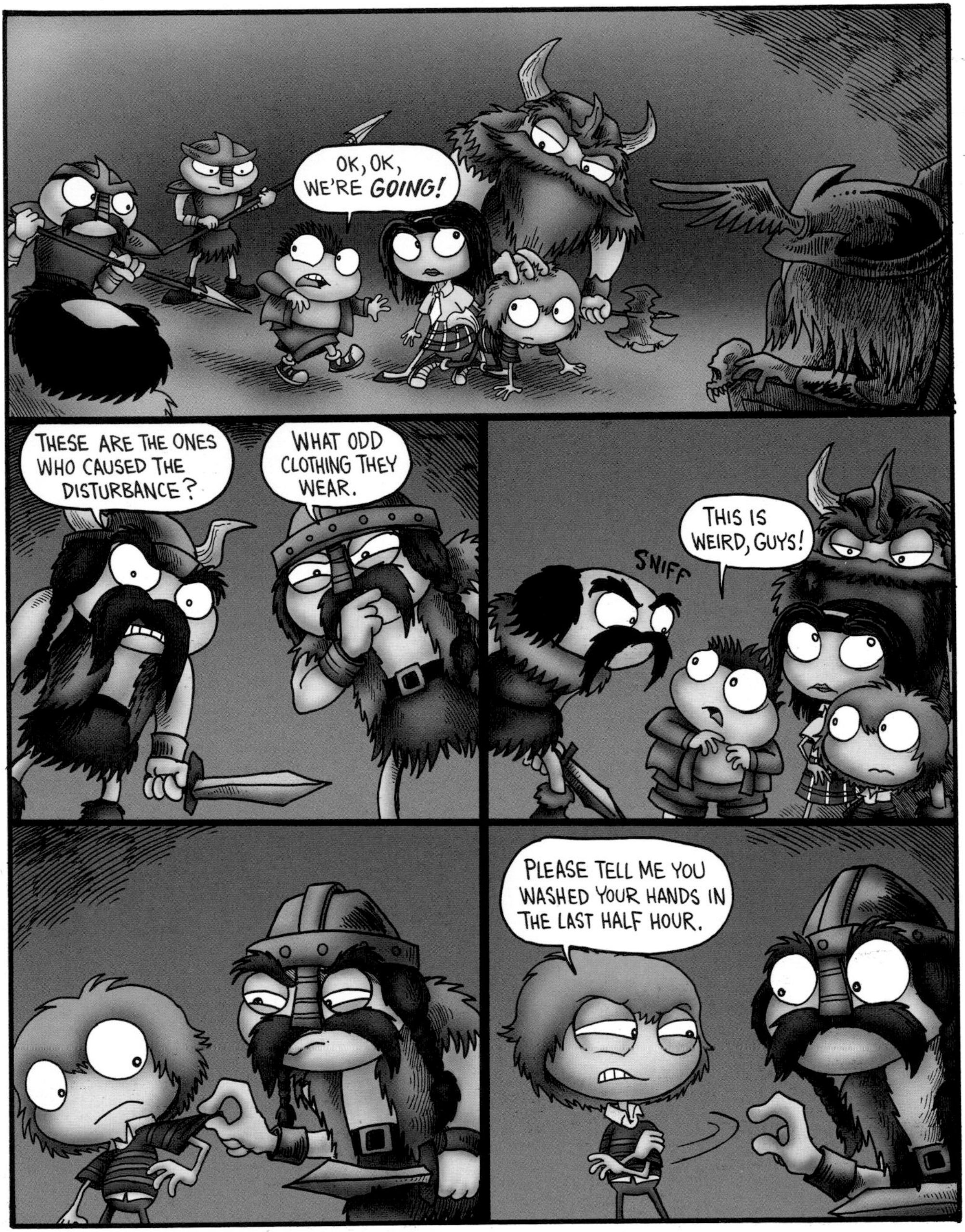
OK, OK,
WE'RE *GOING!*
THESE ARE THE ONES WHO CAUSED THE DISTURBANCE?
WHAT ODD CLOTHING THEY WEAR.
SNIFF
THIS IS WEIRD, GUYS!
PLEASE TELL ME YOU WASHED YOUR HANDS IN THE LAST HALF HOUR.

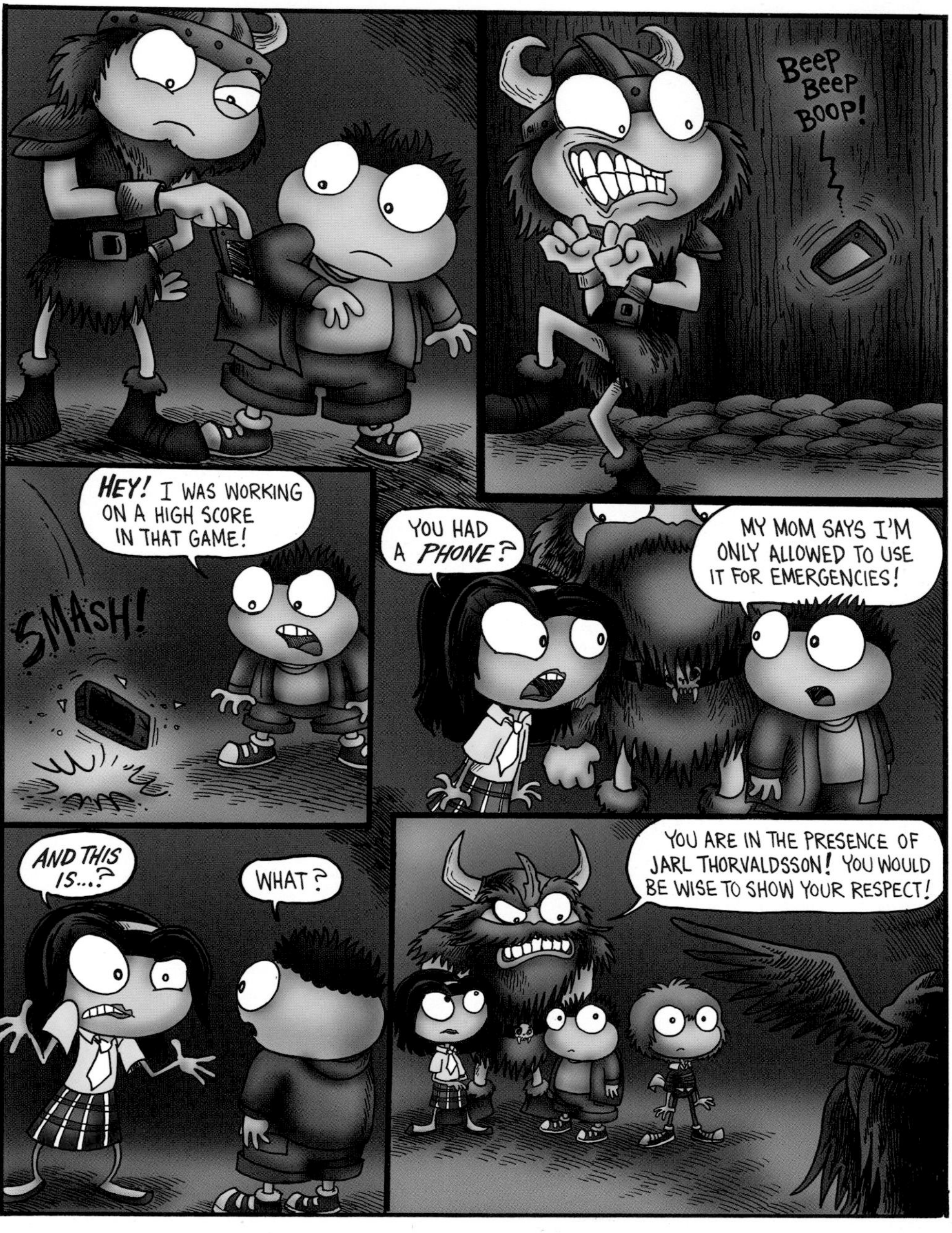
Beep Beep Boop!
HEY! I WAS WORKING ON A HIGH SCORE IN THAT GAME!
SMASH!
YOU HAD A PHONE?
MY MOM SAYS I'M ONLY ALLOWED TO USE IT FOR EMERGENCIES!
AND THIS IS...?
WHAT?
YOU ARE IN THE PRESENCE OF JARL THORVALDSSON! YOU WOULD BE WISE TO SHOW YOUR RESPECT!

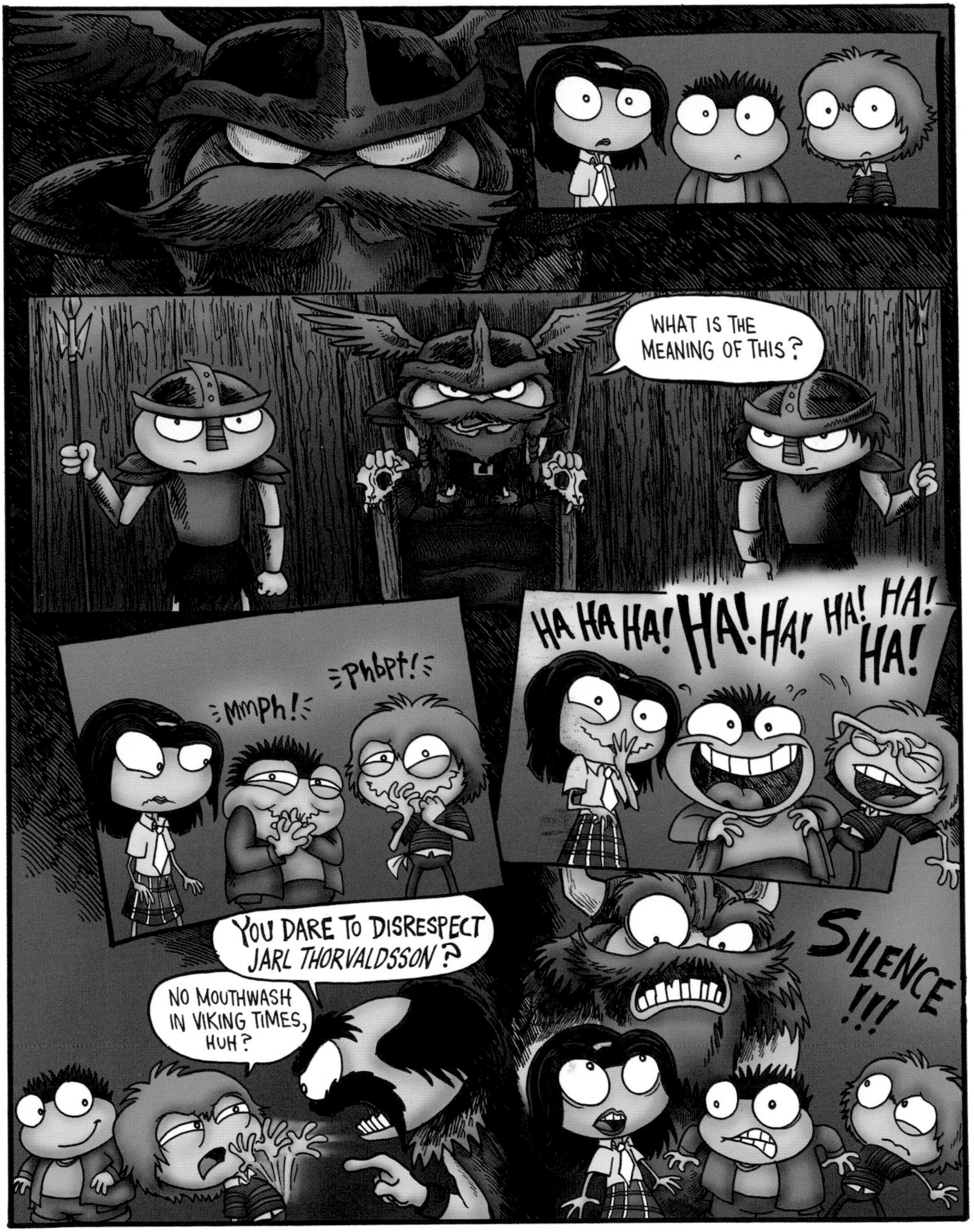
WHAT IS THE MEANING OF THIS?
Mmph!
Phbpt!
HA HA HA! HA! HA! HA! HA! HA!
YOU DARE TO DISRESPECT JARL THORVALDSSON?
NO MOUTHWASH IN VIKING TIMES, HUH?
SILENCE !!!

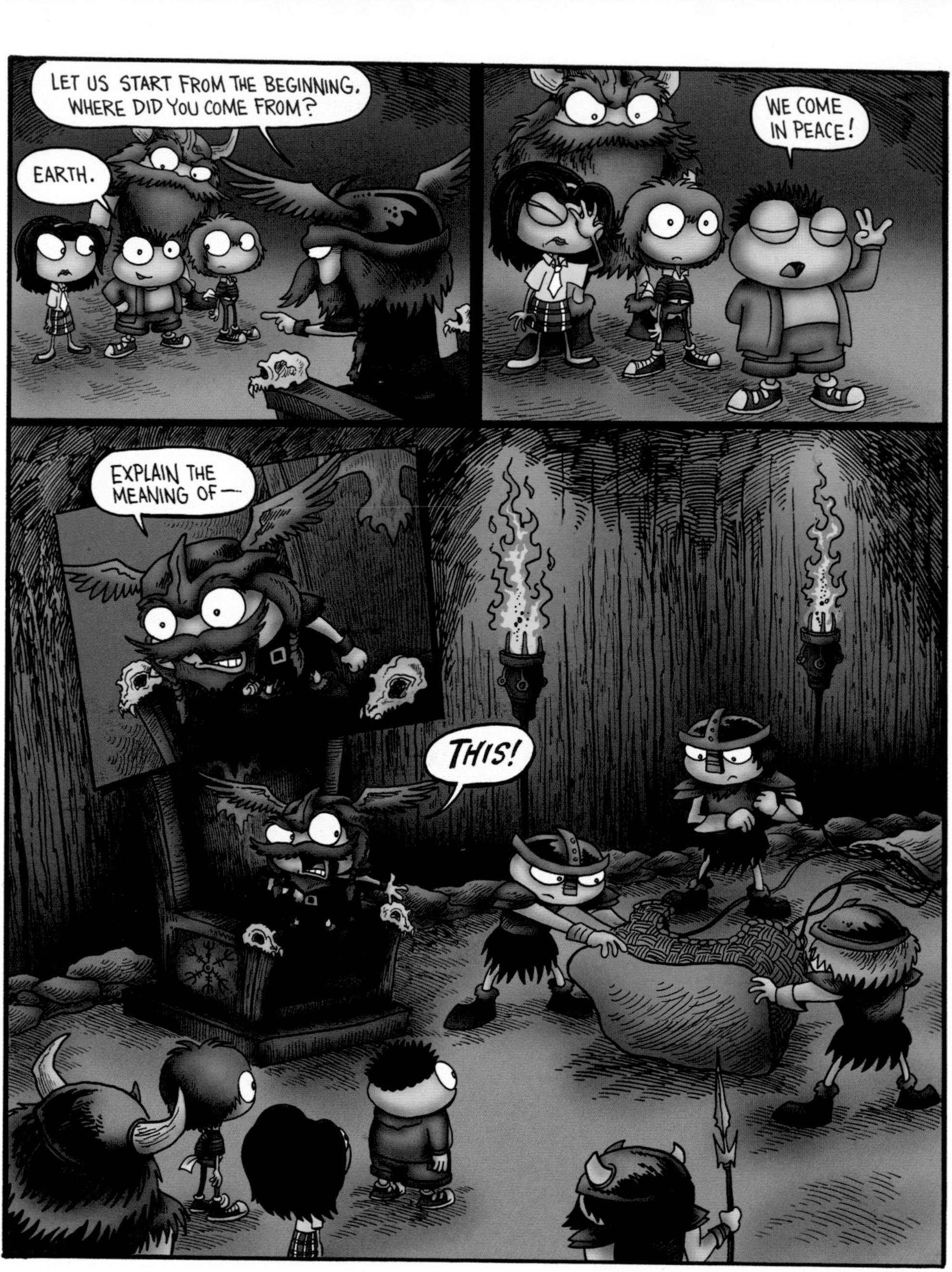
LET US START FROM THE BEGINNING. WHERE DID YOU COME FROM?
EARTH.
WE COME IN PEACE!
EXPLAIN THE MEANING OF—
THIS!

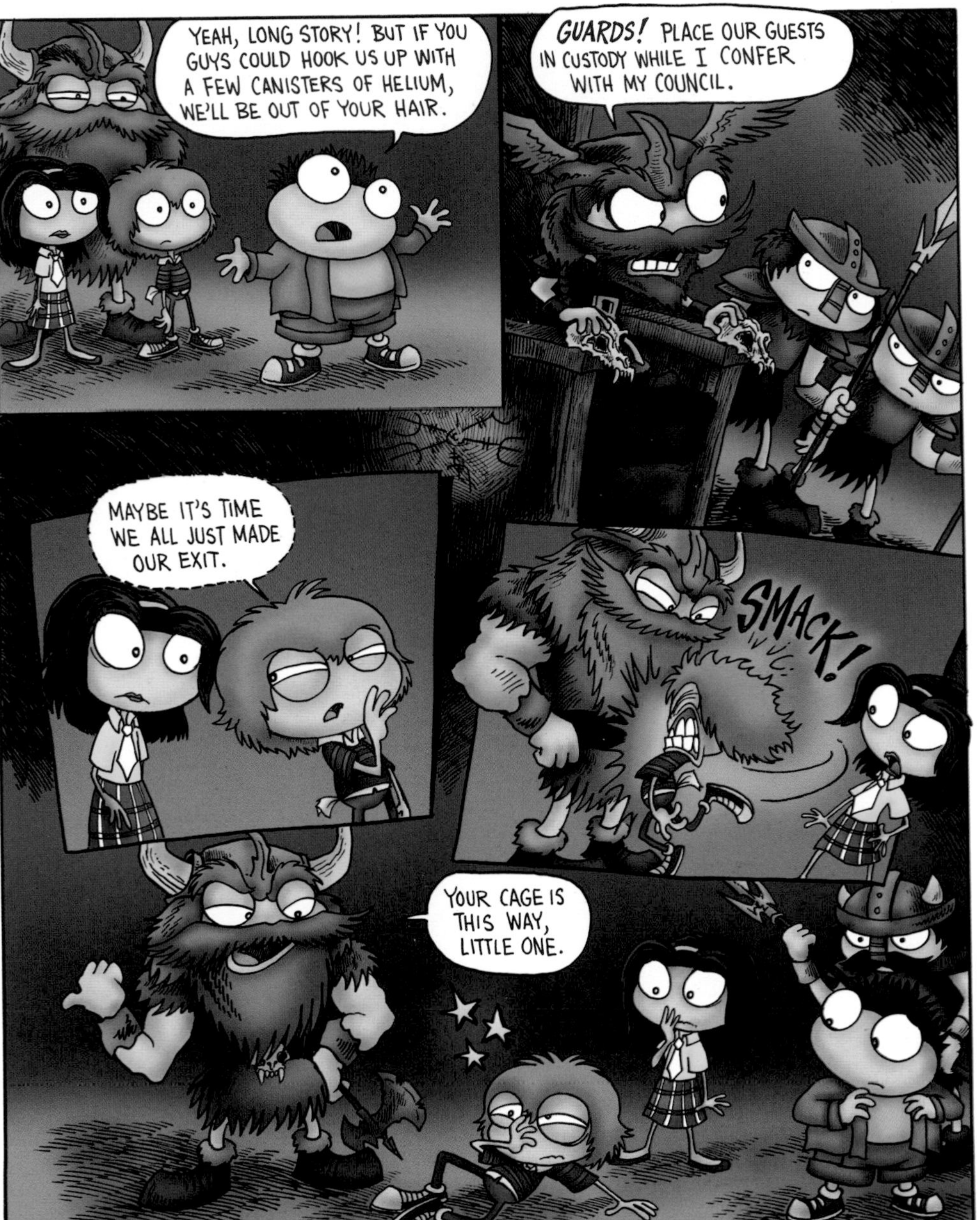
YEAH, LONG STORY! BUT IF YOU GUYS COULD HOOK US UP WITH A FEW CANISTERS OF HELIUM, WE'LL BE OUT OF YOUR HAIR.
GUARDS! PLACE OUR GUESTS IN CUSTODY WHILE I CONFER WITH MY COUNCIL.
MAYBE IT'S TIME WE ALL JUST MADE OUR EXIT.
SMACK!
YOUR CAGE IS THIS WAY, LITTLE ONE.

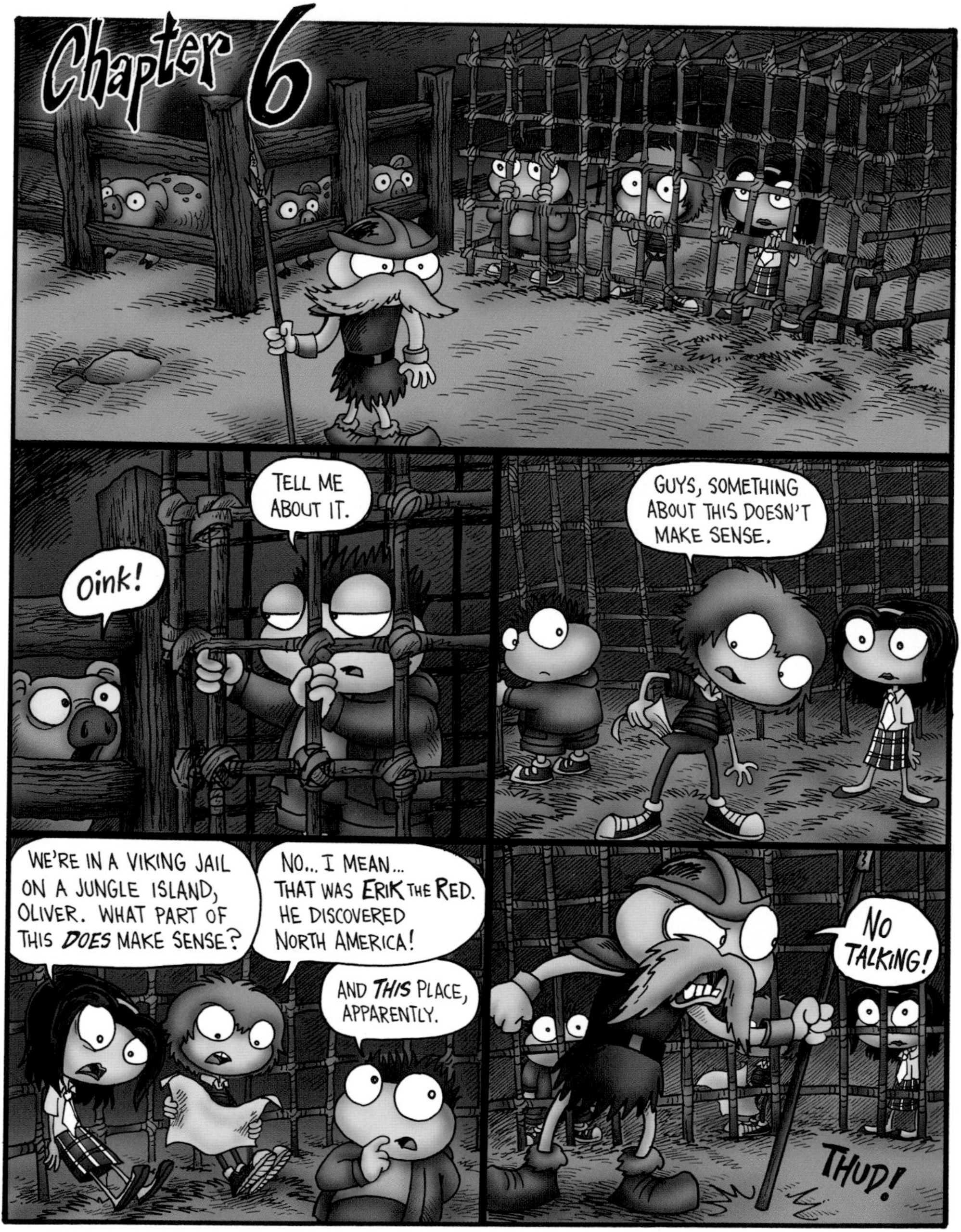
Chapter 6
Oink!
TELL ME ABOUT IT.
GUYS, SOMETHING ABOUT THIS DOESN'T MAKE SENSE.
WE'RE IN A VIKING JAIL ON A JUNGLE ISLAND, OLIVER. WHAT PART OF THIS DOES MAKE SENSE?
NO... I MEAN... THAT WAS ERIK THE RED. HE DISCOVERED NORTH AMERICA!
AND THIS PLACE, APPARENTLY.
NO TALKING!
THUD!

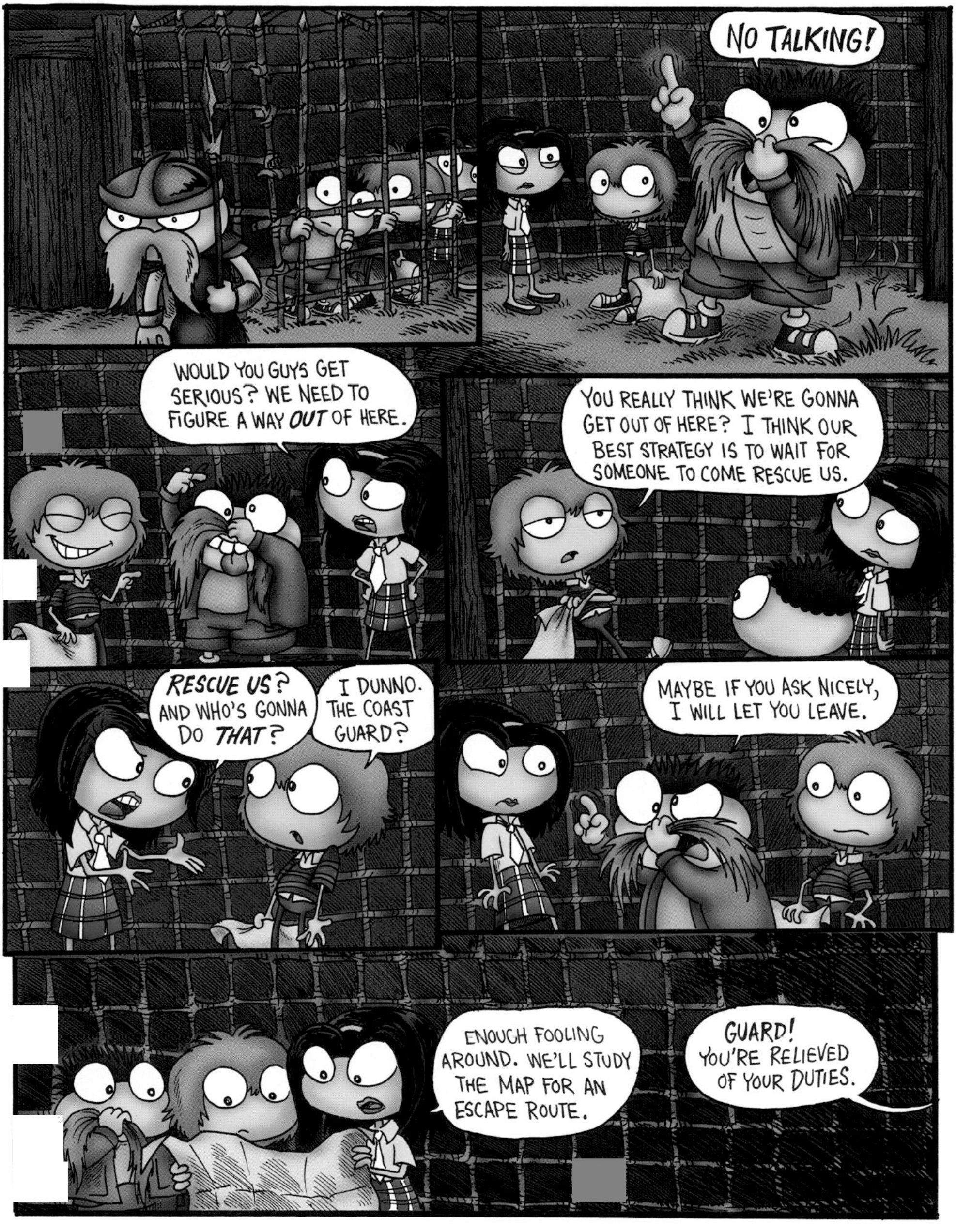
NO TALKING!
WOULD YOU GUYS GET SERIOUS? WE NEED TO FIGURE A WAY OUT OF HERE.
YOU REALLY THINK WE'RE GONNA GET OUT OF HERE? I THINK OUR BEST STRATEGY IS TO WAIT FOR SOMEONE TO COME RESCUE US.
RESCUE US? AND WHO'S GONNA DO THAT?
I DUNNO. THE COAST GUARD?
MAYBE IF YOU ASK NICELY, I WILL LET YOU LEAVE.
ENOUGH FOOLING AROUND. WE'LL STUDY THE MAP FOR AN ESCAPE ROUTE.
GUARD! YOU'RE RELIEVED OF YOUR DUTIES.

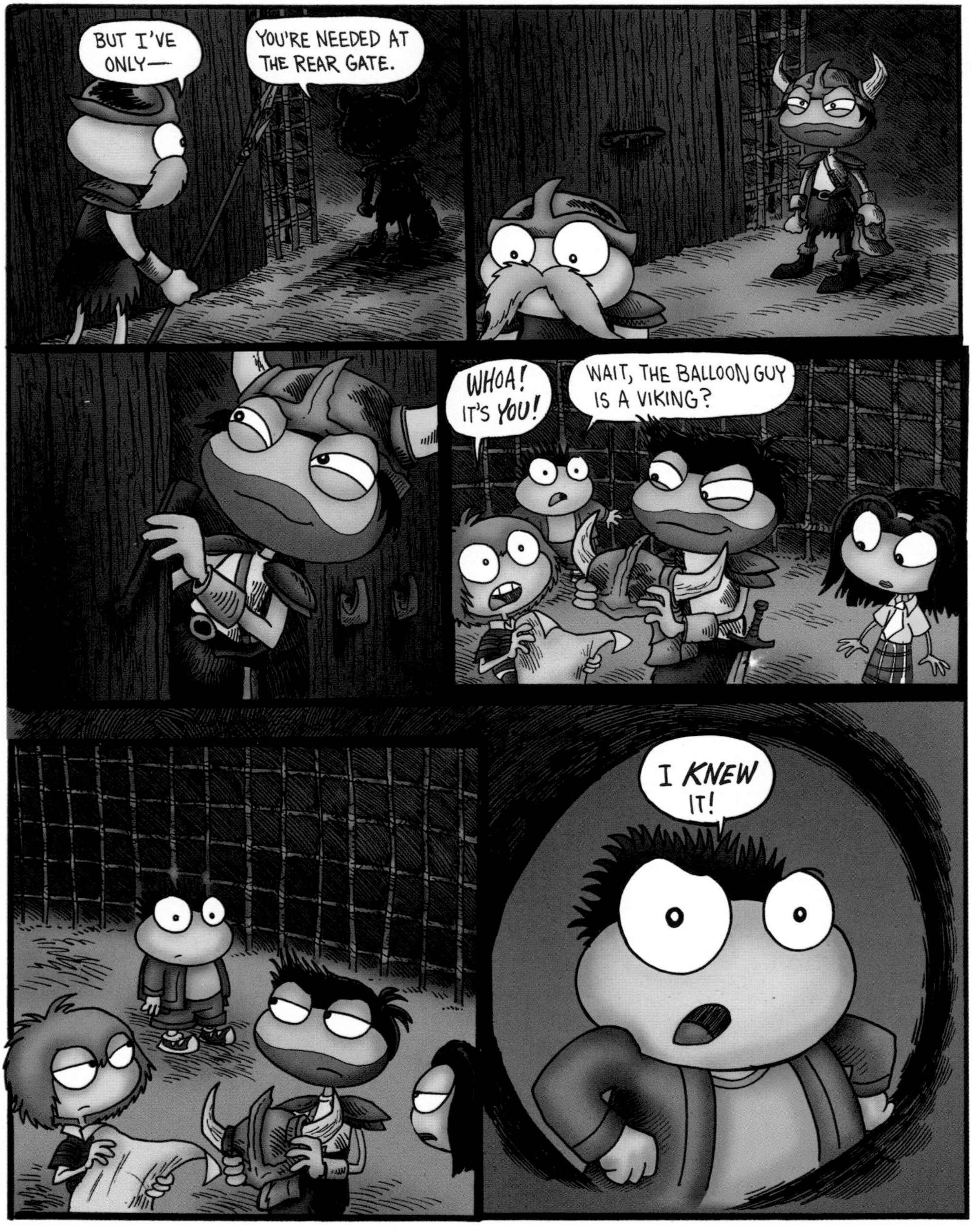
BUT I'VE ONLY—
YOU'RE NEEDED AT THE REAR GATE.
WHOA! IT'S YOU!
WAIT, THE BALLOON GUY IS A VIKING?
I KNEW IT!

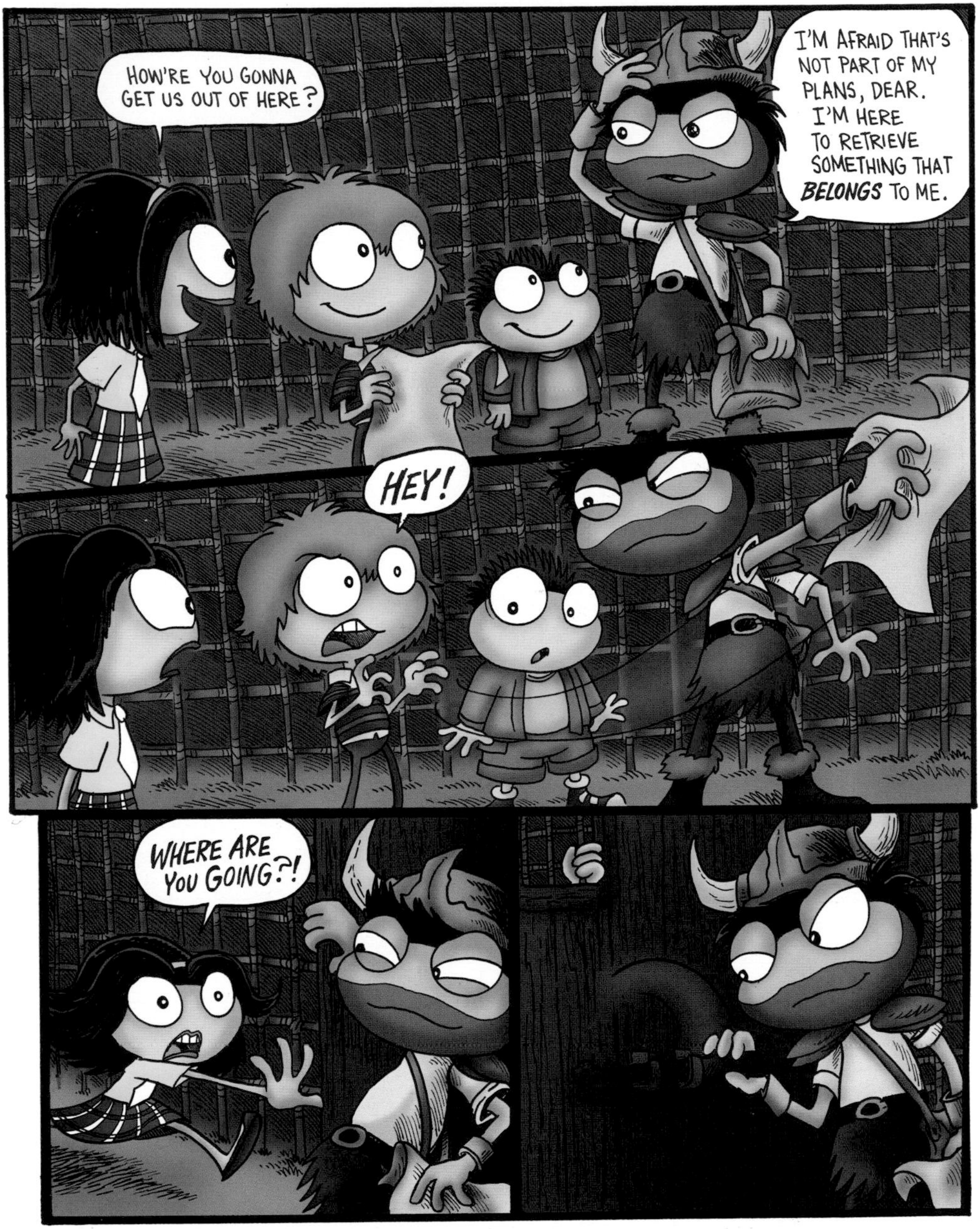
HOW'RE YOU GONNA GET US OUT OF HERE?
I'M AFRAID THAT'S NOT PART OF MY PLANS, DEAR. I'M HERE TO RETRIEVE SOMETHING THAT BELONGS TO ME.
HEY!
WHERE ARE YOU GOING?!

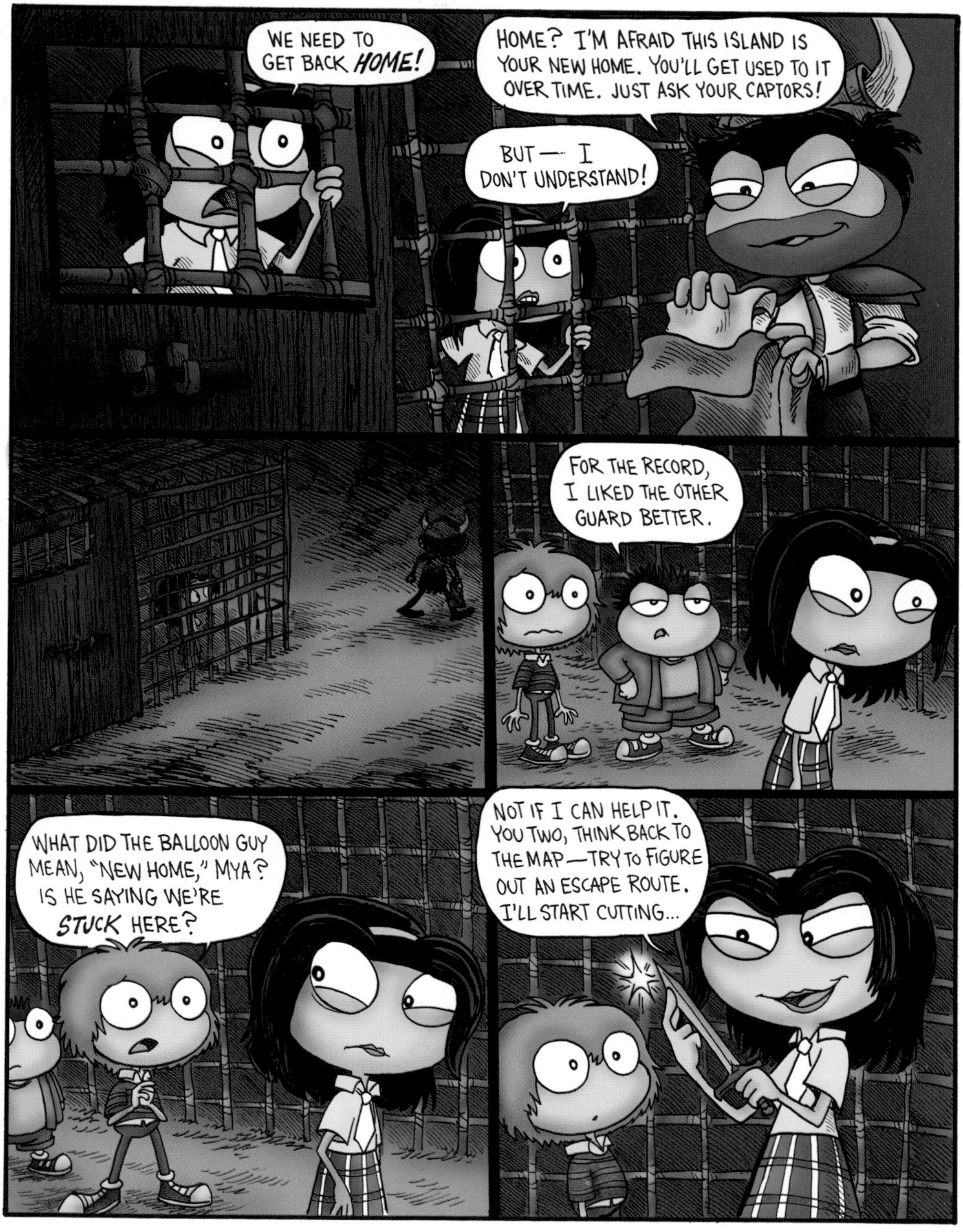
WE NEED TO GET BACK HOME!
HOME? I'M AFRAID THIS ISLAND IS YOUR NEW HOME. YOU'LL GET USED TO IT OVER TIME. JUST ASK YOUR CAPTORS!
BUT— I DON'T UNDERSTAND!
FOR THE RECORD, I LIKED THE OTHER GUARD BETTER.
WHAT DID THE BALLOON GUY MEAN, "NEW HOME," MYA? IS HE SAYING WE'RE STUCK HERE?
NOT IF I CAN HELP IT. YOU TWO, THINK BACK TO THE MAP—TRY TO FIGURE OUT AN ESCAPE ROUTE. I'LL START CUTTING...

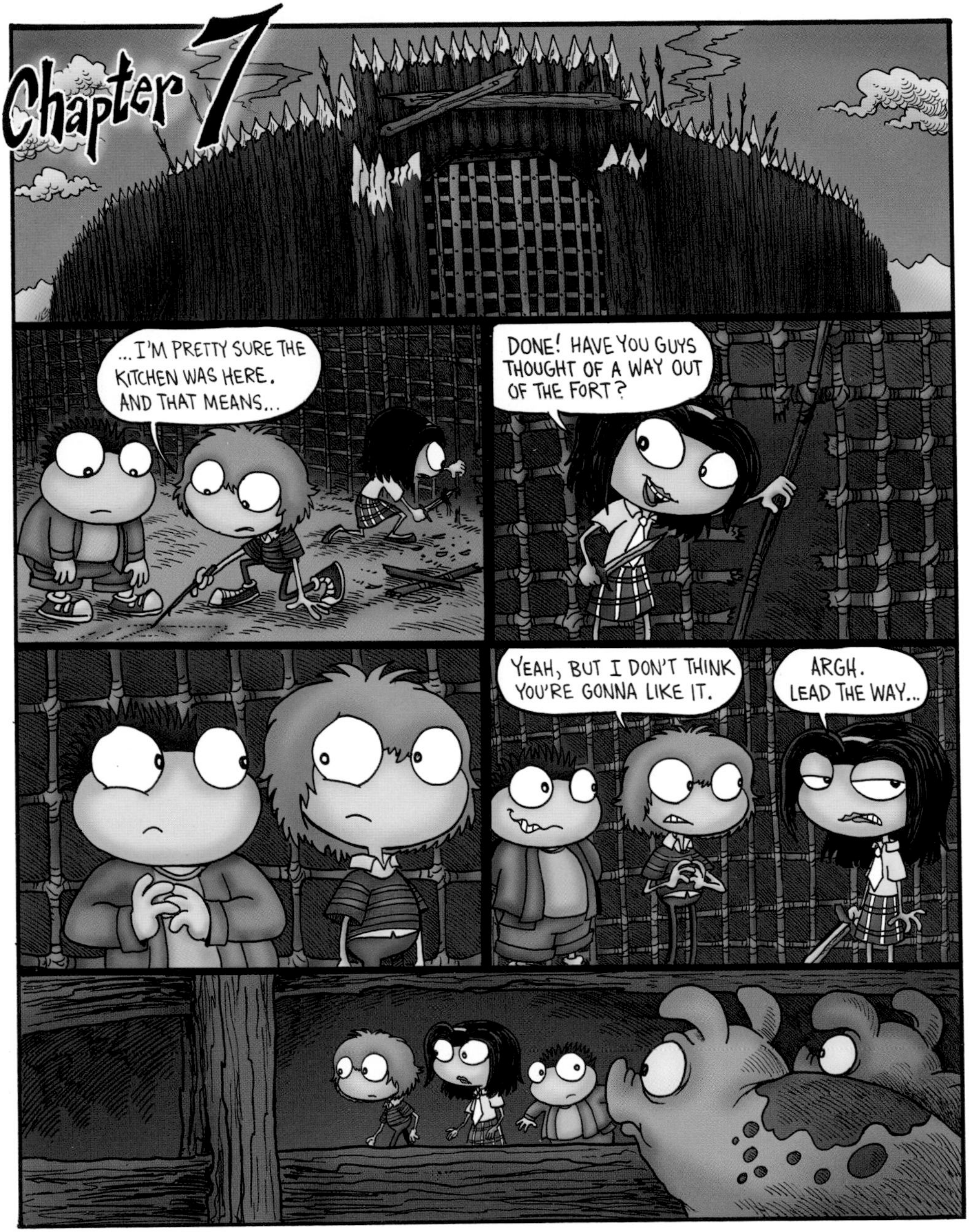
Chapter 7
... I'M PRETTY SURE THE KITCHEN WAS HERE. AND THAT MEANS...
DONE! HAVE YOU GUYS THOUGHT OF A WAY OUT OF THE FORT?
YEAH, BUT I DON'T THINK YOU'RE GONNA LIKE IT.
ARGH. LEAD THE WAY...

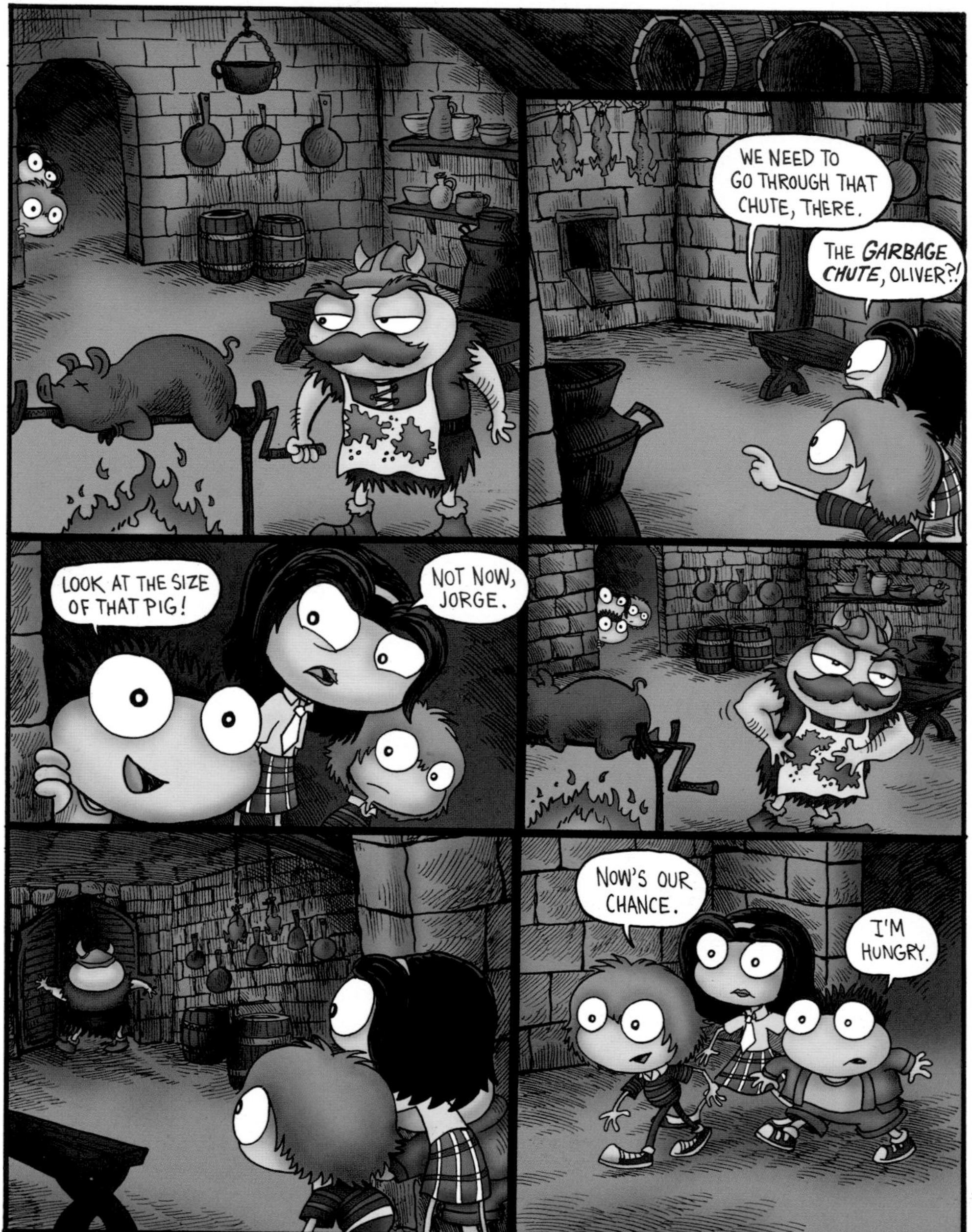
WE NEED TO GO THROUGH THAT CHUTE, THERE.
THE GARBAGE CHUTE, OLIVER?!
LOOK AT THE SIZE OF THAT PIG!
NOT NOW, JORGE.
NOW'S OUR CHANCE.
I'M HUNGRY.

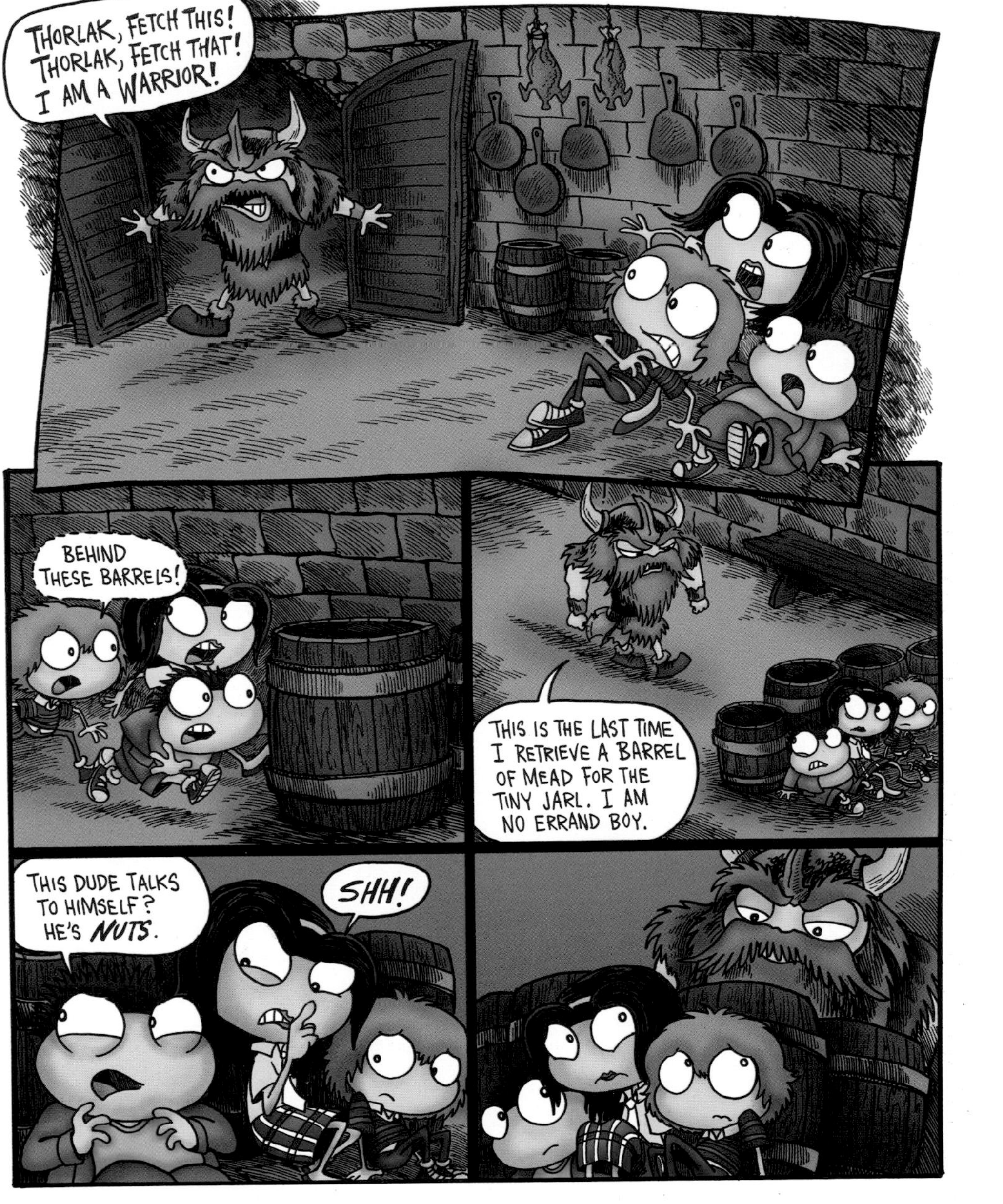
THORLAK, FETCH THIS! THORLAK, FETCH THAT! I AM A WARRIOR!
BEHIND THESE BARRELS!
THIS IS THE LAST TIME I RETRIEVE A BARREL OF MEAD FOR THE TINY JARL. I AM NO ERRAND BOY.
THIS DUDE TALKS TO HIMSELF? HE'S NUTS.
SHH!

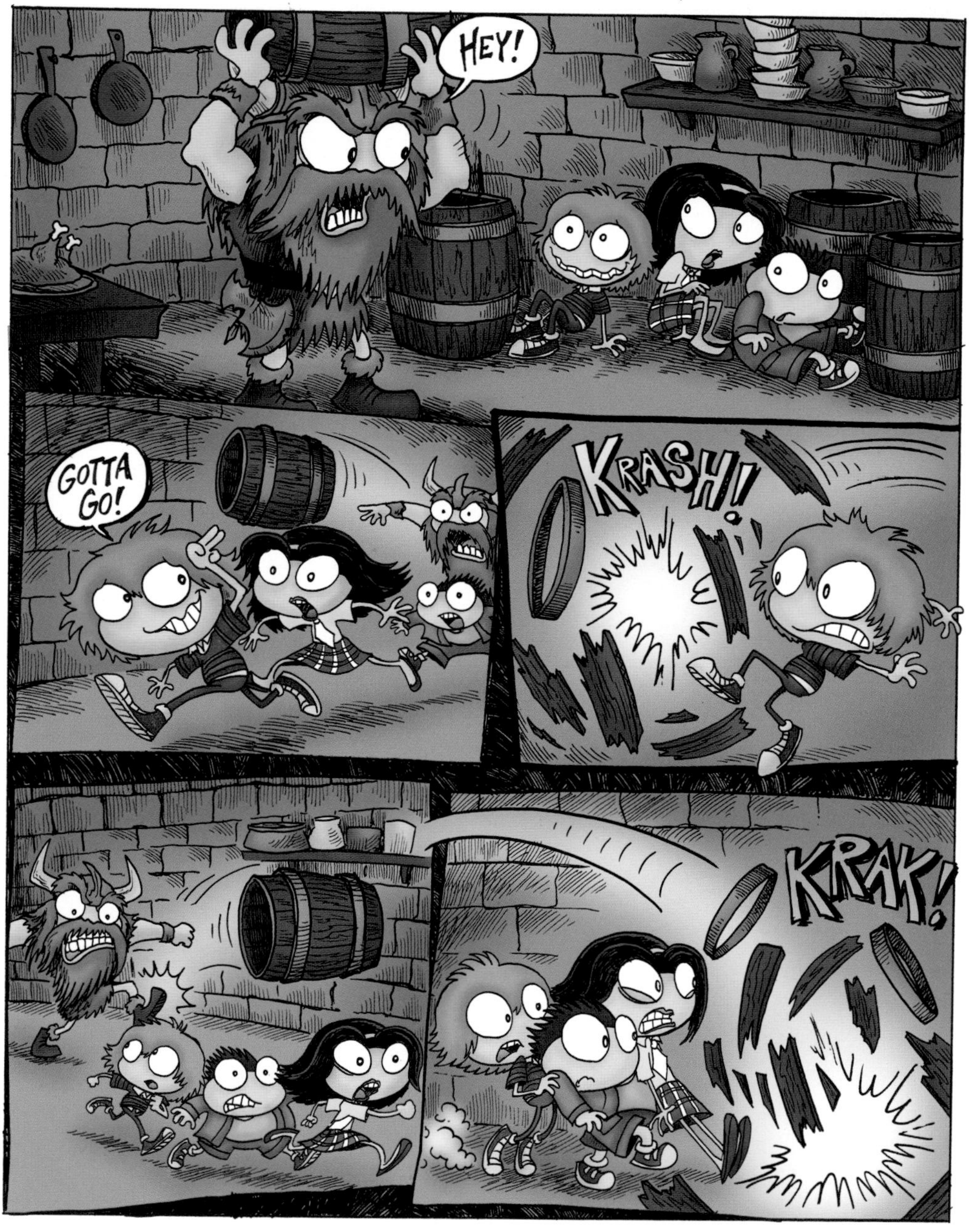
HEY!
GOTTA GO!
KRASH!
KRAK!

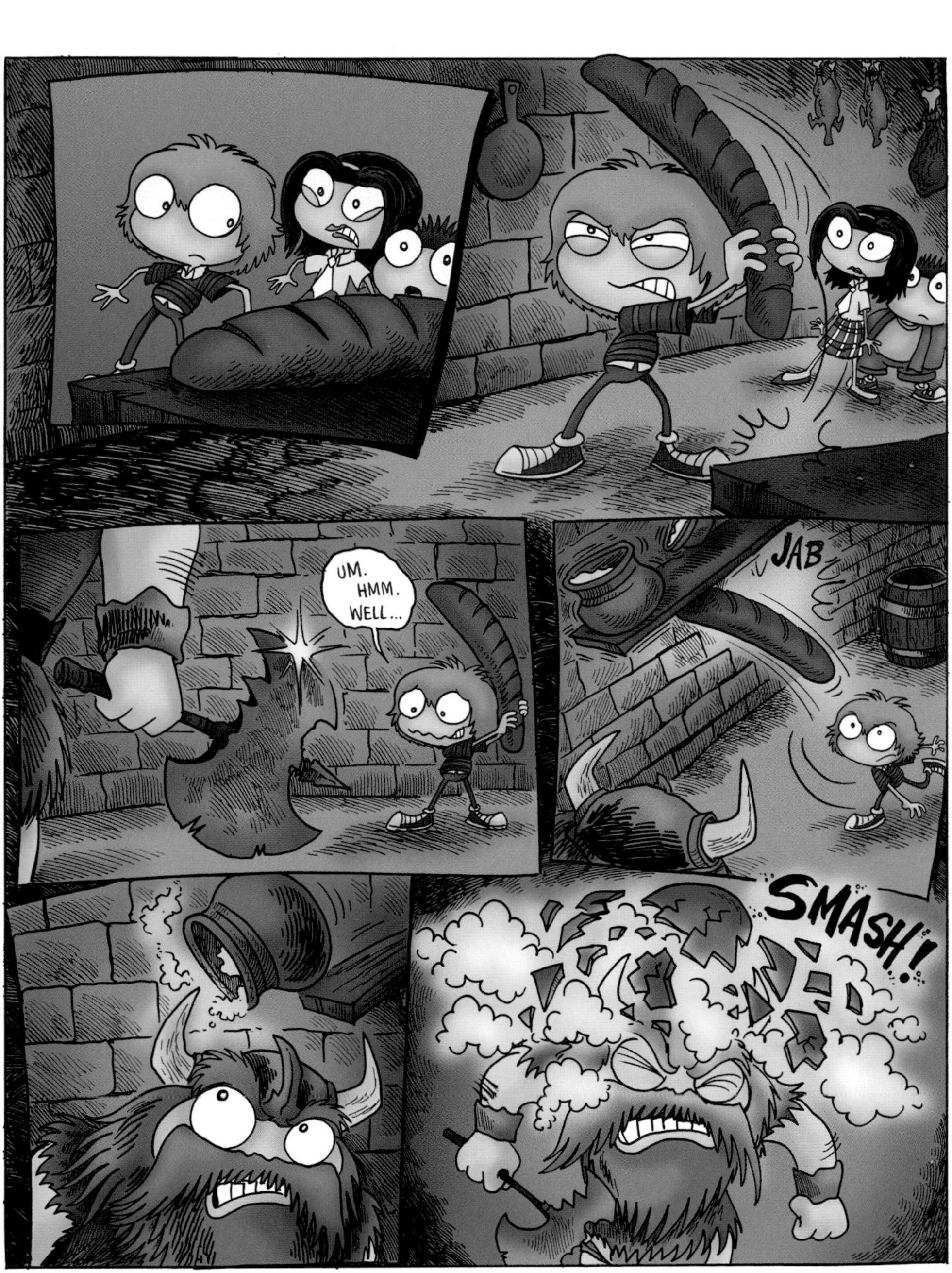
UM.
HMM.
WELL...
JAB
SMASH!

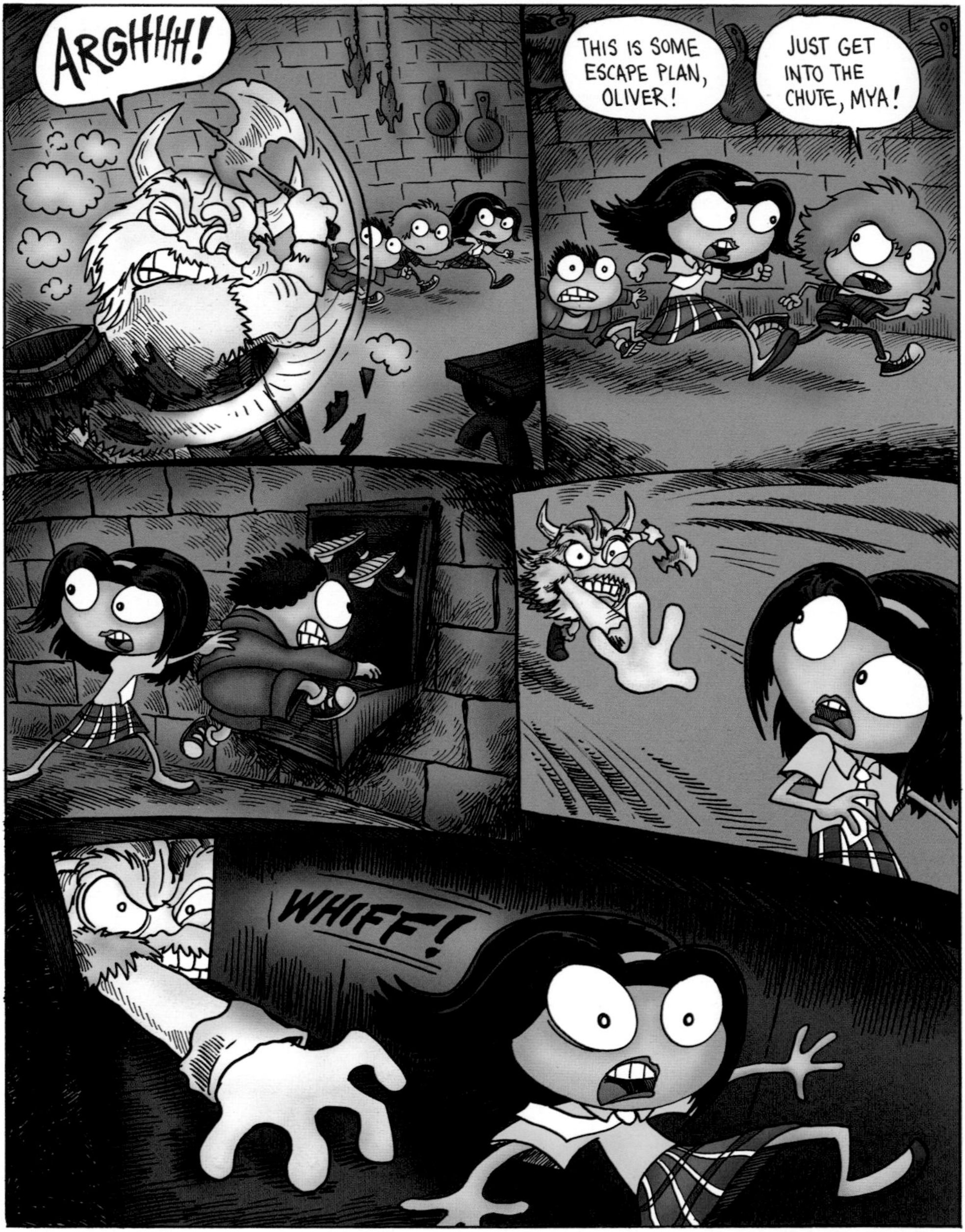
ARGHHH!
THIS IS SOME ESCAPE PLAN, OLIVER!
JUST GET INTO THE CHUTE, MYA!
WHIFF!

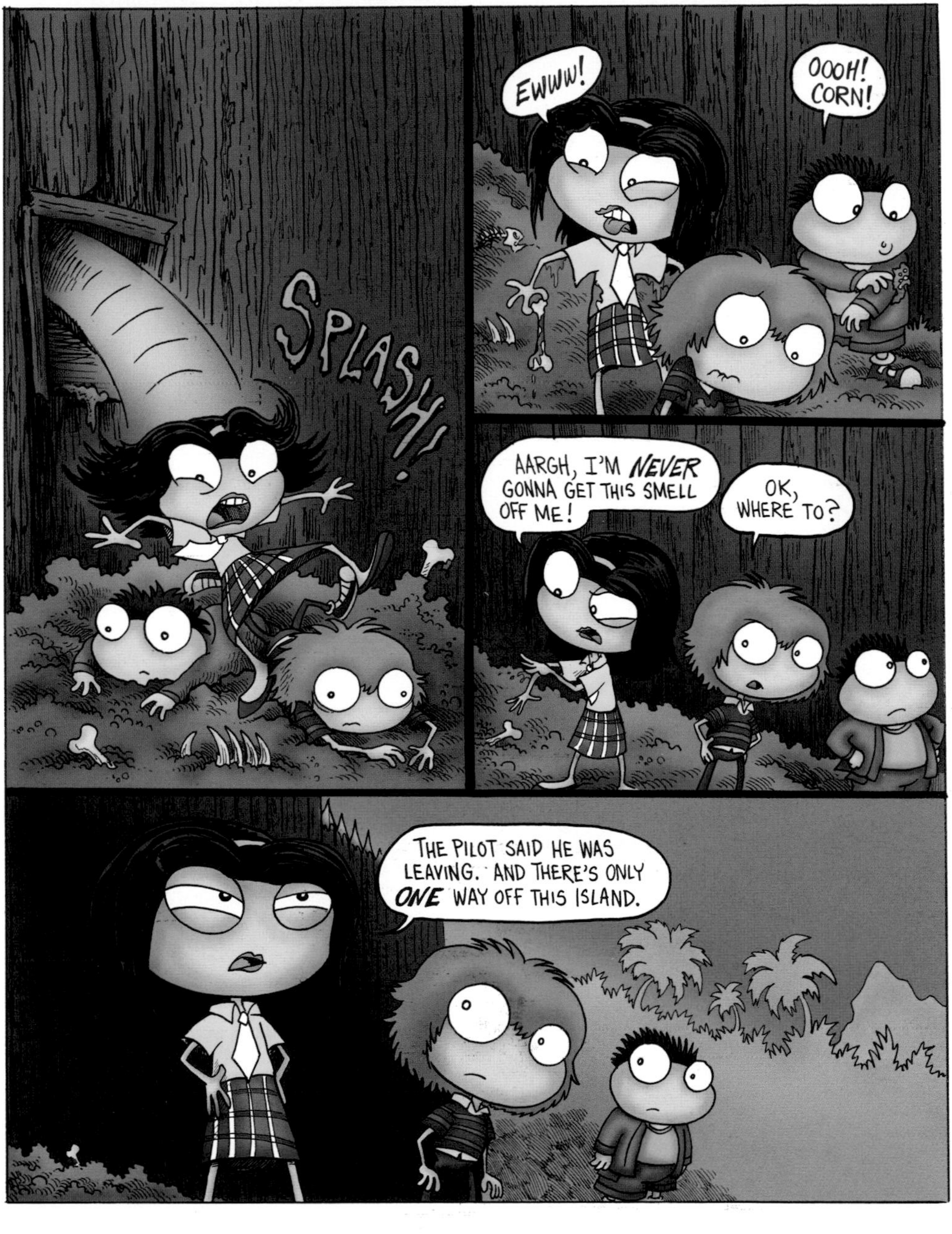
SPLASH!!
EWWW!
OOOH! CORN!
AARGH, I'M NEVER GONNA GET THIS SMELL OFF ME!
OK, WHERE TO?
THE PILOT SAID HE WAS LEAVING. AND THERE'S ONLY ONE WAY OFF THIS ISLAND.

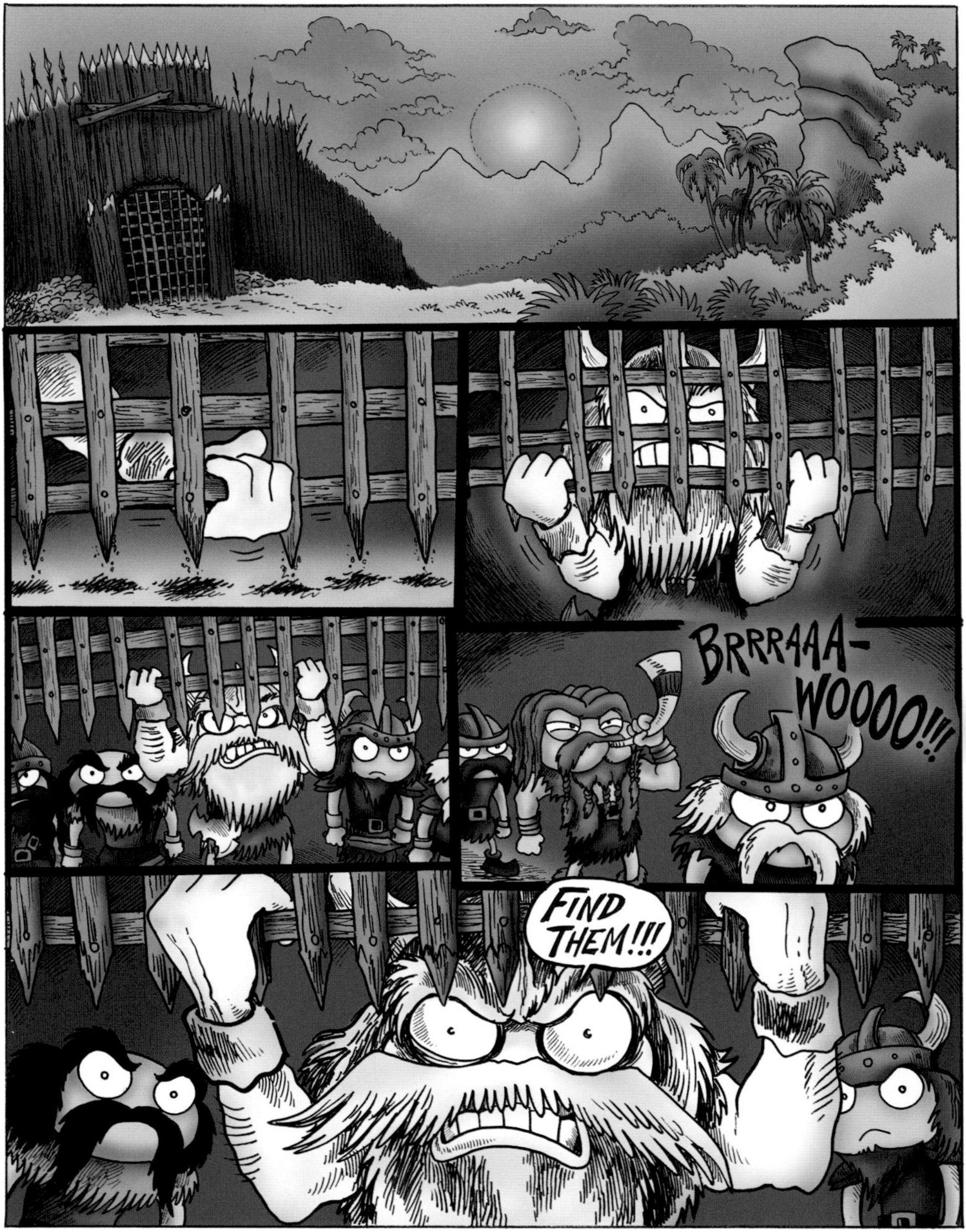
BRRRAAA-
WOOOO!!!
FIND THEM!!!

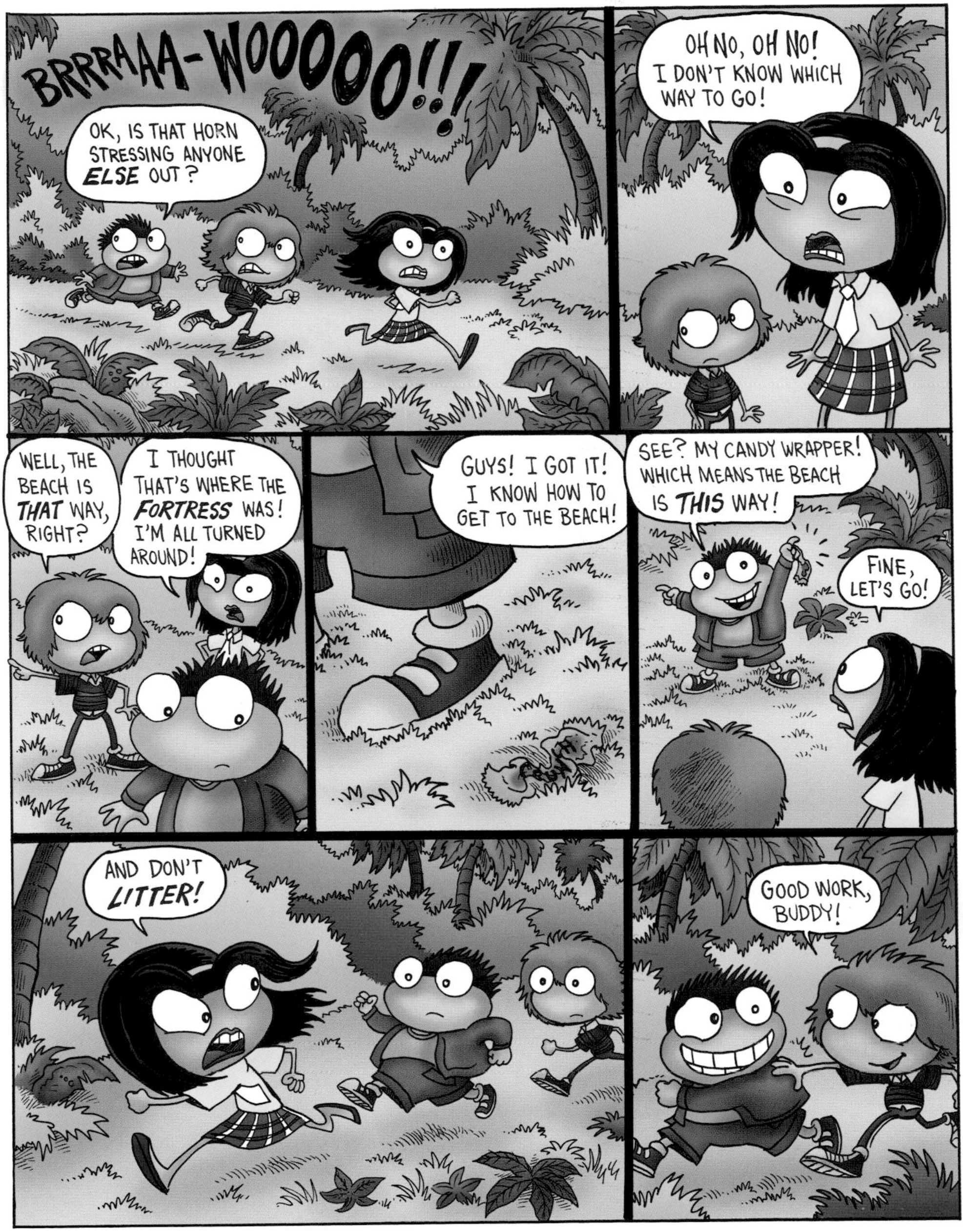
BRRRAAA-WOOOOO!!!
OK, IS THAT HORN STRESSING ANYONE ELSE OUT?
OH NO, OH NO! I DON'T KNOW WHICH WAY TO GO!
WELL, THE BEACH IS THAT WAY, RIGHT?
I THOUGHT THAT'S WHERE THE FORTRESS WAS! I'M ALL TURNED AROUND!
GUYS! I GOT IT! I KNOW HOW TO GET TO THE BEACH!
SEE? MY CANDY WRAPPER! WHICH MEANS THE BEACH IS THIS WAY!
FINE, LET'S GO!
AND DON'T LITTER!
GOOD WORK, BUDDY!

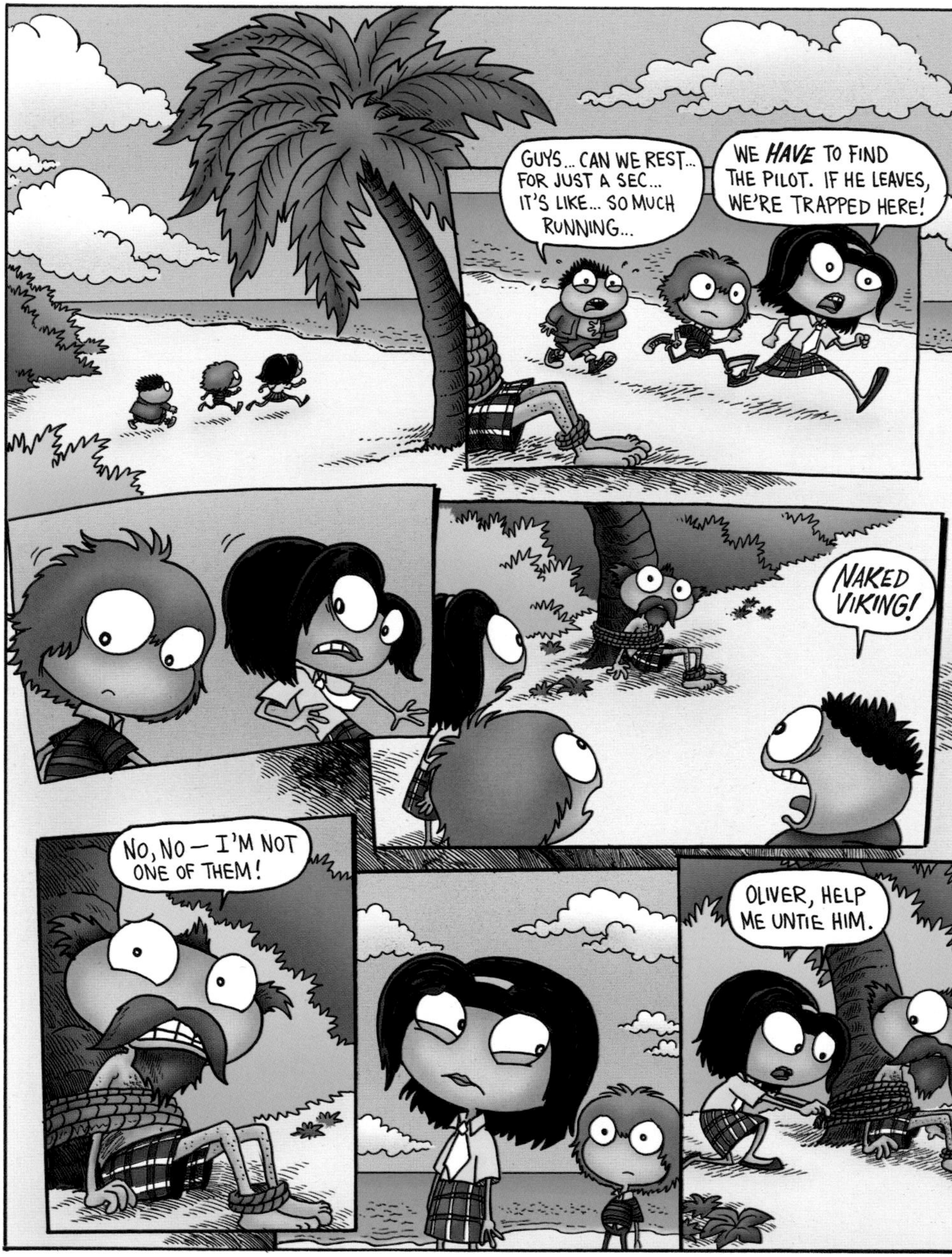
GUYS... CAN WE REST... FOR JUST A SEC... IT'S LIKE... SO MUCH RUNNING...
WE HAVE TO FIND THE PILOT. IF HE LEAVES, WE'RE TRAPPED HERE!
NAKED VIKING!
NO, NO — I'M NOT ONE OF THEM!
OLIVER, HELP ME UNTIE HIM.

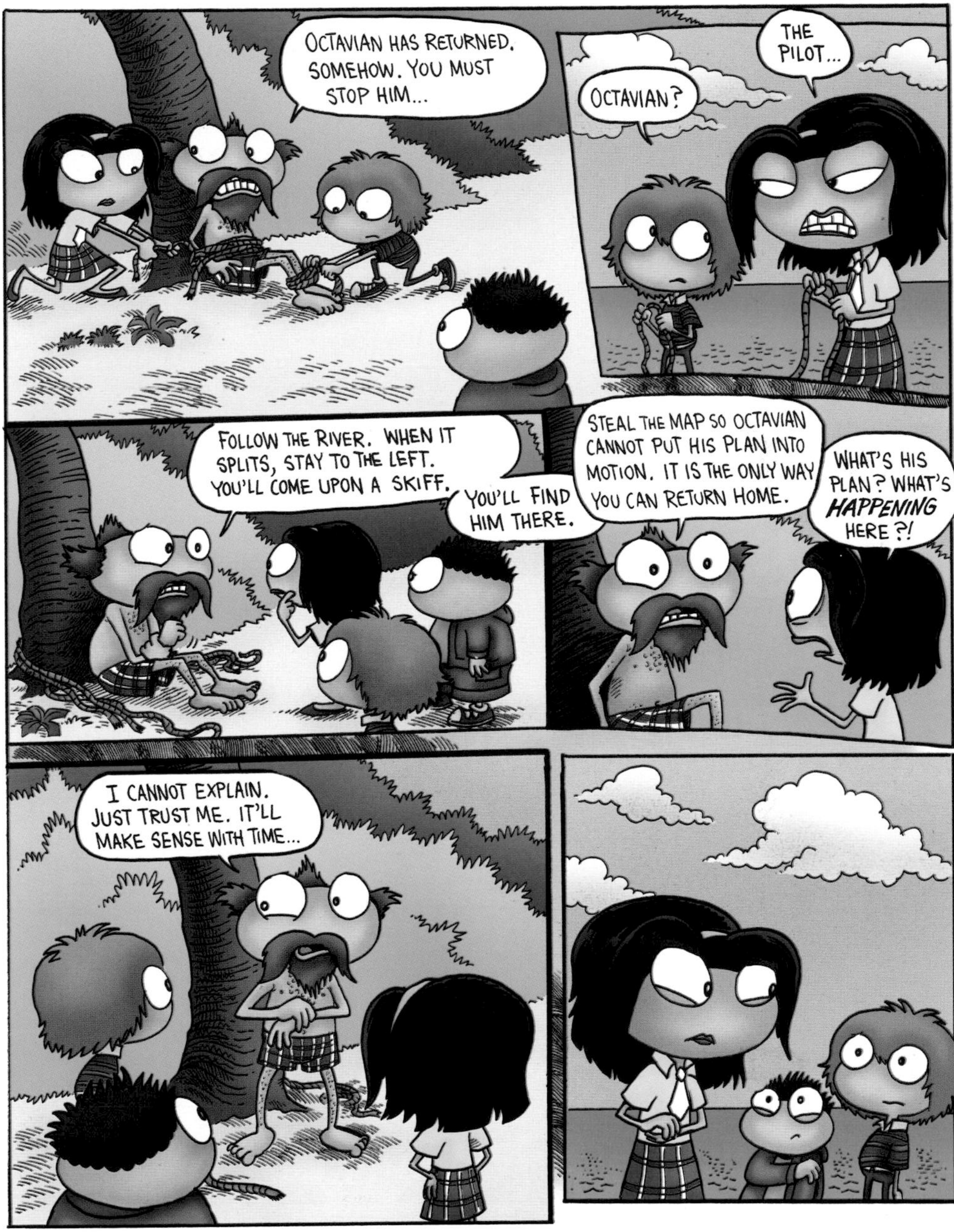
OCTAVIAN HAS RETURNED. SOMEHOW. YOU MUST STOP HIM...
THE PILOT...
OCTAVIAN?
FOLLOW THE RIVER. WHEN IT SPLITS, STAY TO THE LEFT. YOU'LL COME UPON A SKIFF.
YOU'LL FIND HIM THERE.
STEAL THE MAP SO OCTAVIAN CANNOT PUT HIS PLAN INTO MOTION. IT IS THE ONLY WAY YOU CAN RETURN HOME.
WHAT'S HIS PLAN? WHAT'S HAPPENING HERE?!
I CANNOT EXPLAIN. JUST TRUST ME. IT'LL MAKE SENSE WITH TIME...

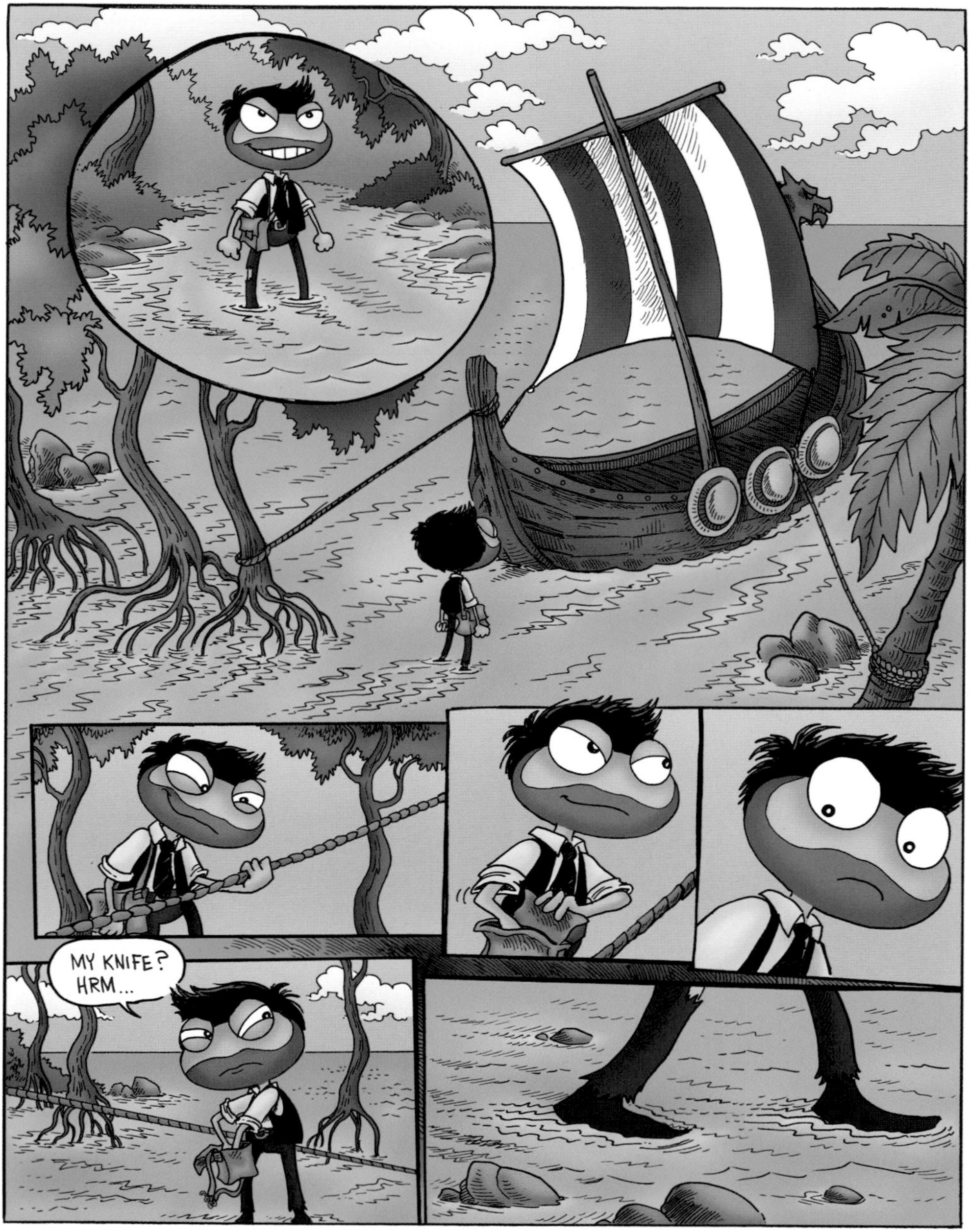
MY KNIFE? HRM...

# Chapter 8

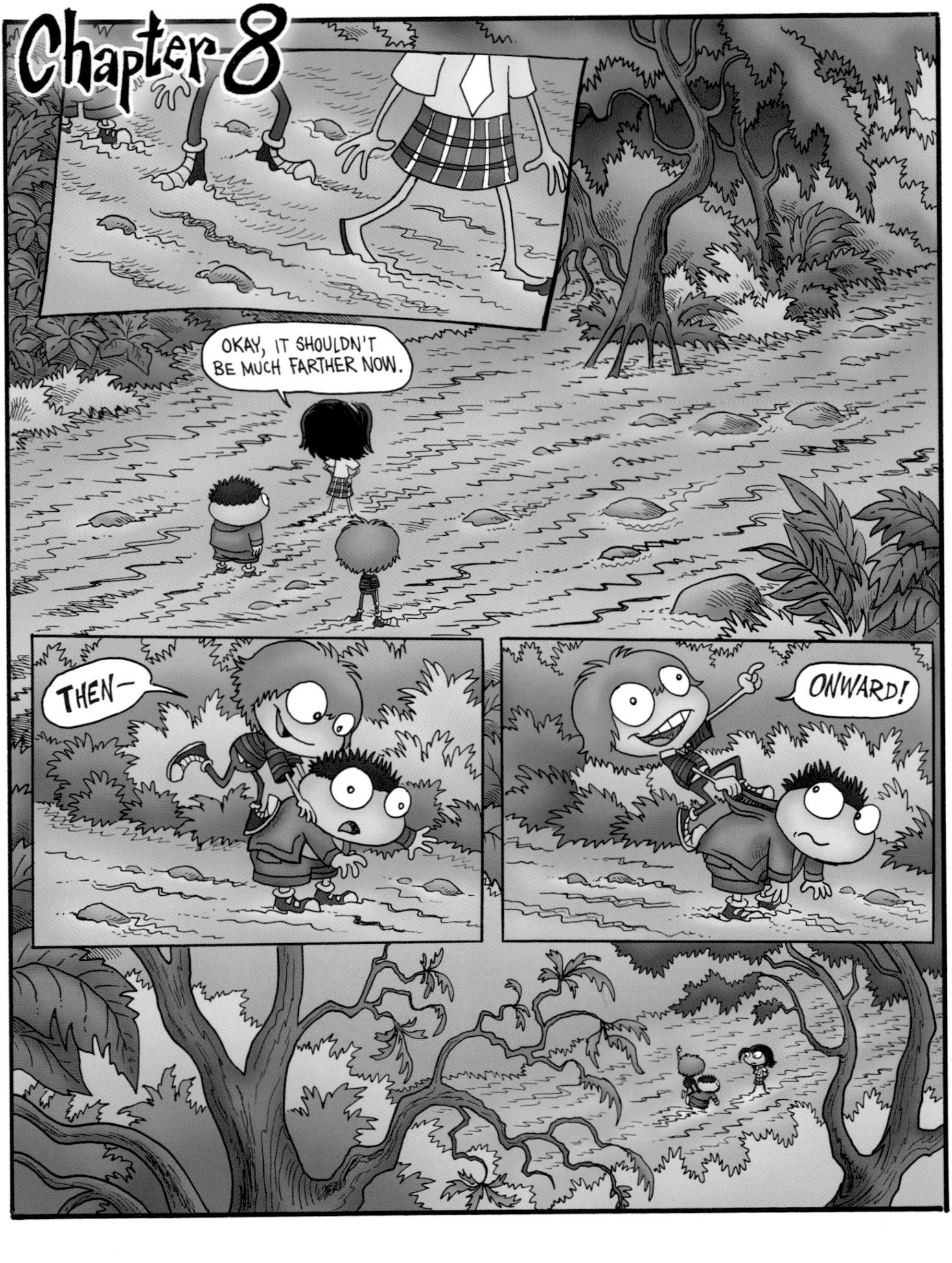
OKAY, IT SHOULDN'T BE MUCH FARTHER NOW.
THEN—
ONWARD!

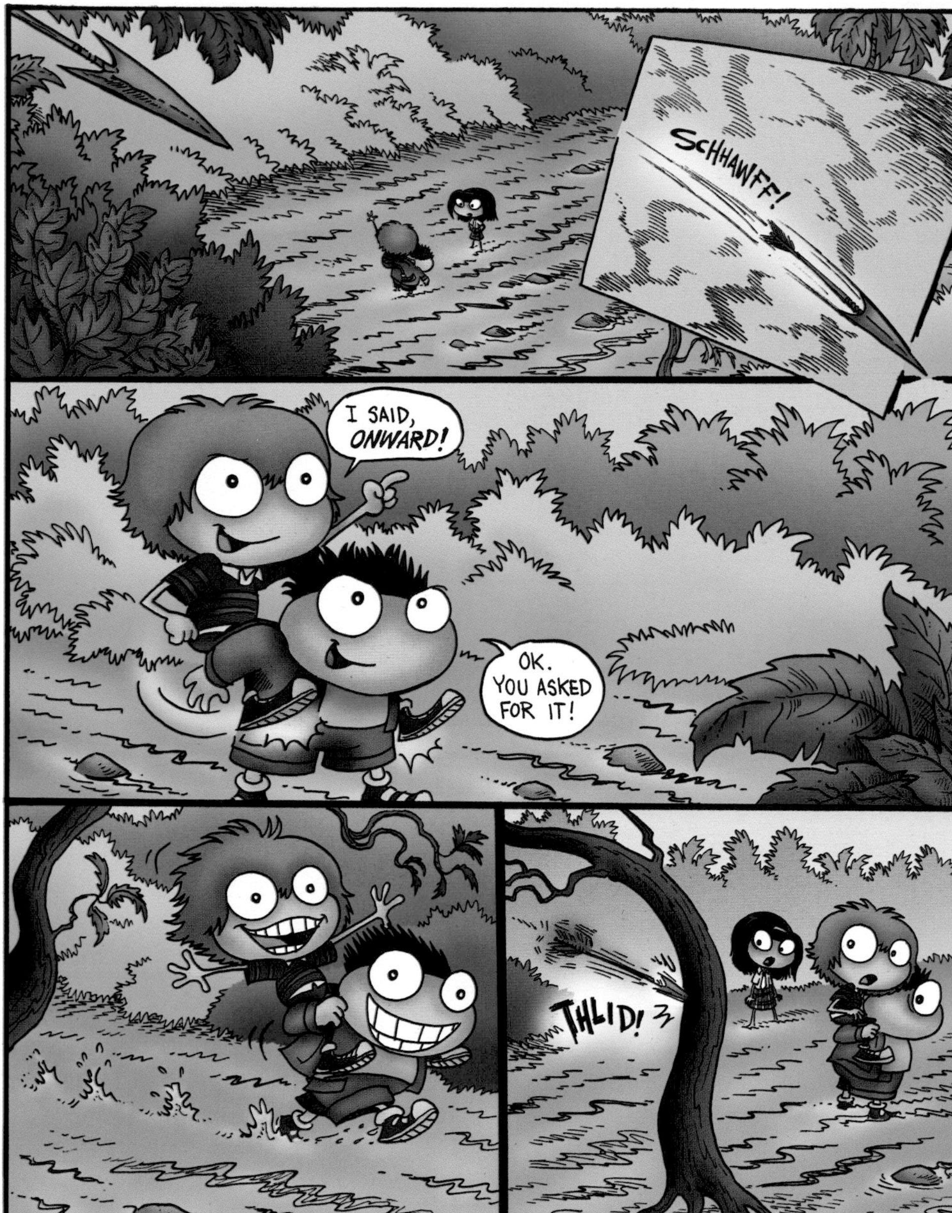

SCHHAWFF!
I SAID, ONWARD!
OK. YOU ASKED FOR IT!
THLID!

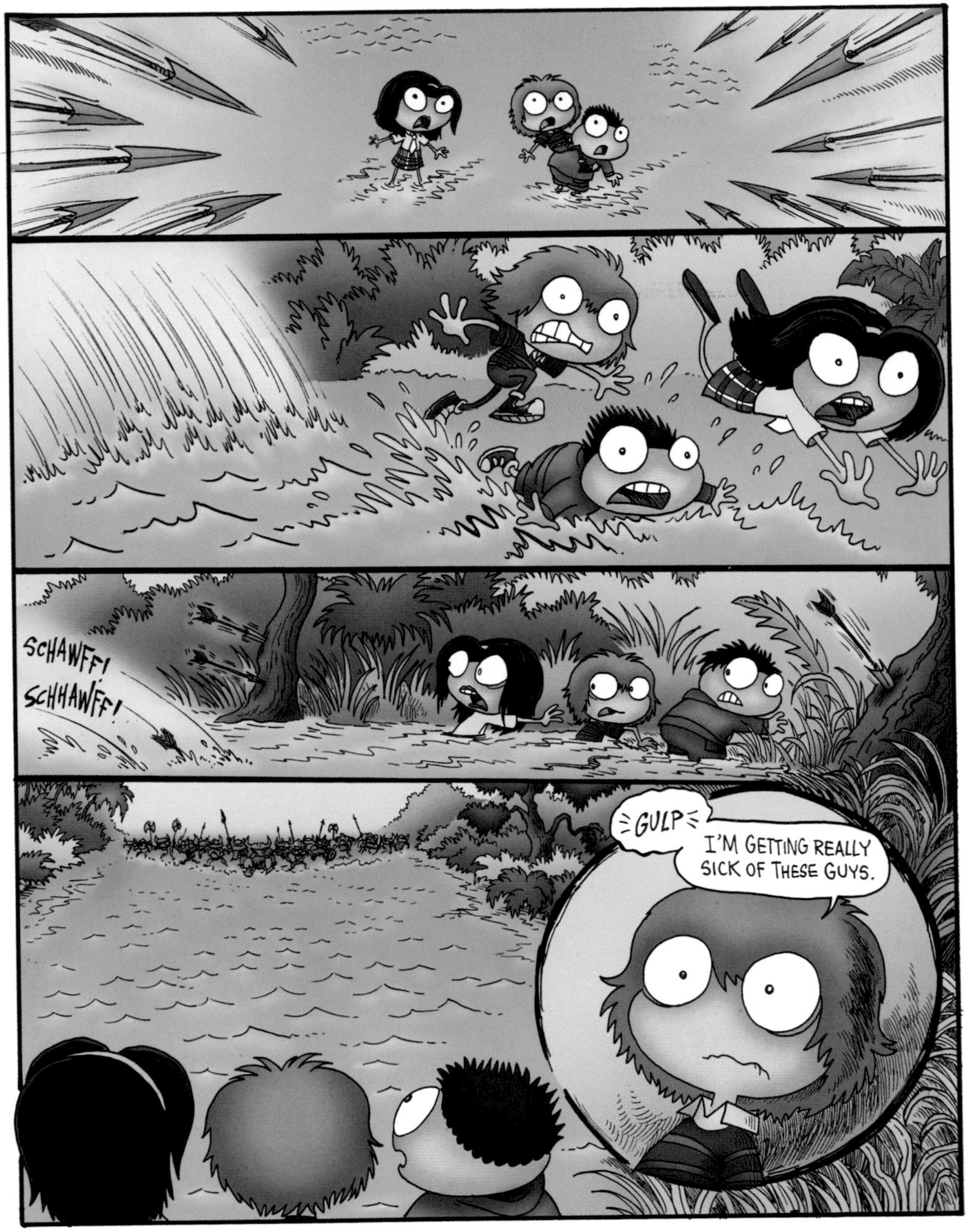
SCHAWFF!
SCHHAWFF!
GULP
I'M GETTING REALLY SICK OF THESE GUYS.

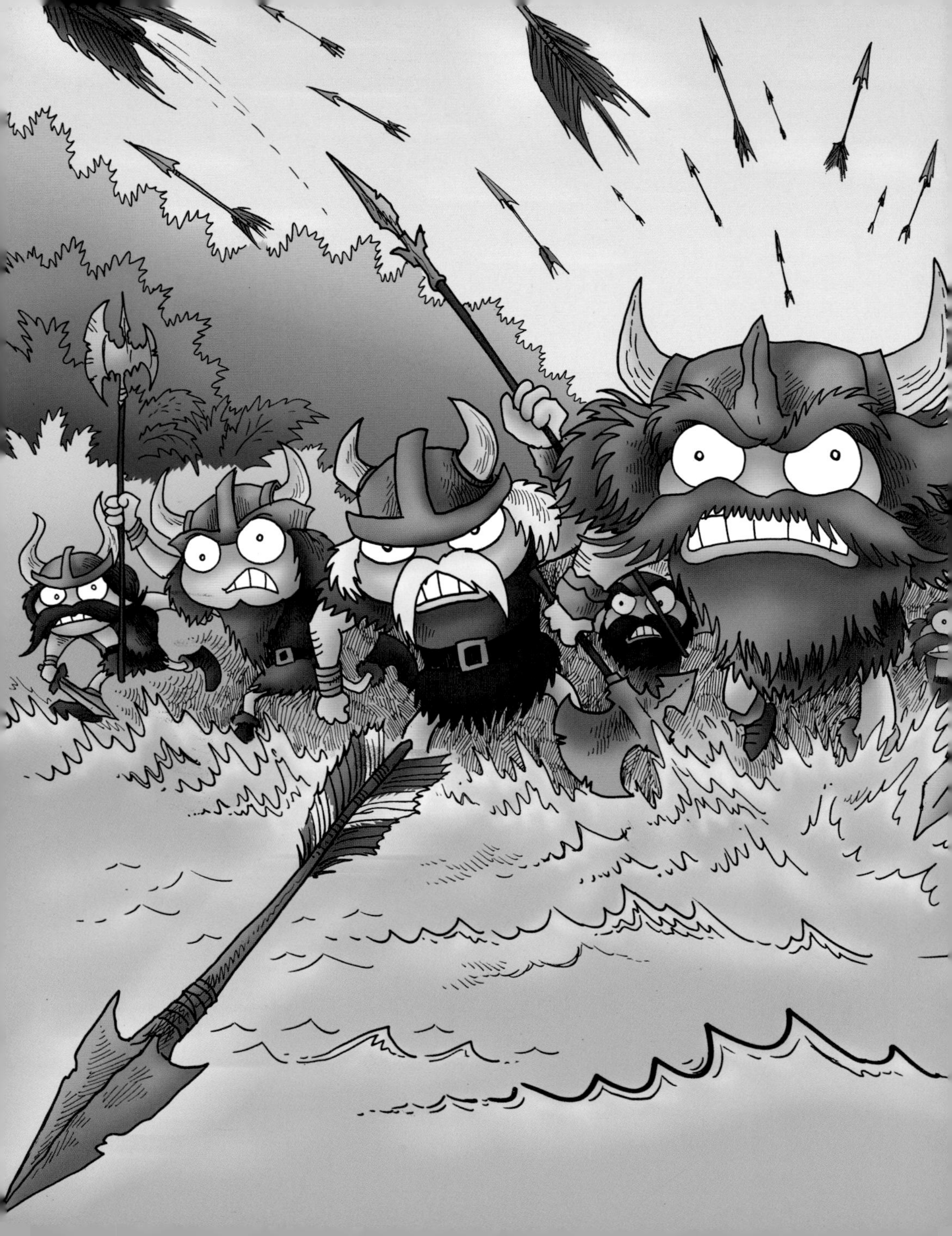

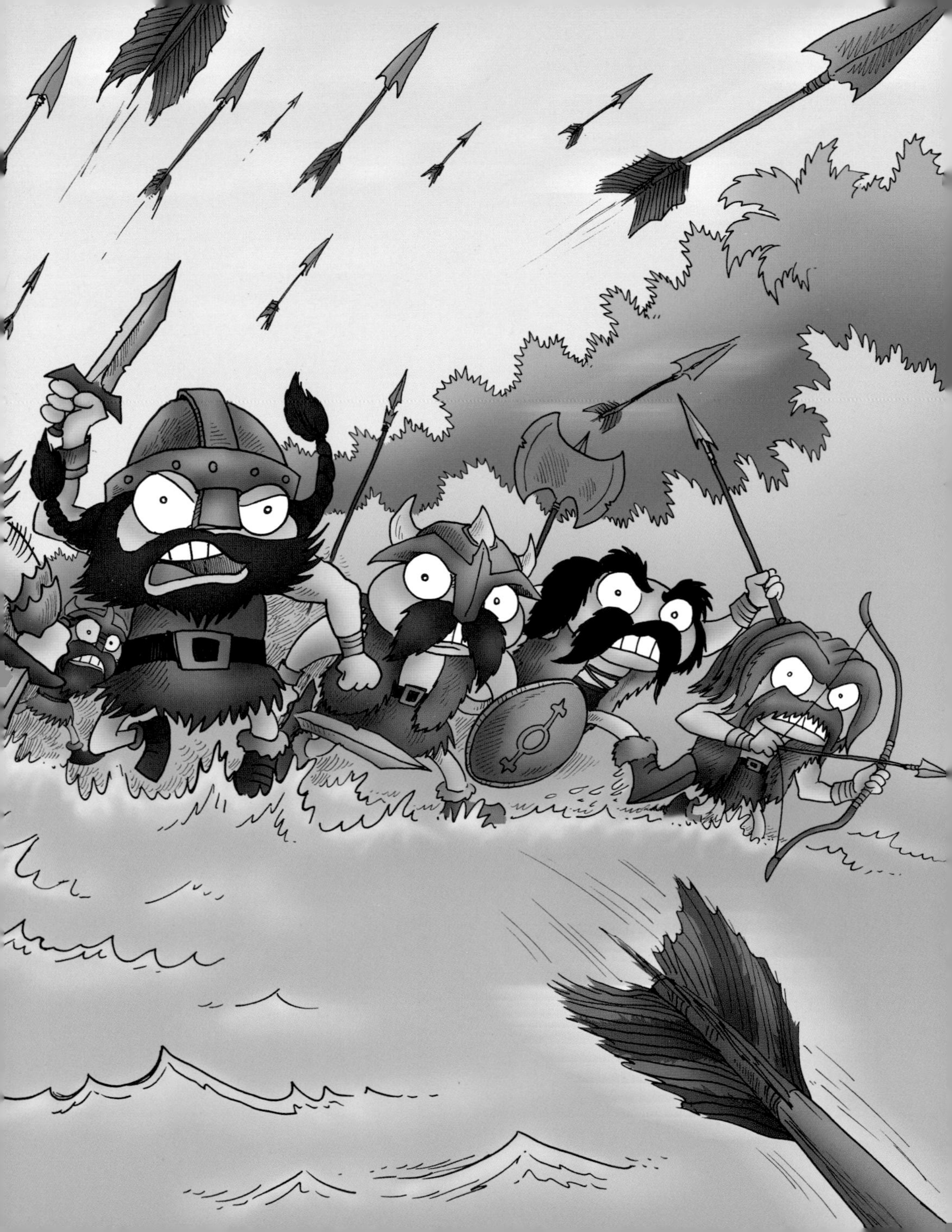

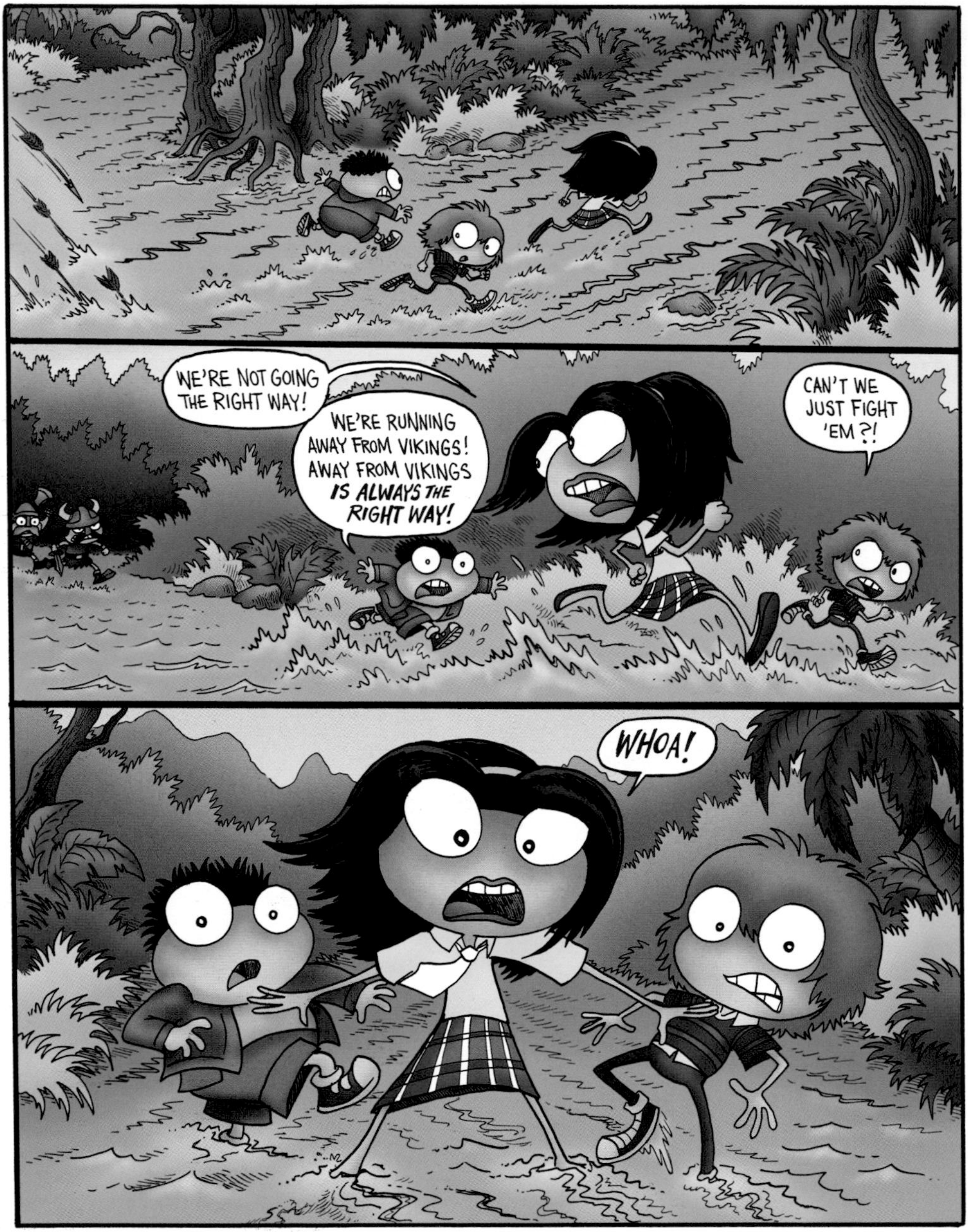
WE'RE NOT GOING THE RIGHT WAY!
WE'RE RUNNING AWAY FROM VIKINGS! AWAY FROM VIKINGS IS ALWAYS THE RIGHT WAY!
CAN'T WE JUST FIGHT 'EM?!
WHOA!

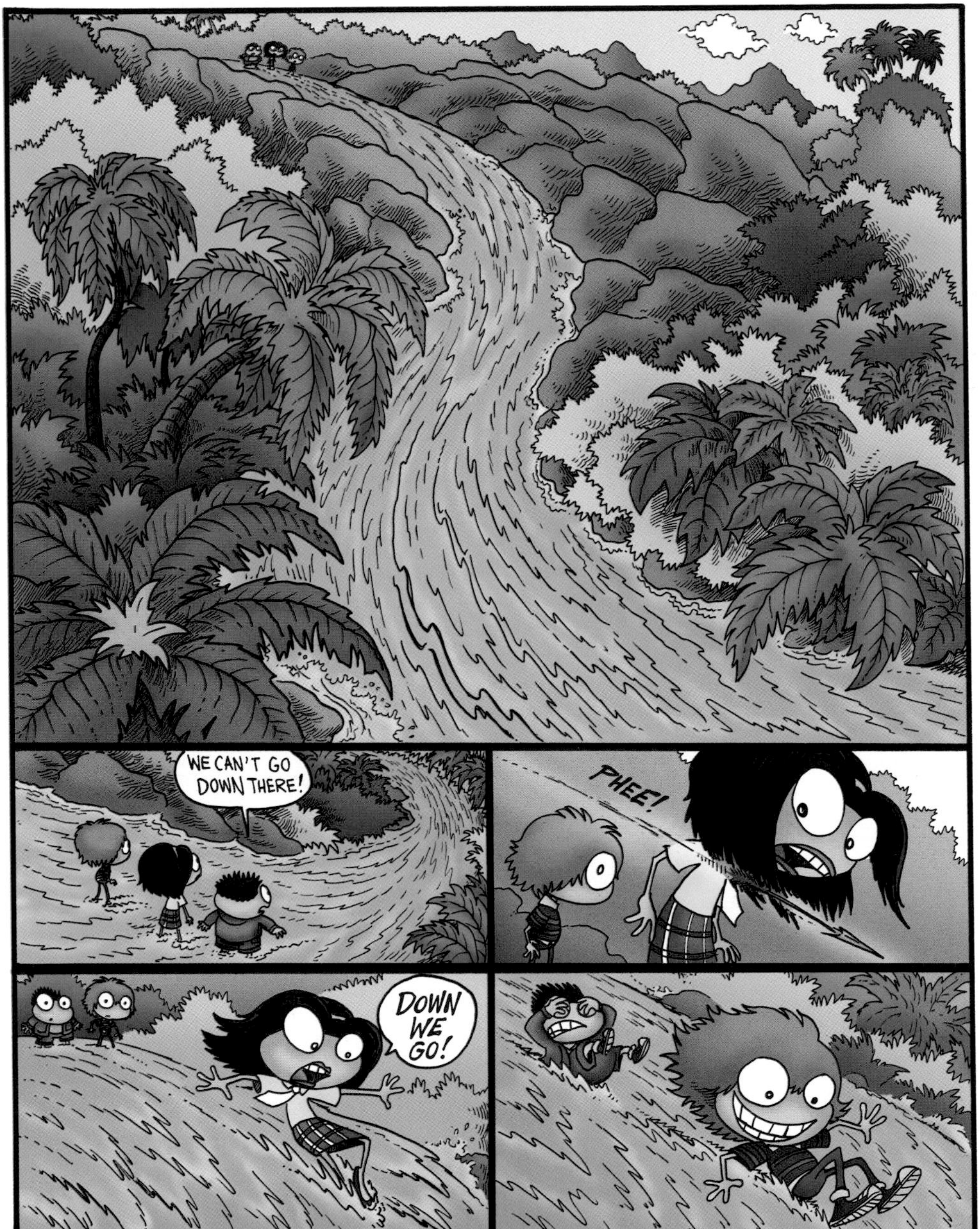
WE CAN'T GO DOWN THERE!
PHEE!
DOWN WE GO!

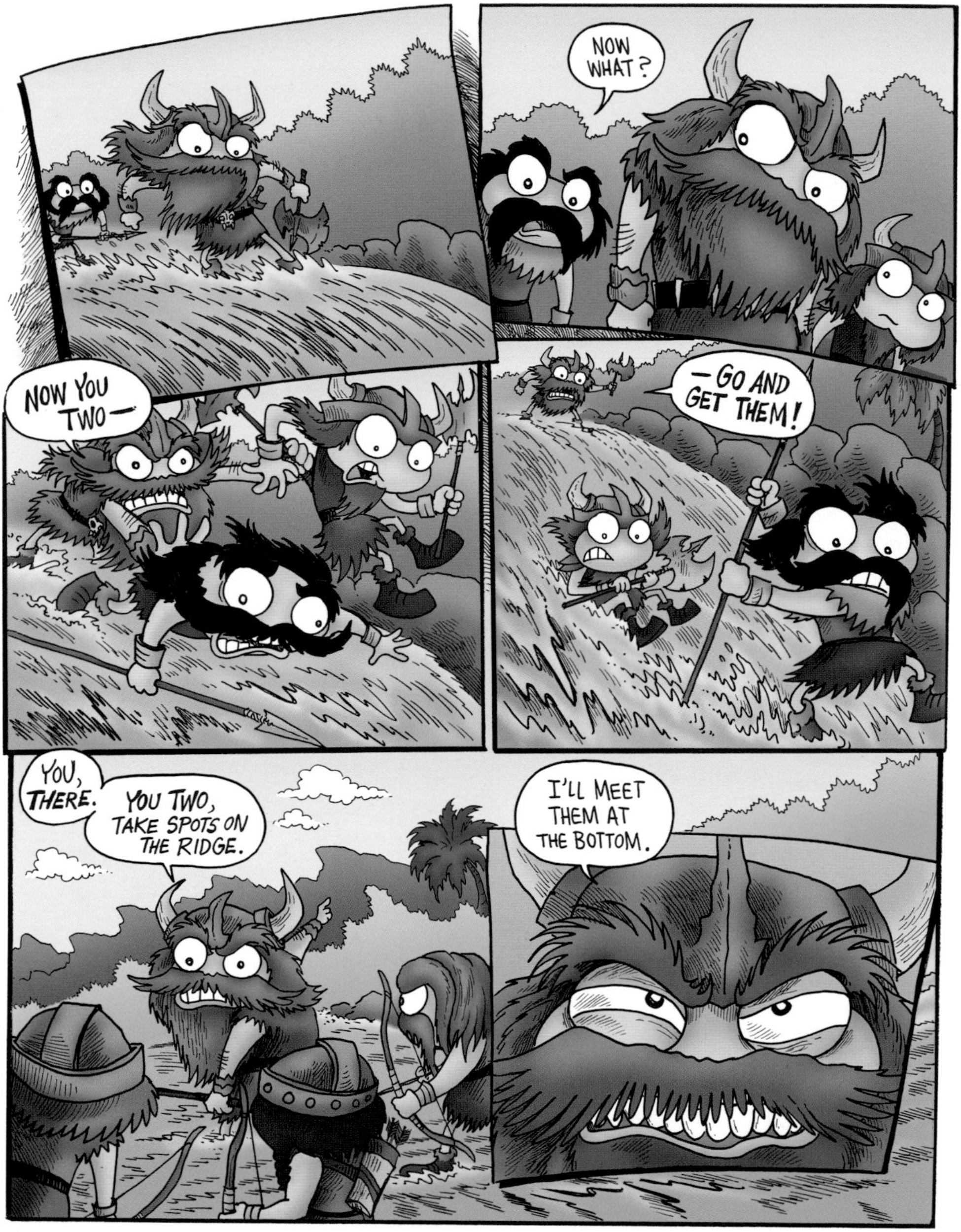
NOW WHAT?
NOW YOU TWO—
—GO AND GET THEM!
YOU, THERE.
YOU TWO, TAKE SPOTS ON THE RIDGE.
I'LL MEET THEM AT THE BOTTOM.

# Chapter 9

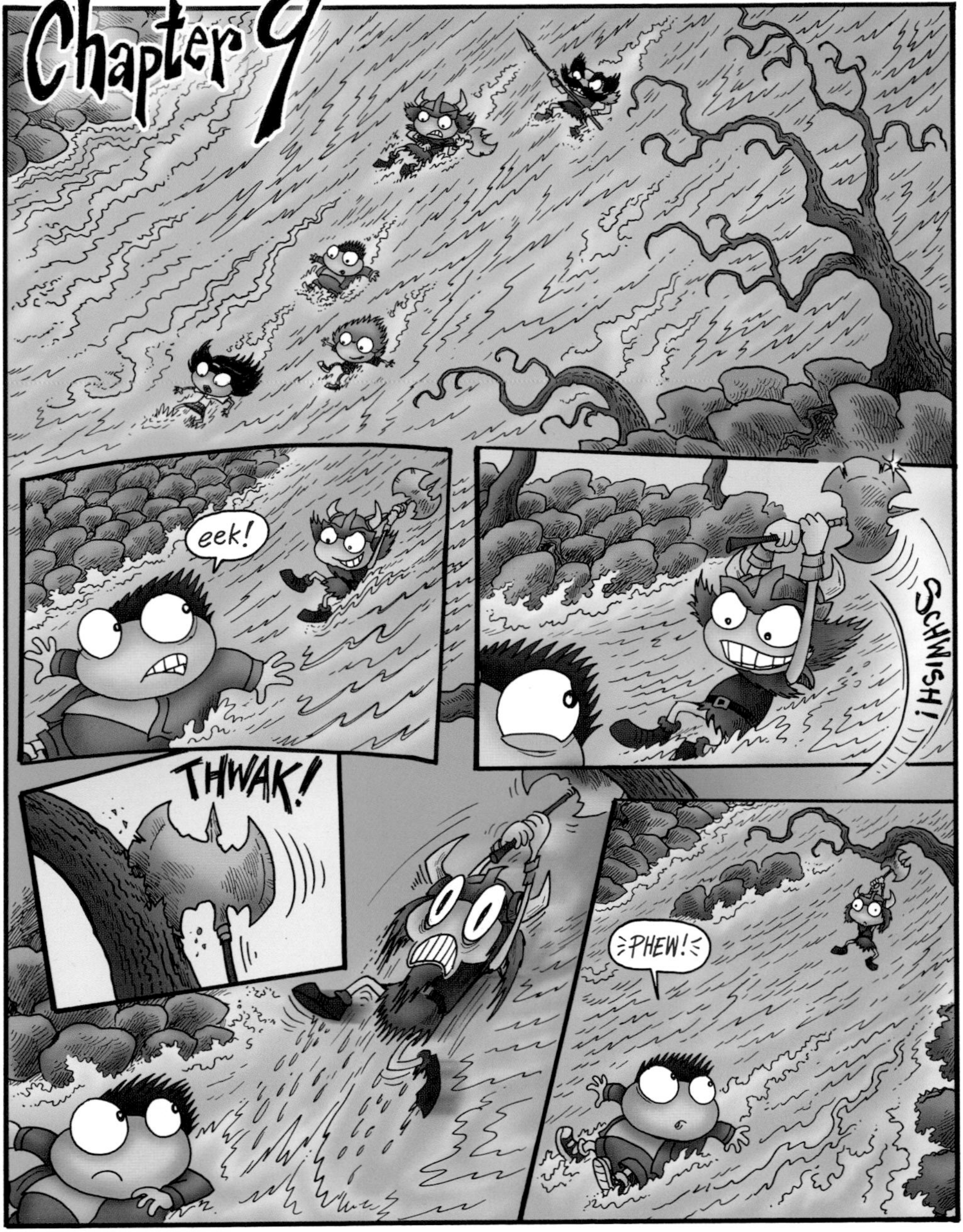
eek!
SCHWISH!
THWAK!
PHEW!

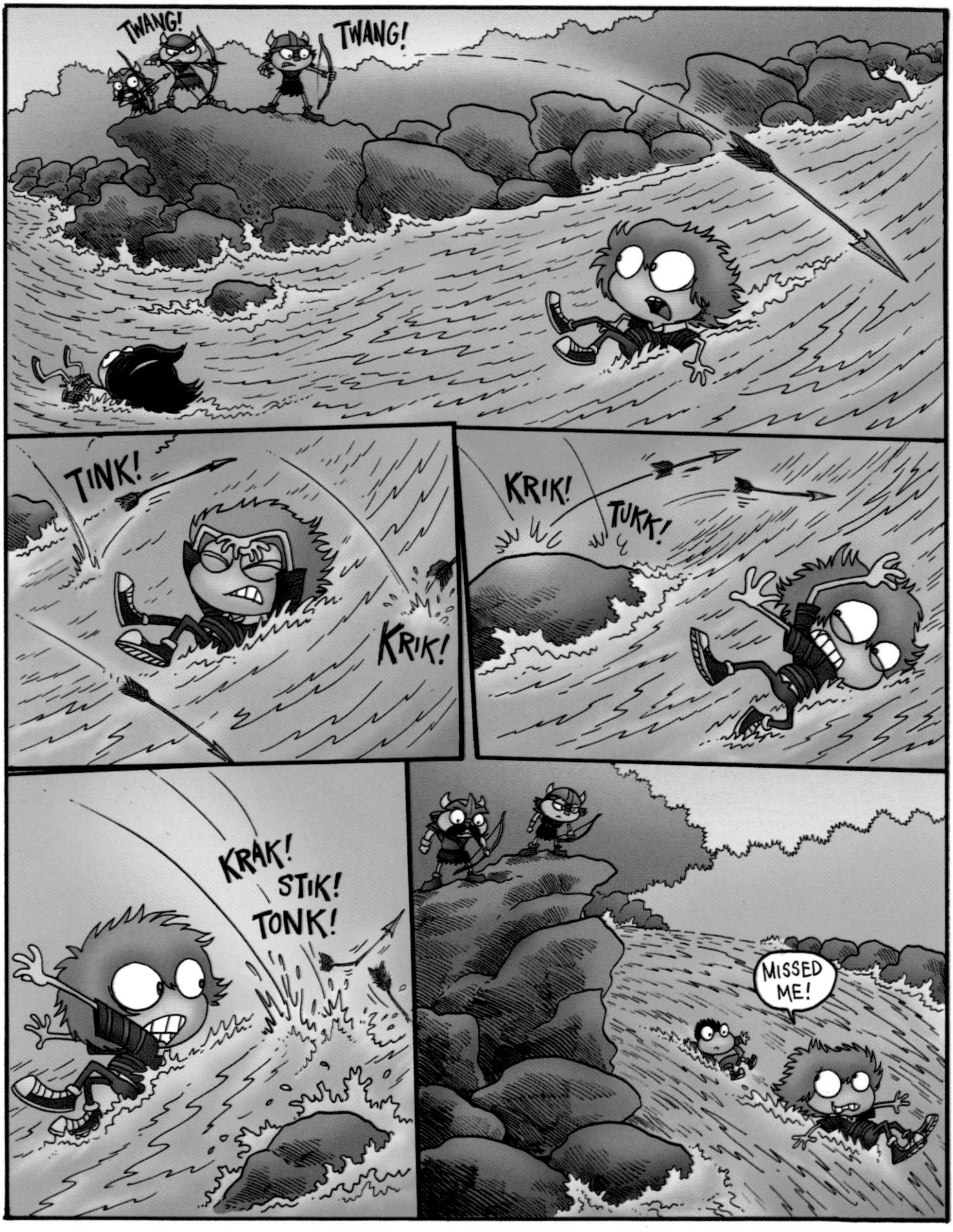
TWANG!
TWANG!
TINK!
KRIK!
KRIK!
TUKK!
KRAK!
STIK!
TONK!
MISSED ME!

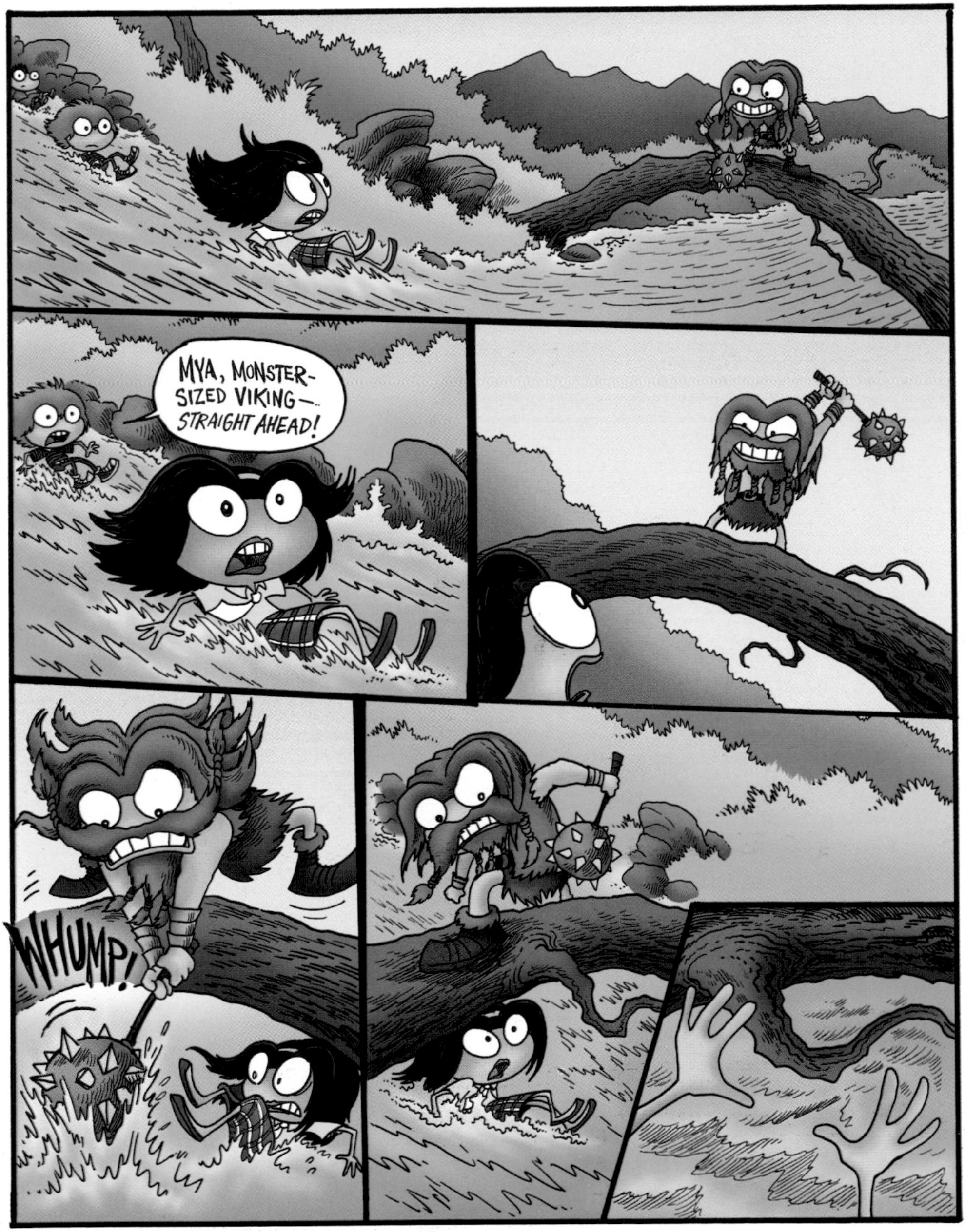
MYA, MONSTER-SIZED VIKING— STRAIGHT AHEAD!
WHUMP!

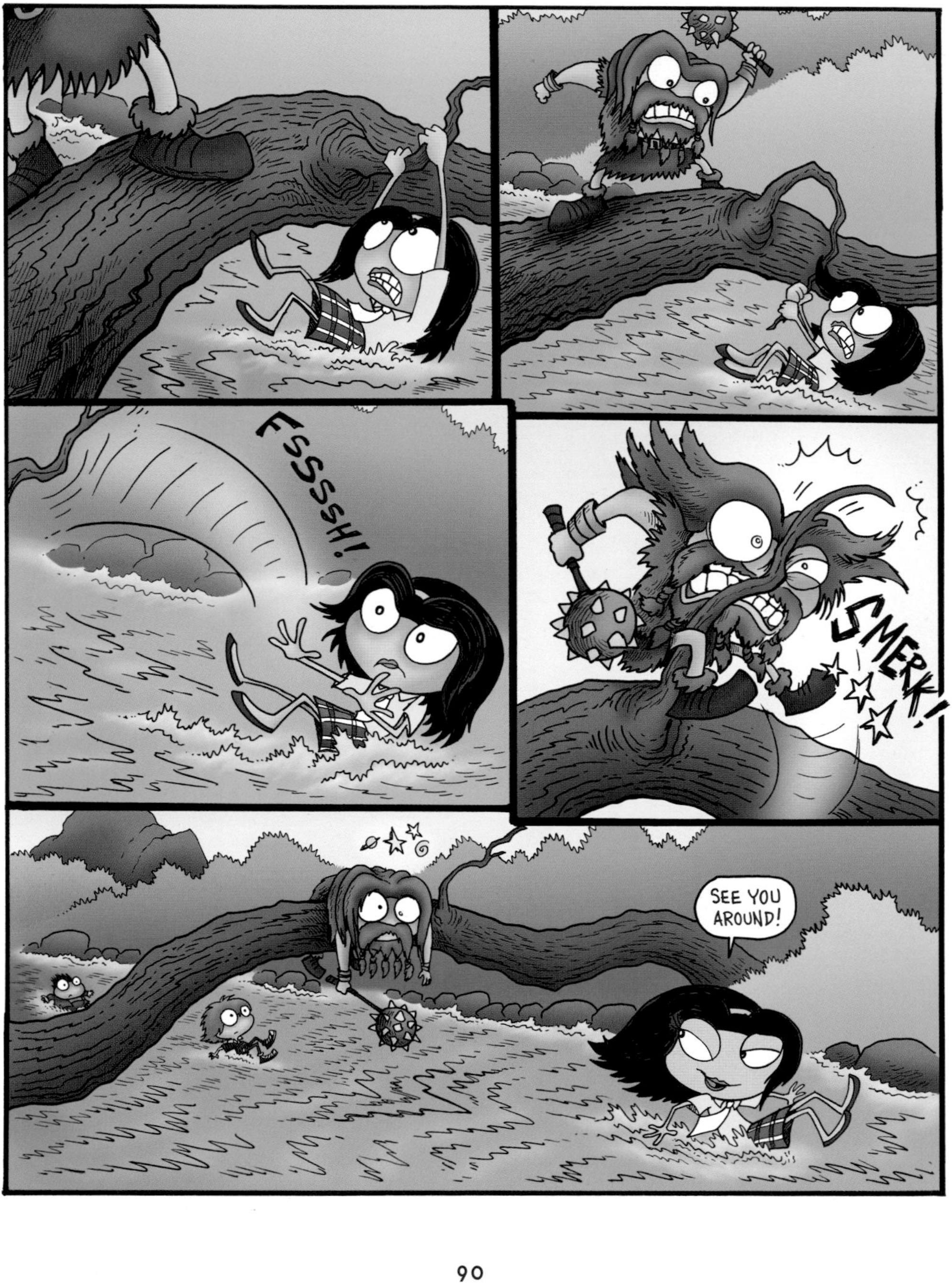
FSSSSH!
SMERK!
SEE YOU AROUND!

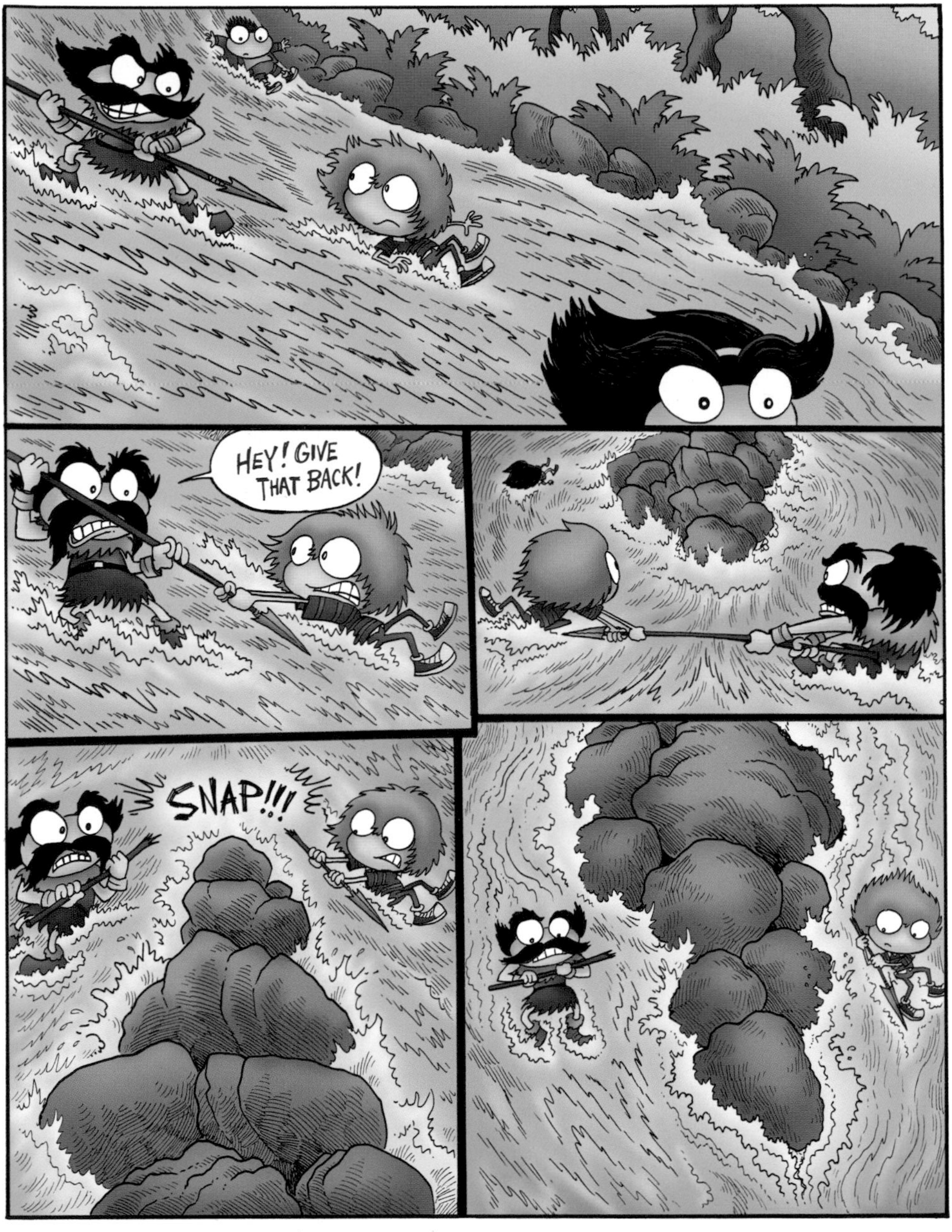
HEY! GIVE THAT BACK!
SNAP!!!

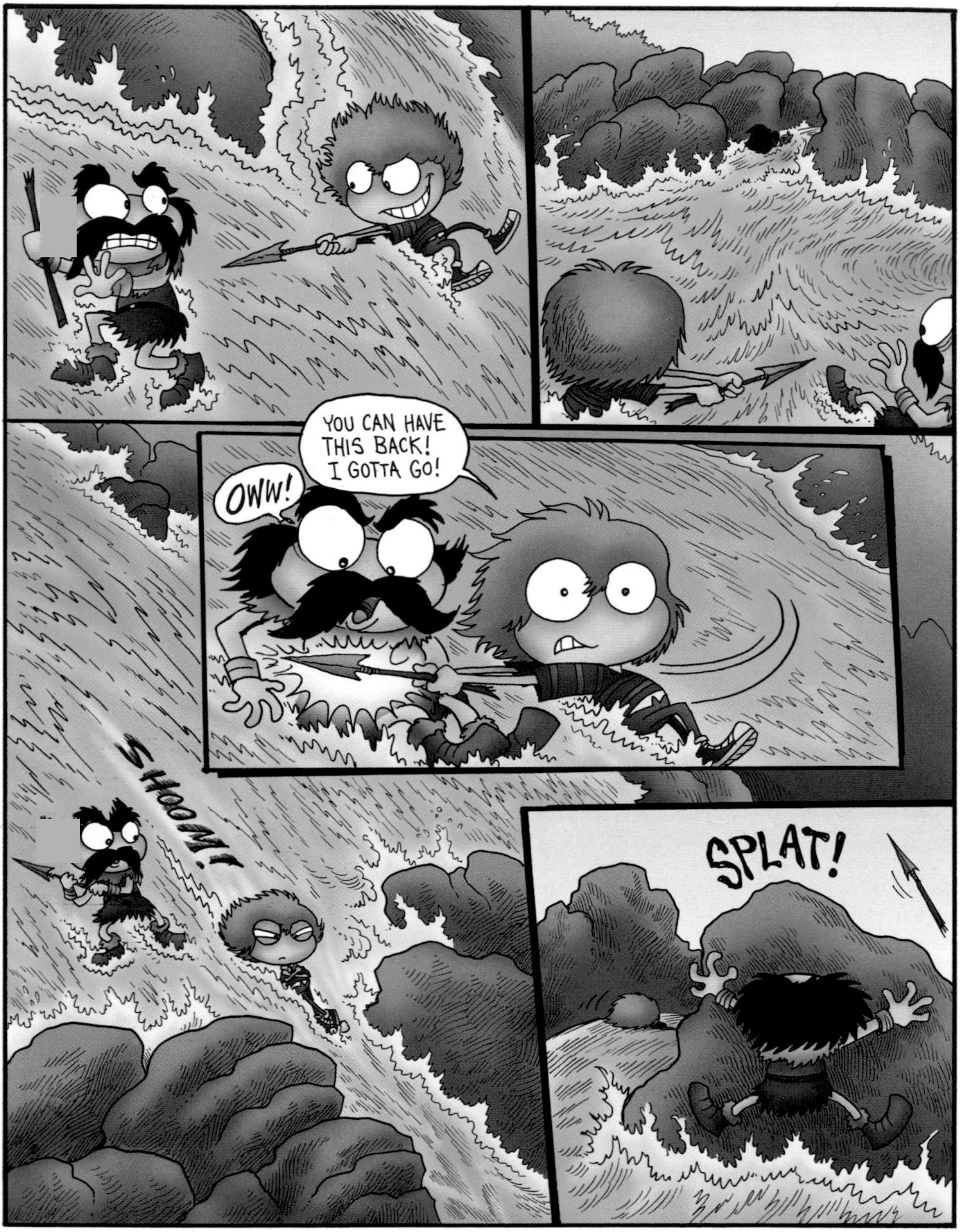
YOU CAN HAVE THIS BACK! I GOTTA GO!
OWW!
SHOOM!
SPLAT!

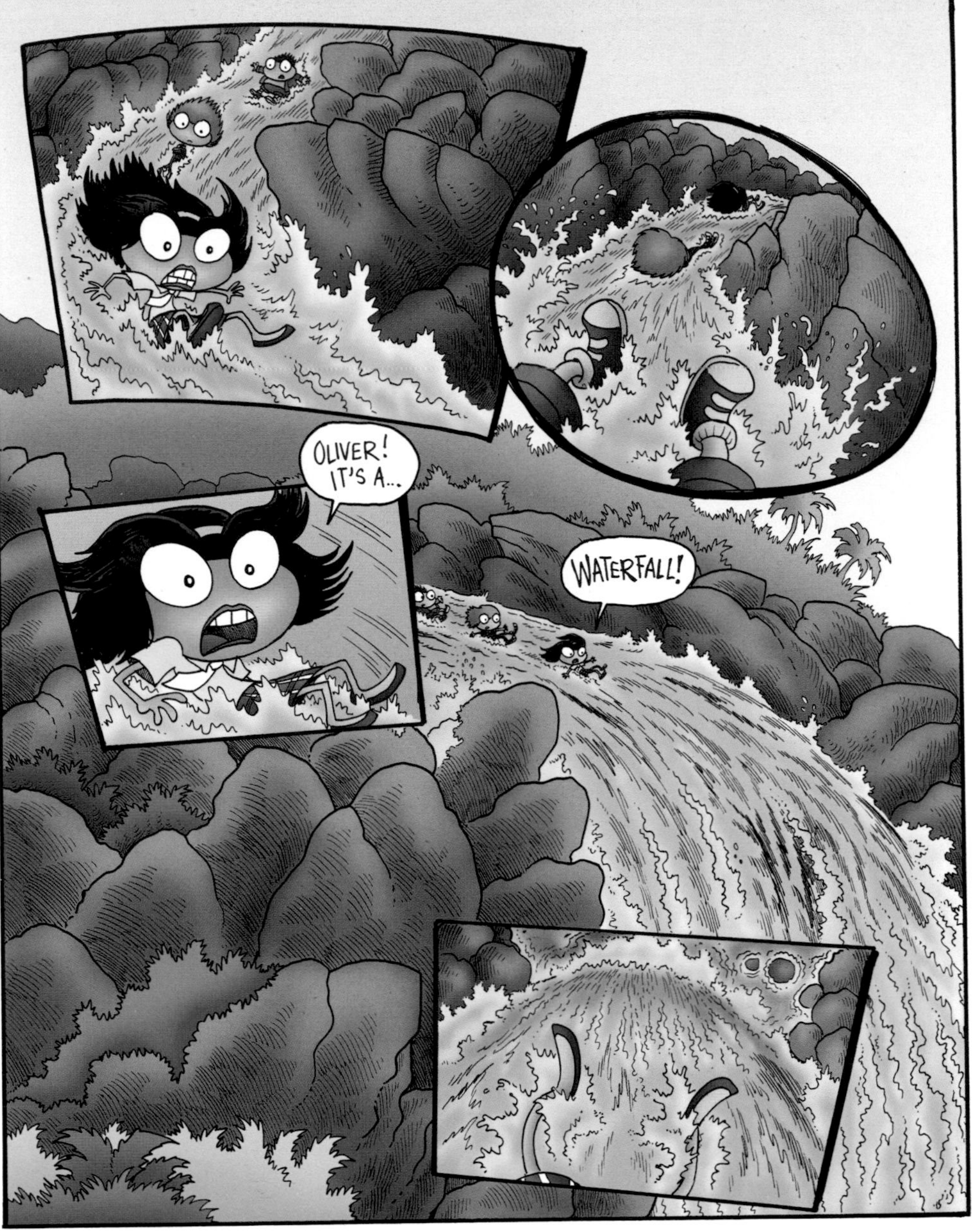
OLIVER! IT'S A...
WATERFALL!

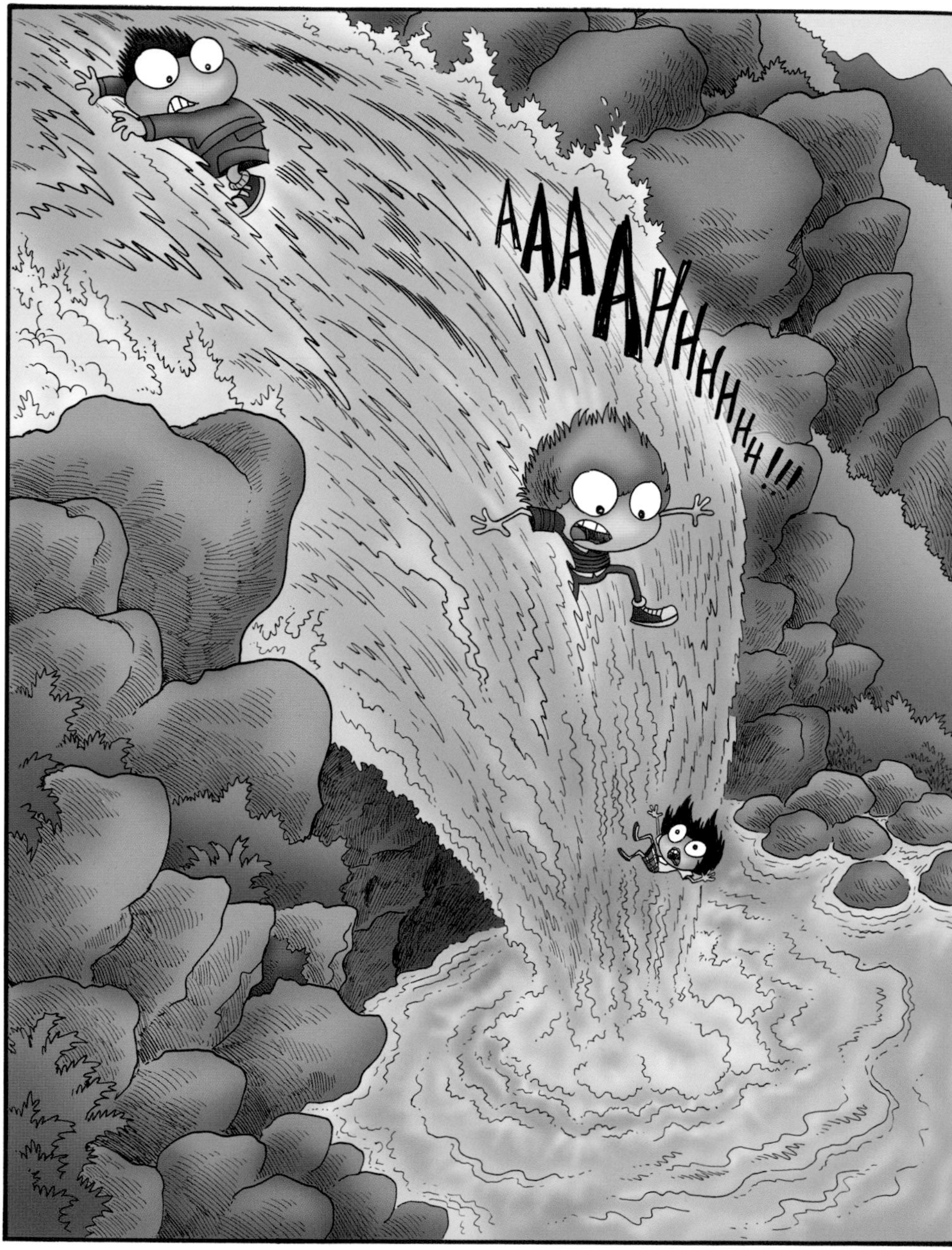
AAAAHHHHHHH!!!

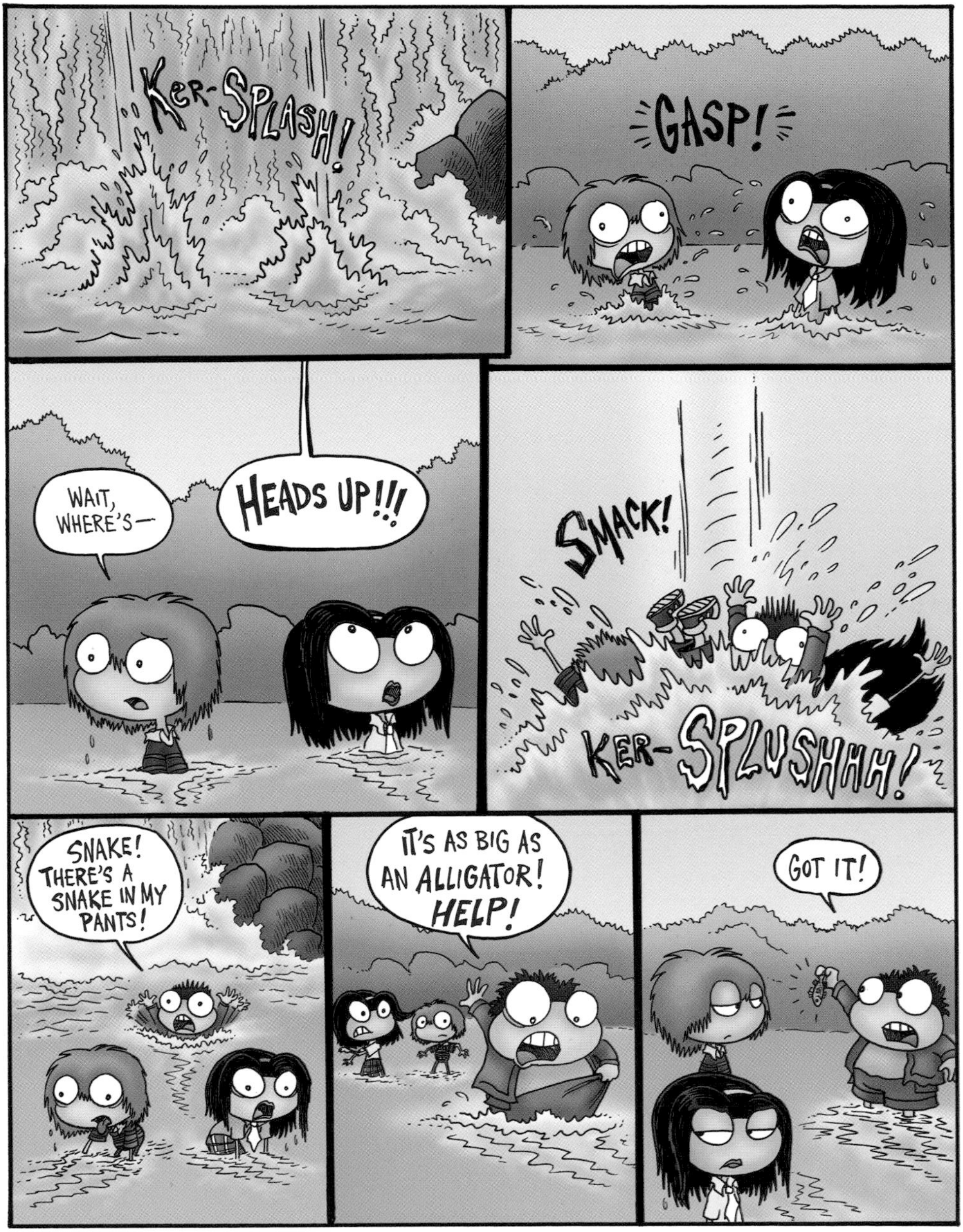
KER-SPLASH!
GASP!
WAIT, WHERE'S—
HEADS UP!!!
SMACK!
KER-SPLUSHHH!
SNAKE! THERE'S A SNAKE IN MY PANTS!
IT'S AS BIG AS AN ALLIGATOR! HELP!
GOT IT!

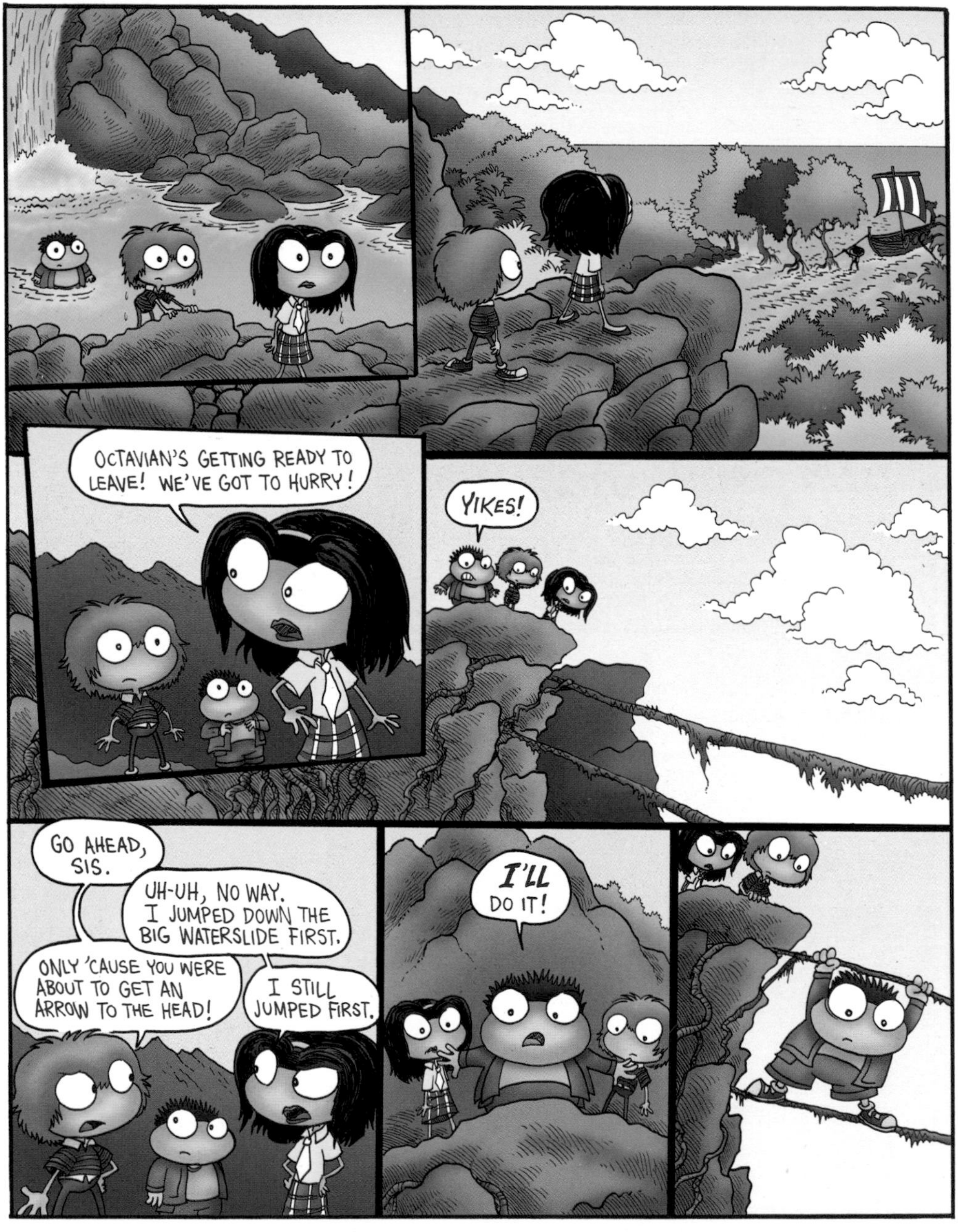
OCTAVIAN'S GETTING READY TO LEAVE! WE'VE GOT TO HURRY!
YIKES!
GO AHEAD, SIS.
UH-UH, NO WAY. I JUMPED DOWN THE BIG WATERSLIDE FIRST.
ONLY 'CAUSE YOU WERE ABOUT TO GET AN ARROW TO THE HEAD!
I STILL JUMPED FIRST.
I'LL DO IT!

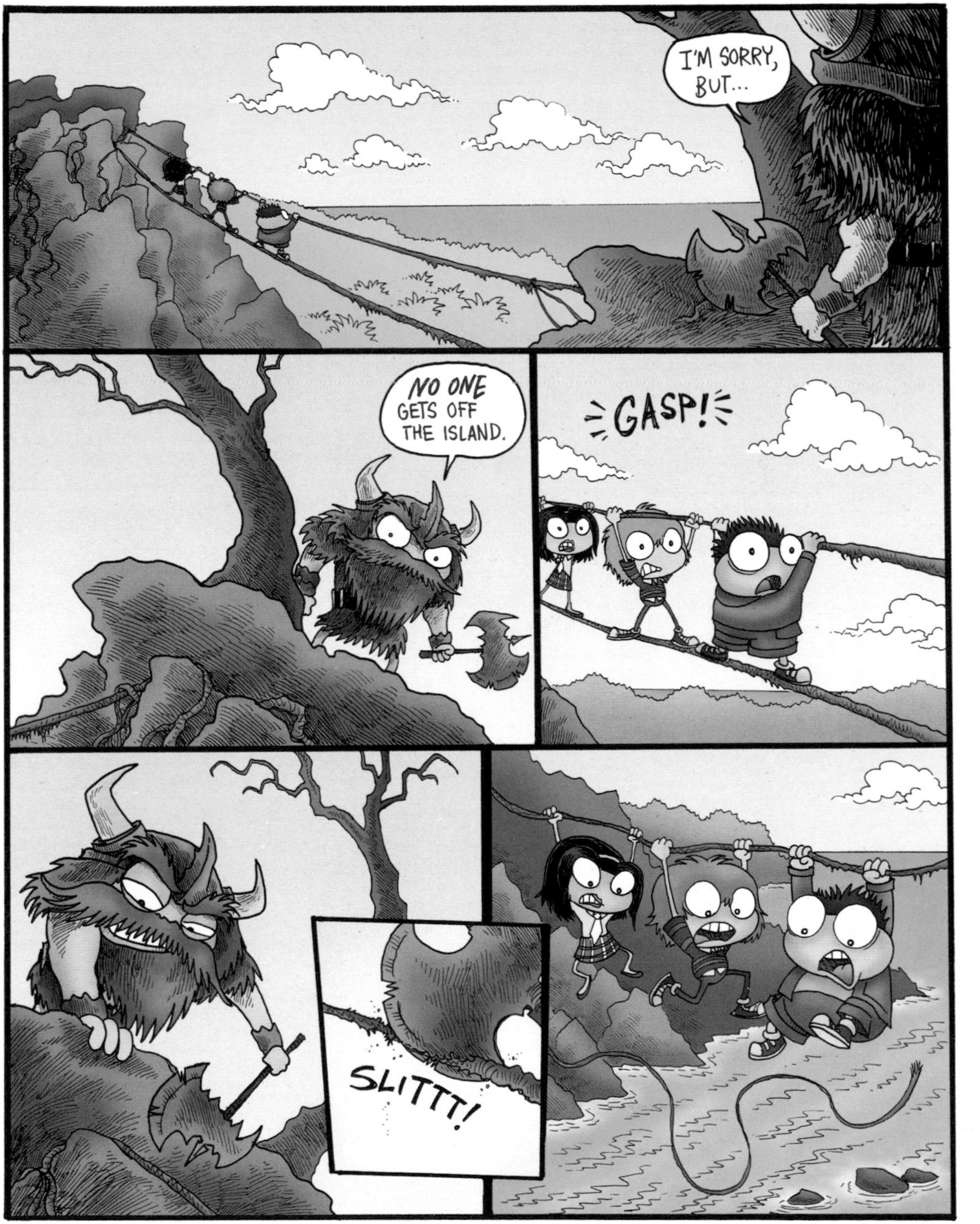
I'M SORRY, BUT...
NO ONE GETS OFF THE ISLAND.
GASP!
SLITTT!

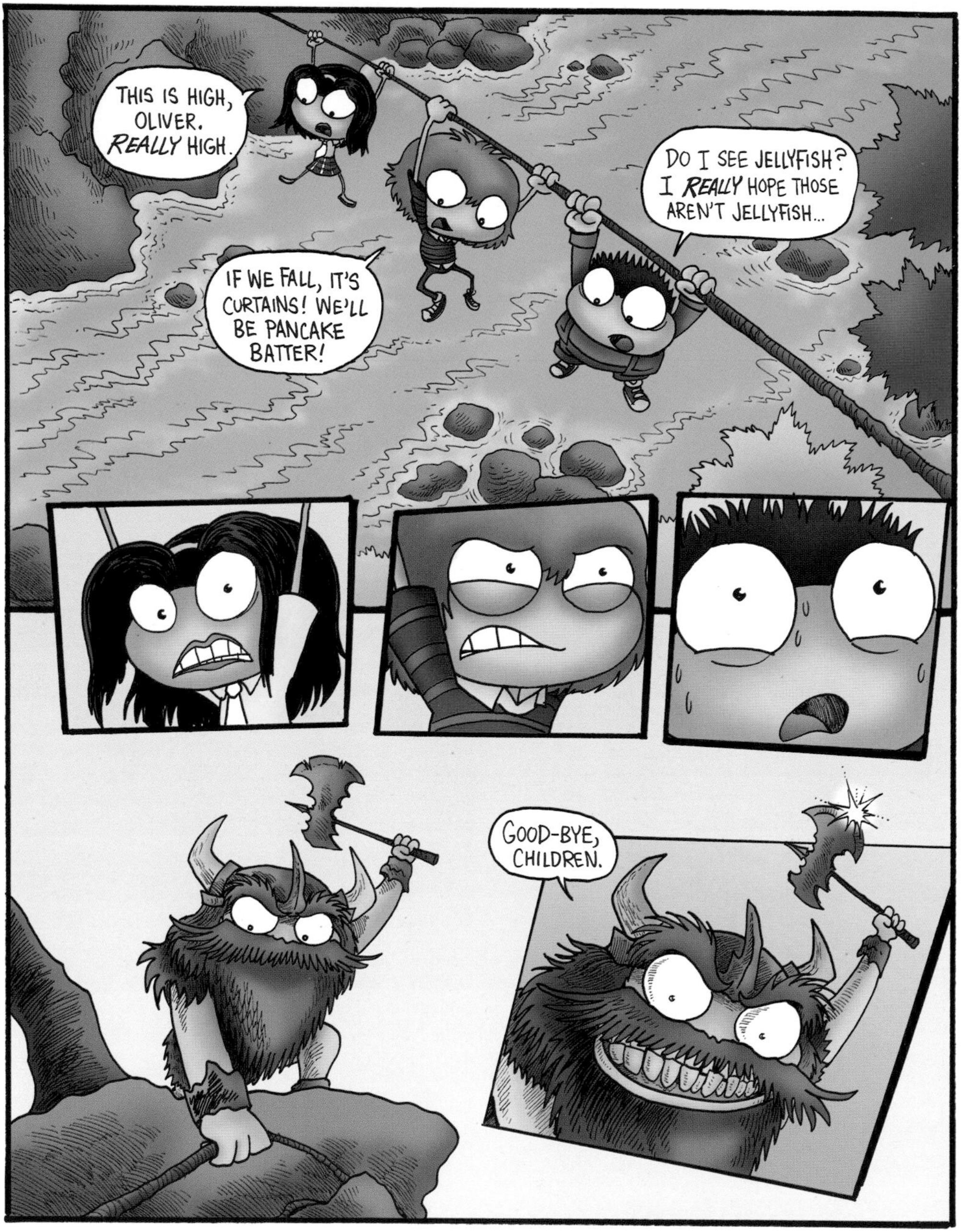
THIS IS HIGH, OLIVER. REALLY HIGH.
DO I SEE JELLYFISH? I REALLY HOPE THOSE AREN'T JELLYFISH...
IF WE FALL, IT'S CURTAINS! WE'LL BE PANCAKE BATTER!
GOOD-BYE, CHILDREN.

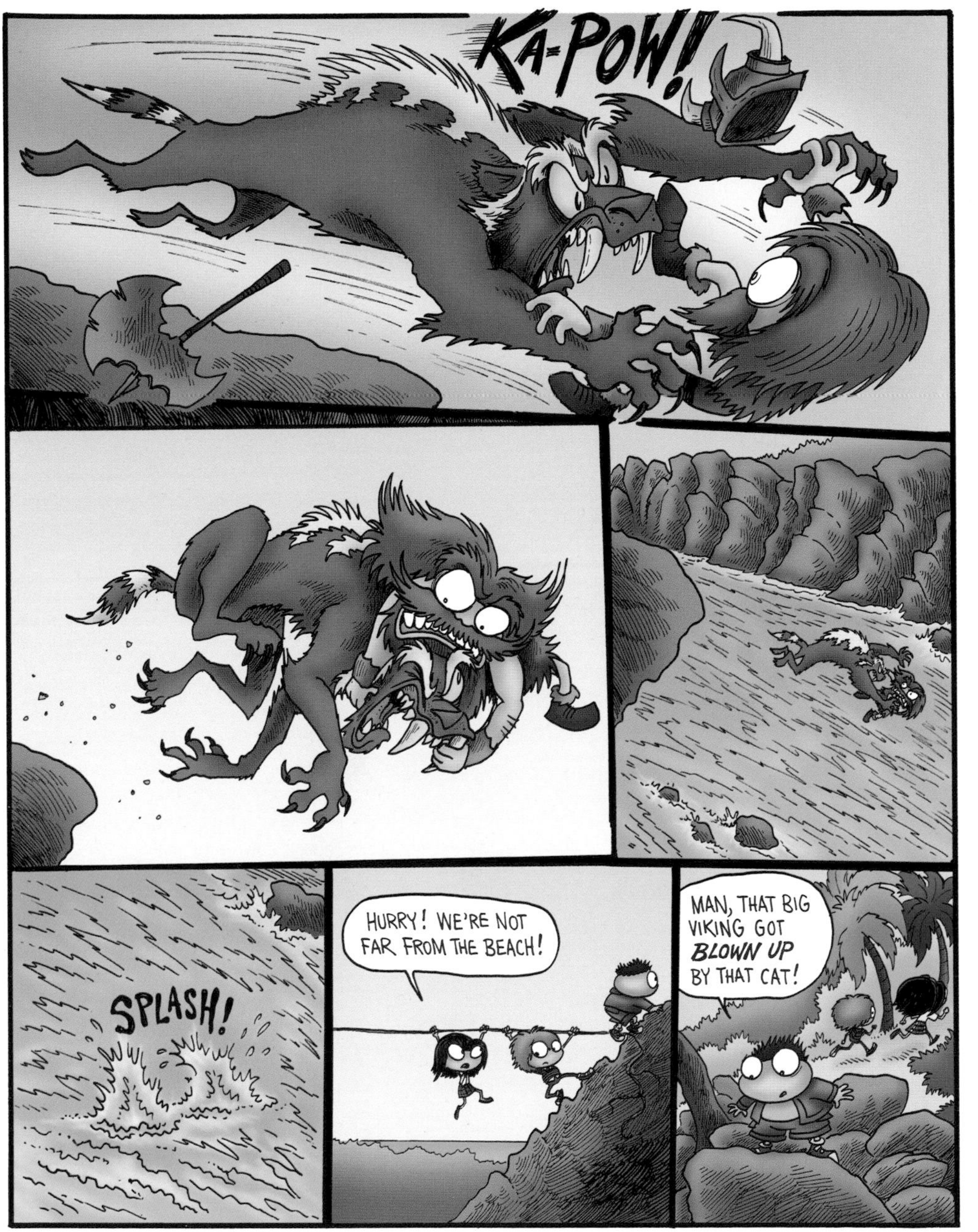
KA-POW!
SPLASH!
HURRY! WE'RE NOT FAR FROM THE BEACH!
MAN, THAT BIG VIKING GOT *BLOWN UP* BY THAT CAT!

# Chapter 10

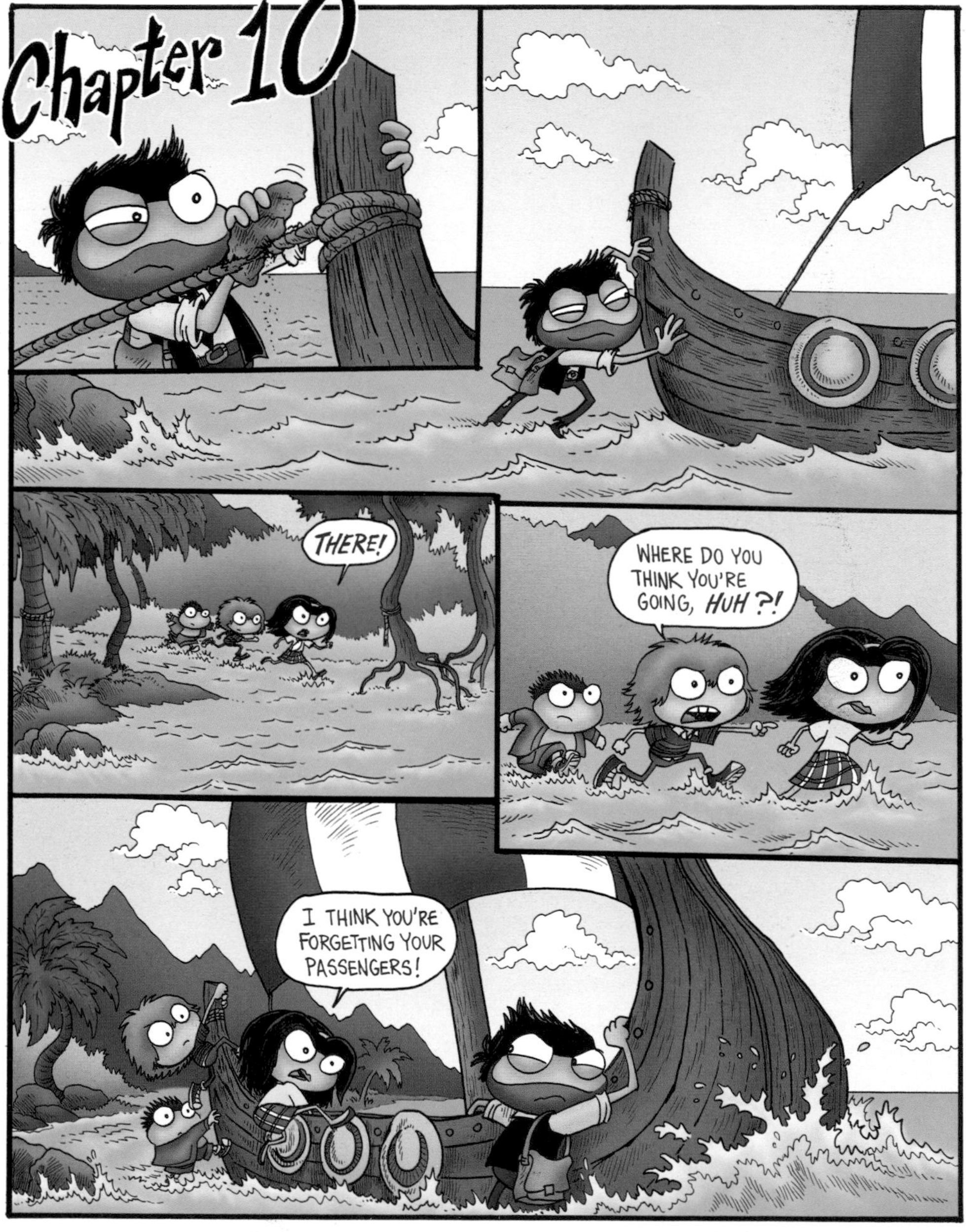
THERE!
WHERE DO YOU THINK YOU'RE GOING, HUH?!
I THINK YOU'RE FORGETTING YOUR PASSENGERS!

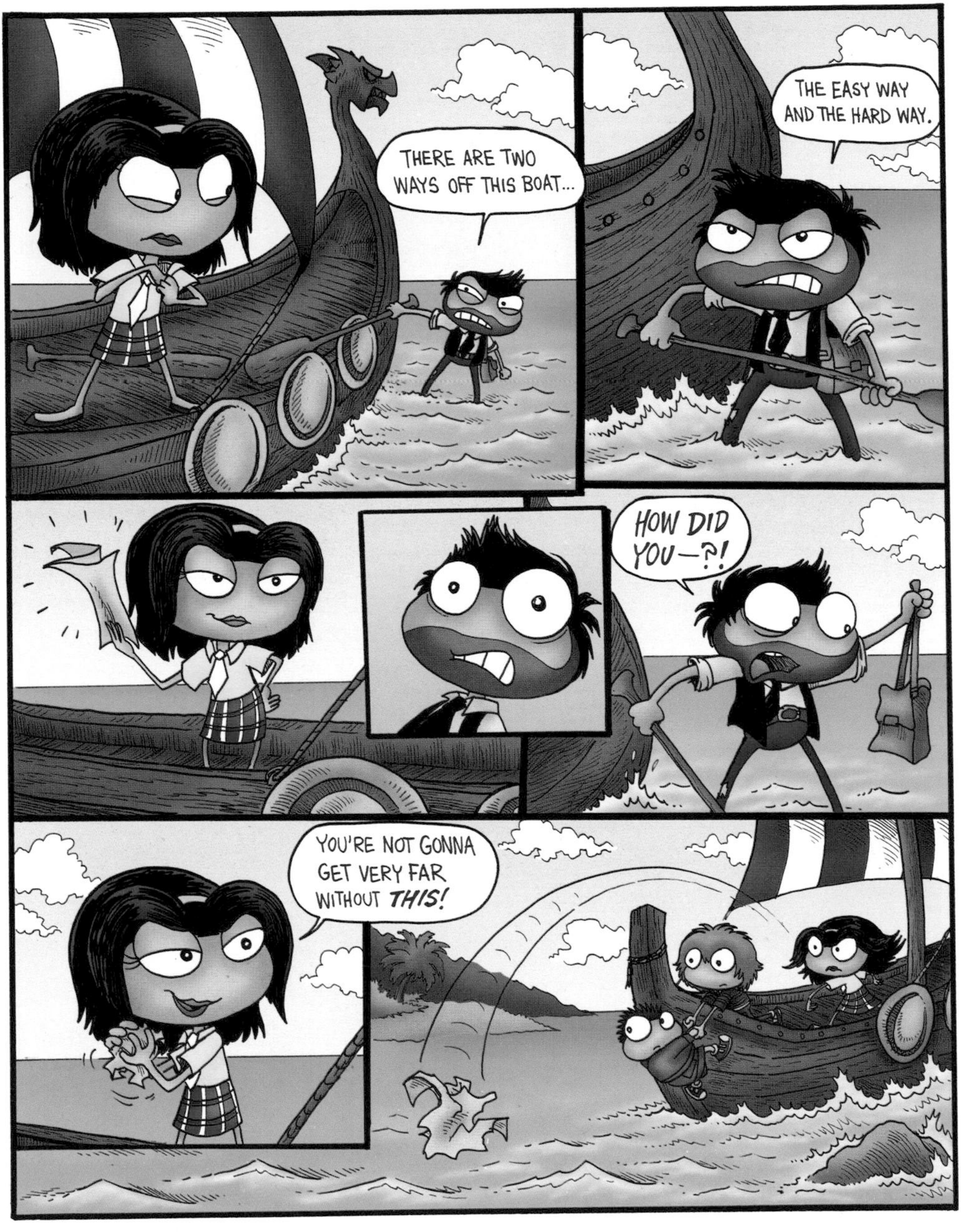
THERE ARE TWO WAYS OFF THIS BOAT...
THE EASY WAY AND THE HARD WAY.
HOW DID YOU—?!
YOU'RE NOT GONNA GET VERY FAR WITHOUT THIS!

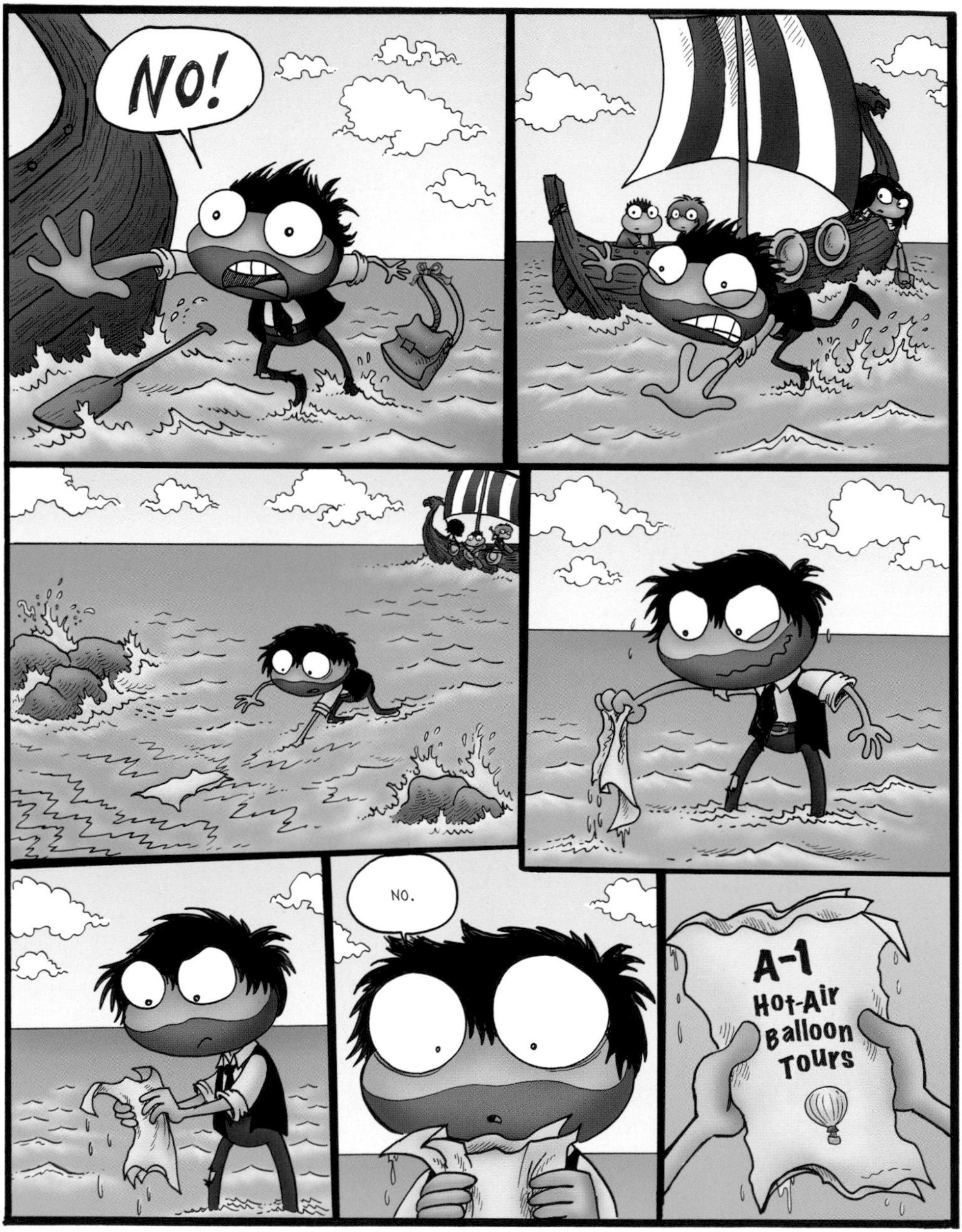
NO!
NO.
A-1
Hot-Air
Balloon
Tours

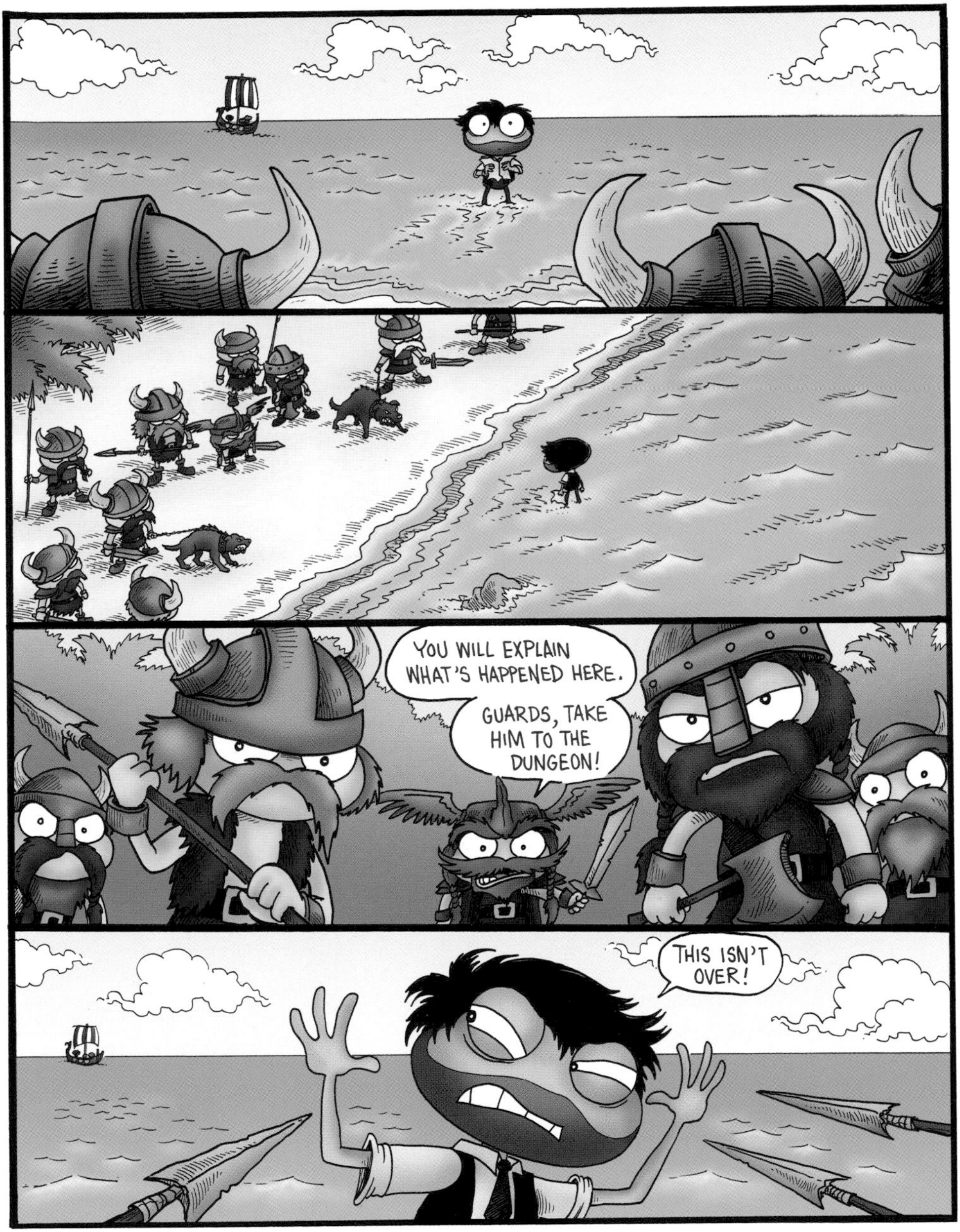
YOU WILL EXPLAIN WHAT'S HAPPENED HERE.
GUARDS, TAKE HIM TO THE DUNGEON!
THIS ISN'T OVER!

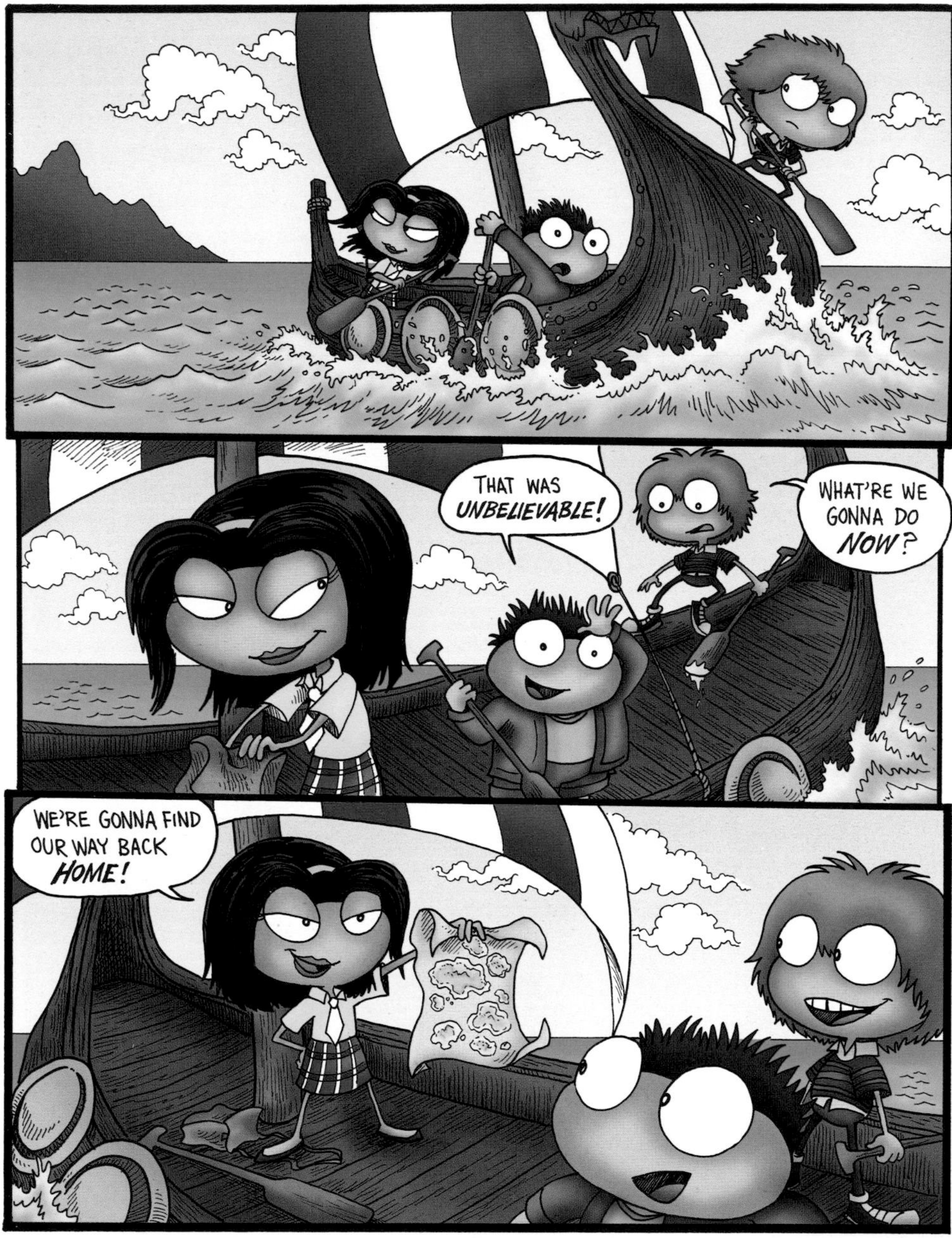
THAT WAS UNBELIEVABLE!
WHAT'RE WE GONNA DO NOW?
WE'RE GONNA FIND OUR WAY BACK HOME!

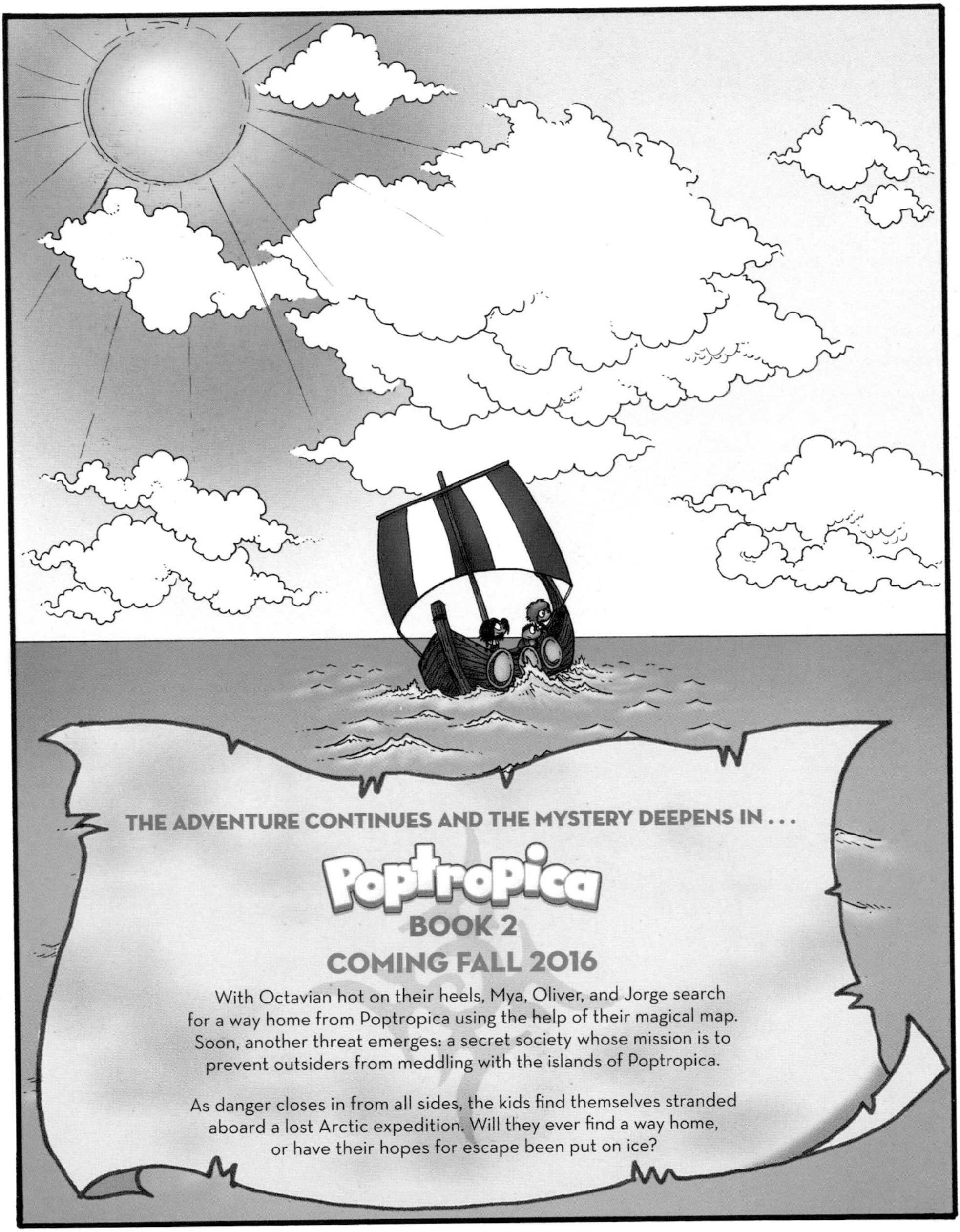
THE ADVENTURE CONTINUES AND THE MYSTERY DEEPENS IN . . .
Poptropica
BOOK 2
COMING FALL 2016
With Octavian hot on their heels, Mya, Oliver, and Jorge search for a way home from Poptropica using the help of their magical map. Soon, another threat emerges: a secret society whose mission is to prevent outsiders from meddling with the islands of Poptropica.
As danger closes in from all sides, the kids find themselves stranded aboard a lost Arctic expedition. Will they ever find a way home, or have their hopes for escape been put on ice?

THANKS TO JEFF FAULCONER, JEFF KINNEY, CHARLES KOCHMAN,
AND OF COURSE JESS BRALLIER FOR PULLING ME
INTO THIS NUTTY BUSINESS.
—KM

## ABOUT THE AUTHORS

**POPTROPICA** is best known for its website, in which stories are shared via gaming literacy. Every month, millions of kids from around the world are entertained and informed by Poptropica's engaging quests, including those featuring Diary of a Wimpy Kid, Big Nate, Peanuts, Galactic Hot Dogs, Timmy Failure, Magic Tree House, and Charlie and the Chocolate Factory.

**JACK CHABERT** is a game designer for Poptropica, the creator and author of *Eerie Elementary*, and, writing under a different name, the author of more than twenty-five titles including licensed books for *Adventure Time*, *Regular Show*, *Uncle Grandpa*, and *Steven Universe*. Chabert lives in New York with his wife.

**KORY MERRITT** is the co-creator of Poptropica comics. His first book, *The Dreadful Fate of Jonathan York*, will be published in fall 2015. Merritt teaches art for kindergarten through sixth grade in Hammondsport, New York.

Library of Congress Control Number: 2015946885

ISBN: 978-1-4197-2067-3

Book design by Chad W. Beckerman

Printed and bound in China
10 9 8 7 6 5 4 3 2 1

THE ART OF BOOKS SINCE 1949
115 West 18th Street
New York, NY 10011
www.abramsbooks.com

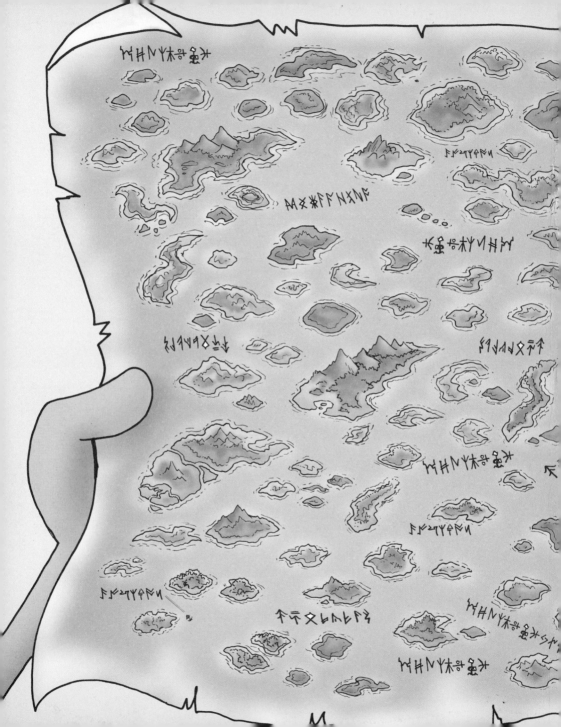